MOTHSTORM

Titles in this series, in reading order:

MOTHSTORM

OR

THE HORROR FROM BEYOND ~~URANUS!~~ Georgium Sidus

OR

A TALE OF TWO SHAPERS

A Rattling Yarn of Danger, Dastardy and Derring-Do
upon the Far Frontiers of British Space!

As Told by ART MUMBY, Esq.
(with the Usual Interpolations by MISS MYRTLE MUMBY) to

PHILIP REEVE

(Purveyor of Scientific Romances to the Discerning Gentry)

& Illuminated Throughout by

DAVID WYATT

('The Devonshire Da Vinci')

BLOOMSBURY

LONDON BERLIN NEW YORK

Bloomsbury Publishing, London, Berlin and New York

First published in Great Britain in 2008 by Bloomsbury Publishing Plc
36 Soho Square, London, W1D 3QY

This paperback edition first published in 2009

A CIP catalogue record of this book is available from the British Library

ISBN 978 0 7475 9416 1

The paper this book is printed on is certified independently in accordance with the rules of the FSC.
It is ancient-forest friendly. The printer holds chain of custody.

FSC
Mixed Sources
Product group from well-managed
forests and other controlled sources
Cert no. SGS - COC - 2061
www.fsc.org
© 1996 Forest Stewardship Council

Typeset by Dorchester Typesetting Group Ltd
Printed in Great Britain by Clays Ltd, St Ives Plc

1 3 5 7 9 10 8 6 4 2

www.larklight.co.uk
www.bloomsbury.com

This book was written with the aid of a
Snagsby & Co. Patent Lexicological Engine.

CONTENTS

Page

*Neither of us noticed the aether-ship that was sailing
silently towards Larklight.*

Chapter One

PEACE AND GOODWILL

IN WHICH LARKLIGHT IS FILLED WITH THE SPIRIT
OF CHRISTMAS, BUT THINGS GO SOMEWHAT AWRY IN
THE PANTRY.

'D underhead!'
        'Clodpole!'
            'Ninnyhammer!'
'Booby!'
'Nitwit!'
'Gumph!'

Yes, 'twas the season of Peace and Goodwill at Larklight,

and my sister Myrtle and I, snug in our fleece-lined, winter-weight spacesuits, were out upon the front porch, decorating our Christmas Tree.

Christmas Trees are a German notion and quite the latest thing, but I doubt whether Prince Albert, who is responsible for introducing this charming festive fad, has ever tried to erect such a tree outside a house like Larklight, which floats about in an eccentric orbit far beyond the Moon. Despite the new Trevithick generator which Mother and Father had lately installed, gravity was still decidedly patchy in the outer reaches of the dear old place, and those baubles, bells and candles with which Myrtle and I were endeavouring to bedeck our tree kept coming undone and drifting off into the inky deeps of space.* It is little wonder that tempers were becoming frayed!

'Numbskull!'

* *Patchy?* I hear you ask. Surely not! Trevithick's make the finest generators that money may buy and have been providing top-quality gravity aboard aether-ships and orbital establishments since 1809. Well, this is true. Unfortunately, ever since her adventures aboard that old Yankee warship *Liberty* in September, Myrtle had been gripped by a silly notion of becoming an alchemist, and Mother had decided to humour her. They had set up a laboratory in one of the spare rooms in the spinward wing, and there, in smoked-glass goggles and a leather

'Jackanapes!'

'Knuckle-headed galoot!'

Dipping into the trunk which held the Christmas decorations, we both seized upon the same pretty chain of silver stars. 'It is mine!' I cried.

'Not so, you brute,' replied my sister. 'I saw it first!'

And thus a tug-of-war commenced, with each of us quite refusing to relinquish our end of the chain.

So angry were we, and each so intent upon gaining victory over the other, that neither of us noticed the aethership that was sailing silently towards Larklight on outspread wings, until the shadow of its space-barnacled hull fell across us. Only then did we look up.

'Why, it is Jack!' cried my sister, and let go her end of the chain in order to tidy her hair and pinch a little more colour into her cheeks. You would be amazed at how calm and

---

apron, Myrtle was learning how to perform the chemical wedding, that complicated alchemical reaction which can drive a ship through space far faster than the speed of tardy old light. Naturally, since Myrtle is a girl, and not an especially bright one, these experiments had resulted in a number of horrible smells, a deal of smoke and a couple of rather spectacular explosions. One of the latter had affected our gravity generator, and it has never been quite the same since.

dignified she looked as the good ship *Sophronia* drew alongside, with our old friend Jack Havock beaming down at her from the star deck. He could never have guessed that a few moments before she had been bellowing at her innocent younger brother (i.e. me) in a manner that would have made a fish-wife blush!

Meanwhile, I had been taken all aback at the sudden way Myrtle let go her end of the starry chain and, still tugging upon my end, I went hurtling backwards off the balcony and seemed set to follow so many of our decorations out into the endless wastes of the interplanetary aether.

I daresay I should have drifted halfway to the Moon had not Mr Munkulus, the *Sophronia*'s mate, seen my predicament and thrown me a line. 'There now, young Master Art,' he cautioned, reeling me in through the *Sophronia*'s main hatch a minute later, 'this is no time for gymnastics and ballyhoo!'

And it would hardly have been gentlemanly of me to say, ''Tis all Myrtle's fault', would it?

The *Sophronia* was soon tied up at Larklight's mooring platform, and I greeted her crew as they made ready to disembark. I was pleased to see that they all bore heaps of brightly wrapped gifts, and that the Tentacle Twins were bearing between them a hamper from which the scents of cooked hams and game pies wafted. But better than anything was just to be there among them again, and to see the friendly way they smiled at me and clapped me on the back as they made their way ashore.

I had not seen any of them since our adventure with the Moobs at Starcross, and since then I had endured a long and dismal season spent cramming Latin, Geography and Arithmetic, for once the Christmas holiday was done I was to be making a start at Vermiform's Academy for the Sons of Space-Faring Gentlefolk, which is a minor public school on Callisto. To be quite honest, I was not much looking forward to leaving home and beginning my education, but the arrival of the *Sophronia* made me forget all my worries. School was next year; for now there would be parlour games, and sing-songs about the pianoforte, and toasted muffins, and Christmas presents, and tales of all the daring things that Jack and his crew had been up to in the wildernesses of space!

I was so happy to see them that I even managed to forgive Myrtle and bestowed a cheerful smile upon her as we gathered outside Larklight's brand-new front door. The others were all busy wishing her a Merry Christmas and teasing her and Jack about their romantic attachment, asking when the engagement was to be announced, etc., and drawing their attention to the large bunch of mistletoe which Nipper held up above their heads.

Myrtle looked somewhat put out at first, for she and Jack had had a squabble at Starcross; Jack had told her that she

was too much the lady to ever be a part of his roistering, adventuring life, and Myrtle had vowed to prove to him that she was every bit as good an aethernaut as he – which is how she came to be having lessons in Alchemy and causing stinks and explosions. But they did not have to look at each other long in the dappled shadow of that mistletoe before they seemed to forget their differences and warm to one another once again.* There was a hearty cheer when Jack kissed her, and then we all joined in a rousing chorus of 'O Come, All Ye Faithful', instead of pulling upon the bell-rope.

But when Father opened the door, he did not look pleased by our carolling. Indeed, he seemed distracted, and his spectacles sat awry, giving him a lop-sided appearance.

'Jack! Sophronias!' he exclaimed in a dreadful whisper. 'Thank Heaven you've arrived! A most vexing thing has happened! The Pudding has gone Rogue!'

Those of you who live in earthly houses, and have no experience of life as it is lived on the further frontiers of

---

* What Jack Havock sees in my sister is one of the Mysteries of Known Space. She is an absolute horror and looks like a loony fish.

Britain's empire, may never have had any difficulty with your Christmas puddings. To you, no doubt, it is a simple matter. Your cook makes you a pudding on 'Stir-up Sunday'; it is left to mature upon a pantry shelf, and on Christmas Day it is delivered to your table piping hot, doused in blazing brandy, with a sprig of holly on the top and a sixpenny-bit in the middle.

Here in space, however, there is an added complication. For all manner of strange beasts haunt these heavenly oceans, and one of them is the dread Pudding Worm. The larva of this charmless insect looks almost exactly like a raisin, and so it oft goes unnoticed as it creeps into our kitchens and burrows its furtive way into a Christmas pud. Once inside, it starts to gorge itself, growing and growing in the heart of the pudding until there is no pudding left, only

fig. 1   *fig. 2*   *fig. 3*

LIFE CYCLE OF THE PUDDING WORM

the worm, a noisome thing in pudding shape. Its antennae look uncannily like a sprig of holly, its eyes glint like the edges of silver sixpennies and within its fat and unctuous body lurk a thousand more raisin-grubs, all itching to sneak out and ruin other puds!*

Such, sad to relate, was the fate that had befallen our pudding at Larklight that year! Only about a month before, Myrtle and I had helped Mother to stir it up, laughing and chatting in a most carefree manner as we cast figs and dates and orange peel into the mixture, and never noticing that worm in raisin's clothing which must have inched its way up the leg of the kitchen table and secreted itself among the other ingredients. But while we were outside decorating the tree that afternoon, Mother had gone down to check once more that our larder was fully stocked in readiness for the arrival of our guests and had happened to peek beneath the pudding cloth. Then, snarling horribly, the vile bug had leapt from its bowl, knocked her to the floor and made off into Larklight's labyrinth of air ducts!

* In seasons when no Christmas puddings are available, the Pudding Worm contents itself by eating up puddings of other sorts – plum duff, spotted dog, jam roly-poly; no pud is safe from this voracious pest. Not only that, but it will snack on cakes and preserves too, if the opportunity arises.

Mother met us in the entrance hall, carrying the patent flame-gun which Father had purchased a few years previously for clearing Nattering Space Moss from the gutterings. Because she is a Superior Being and four-and-a-half-thousand-million years old, she was not too much affected by her nasty encounter with the pudding, and she looked very grim and beautiful with her long hair tied back and smudges of flour upon her face and clothes.

'Oh Sophronias,' she said. 'How pleased I am to see you! But I fear we cannot offer you much hospitality until this pudding is captured and destroyed. From the glimpse I had of it I should say that it is almost ready to reproduce, and if that happens, then the hatchling maggots may infest all our mince pies and fruit cakes too . . .'

The Sophronias, like the devil-may-care space dogs they

are, rose splendidly to the occasion. They at once set down their gifts and hamper, and armed themselves with walking sticks and umbrellas from the hallstand, while Jack drew one of his revolving pistols. No one spoke, as we were all awaiting Mother's orders – but we did not need them, for in that silence we plainly heard the pseudo-pudding go trundling above our heads through one of the air ducts which crosses the hall ceiling!

'The game's afoot!' cried Mother.

'It's making for the Chinese drawing room!' exclaimed Father, brandishing a golf club.*

We ran in a crowd along the hall, through a few panelled passageways and into the room he had spoken of, which has

* It was a mashie niblick, very useful for driving out of the rough and fending off monsters.

been very tastefully redecorated and is a perfect sea of lacquered cabinets and willow-patterned wallpaper, in which the Emperor of China himself might feel at home. Alas, the Pudding Worm seemed at home there too; a large, pudding-shaped hole in the wire-mesh cover of a ventilator showed where it had burst out, seeking a place to cocoon itself and spawn its vile maggots!

'Oh, this would never have happened if we lived in Berkshire or Surrey,' said Myrtle in a complaining undertone.

'Hush!' warned Mr Grindle, the *Sophronia*'s goblin-like master gunner, and by means of pantomime conveyed to us that the pudding was lurking behind a charming screen in the farthest corner of the room. Gripping one of Father's walking sticks like a broadsword, he crept over to the screen and kicked it aside with his space boot. At once the pudding rolled out, flailing its holly at Grindle's shins. He struck at it with the stick, but managed only a glancing blow as the foul pud came trundling across the carpet towards the rest of us, who were ranged between it and the door.

We went down like so many skittles as it crashed into us, and by the time we had picked ourselves up it was clear out of the door and down the passage. A moment later we all heard the *bomp-bomp-bomp* of its fat body rolling down the back stairs.

'Quickly!' urged Mother. 'It is trying to find its way to the kitchens again!'

'Returning to its ancestral breeding ground to spawn, eh?' cried Father.

Myrtle fainted. (Whether it was because of the emergency or because Father had just used the word 'spawn' in mixed company, I could not tell.) Jack hung back to tend to her. The rest of us hared off after the puddingey foe, and I am pleased to say that I had the presence of mind to snatch a decanter of Father's best brandy from the drinks cabinet as I passed, for I knew that it was quite the best weapon against a foe of that sort.

Down the stairs and into the kitchen we went thundering. There we found a trail of crumbs and shattered dishes and a gaggle of startled auto-servants, all bearing mute testimony to the pudding's passage.

The larder door stood ajar. Cautiously, Mother approached it. I went with her, and the others spread out behind us, determined that our quarry should not escape a second time.

'The door, Art, if you please,' Mother breathed.

I slipped in front of her and threw the door wide open. From inside the larder came a horrid shriek. There the pudding crouched at bay. Yellowish blood oozing from the wound that Grindle had inflicted dribbled down its sides like custard. Its holly rattled and upon its flanks seethed whole legions of raisin-maggots!

'Brandy!' cried Mother.

I took her meaning and dashed the contents of the decanter over the brute, leaping back just in time as she depressed the triggers of the flame-gun.

A sheet of blue fire enveloped the evil pudding. It hissed and screeched as its holly blackened and its raisins popped like roasting chestnuts. It lunged towards the door, and for a moment I feared that it would roll past us again and set the whole kitchen ablaze. But in a second more the fire had done its work, and only a heap of black and stinking ashes lay a-smouldering upon the flagstones.

'Jolly well done, Art!' said Mother, and the others gathered around us to look into the smoke-filled larder and add their own words of congratulation. Of course, it felt very fine to have their praise, but even so, I did not feel as bucked as you might think. After all, destroying the pseudo-pudding had not brought our own pudding back to us, and what sort of Christmas could we look forward to without a Christmas pud?

I think the others felt just as subdued as we set the auto-servants to clear up the mess and climbed together back up the stairs, where Jack and Myrtle were awaiting us. But Mother, wiping the soot from her face, said, 'A nice cup of tea is what we all need.' And since she is old enough and wise enough to know almost everything, I decided that she was probably right.

No sooner had we disposed ourselves on the chairs and sofas of the green drawing room and begun to exchange the words of welcome and festive good cheer that the Pudding Worm had so rudely delayed, than another surprise interrupted us. Our auto-butler, Raleigh, came stumping in to announce, 'Sir, madam, there is a large warship approaching from the direction of the Moon and her captain is signalling for permission to dock. Shall I tell him that we are not at home?'

Chapter Two

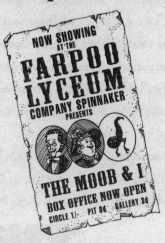

IN WHICH SIR RICHARD BURTON REVEALS A SECRET, AND
THE CHIEF NATURAL PHILOSOPHER PUTS HIS FOOT IN IT.

We all hastened, cups of tea in our hands,* into a
neighbouring room, whose picture windows
looked out over the mooring platform. There,
beyond the masts and rigging of the *Sophronia*, we beheld a
more modern ship making her approach to Larklight, and a

* Or pincers, tentacles, etc.

jolly fierce and warlike spectacle she presented. Jack had his telescope to his eye in a twinkling, and naturally the rest of us clamoured at him to tell us what he saw.

'Hold fast!' he said. 'Don't jostle! I cannot make out her name . . . Oh, yes, I can. She is HMS *Actaeon*. One of the Navy's new "Viper" class of space gunboats. I wonder what brings her out here? Oh, there are some people up there on her star deck . . .'

We could all see the group he meant, clustered about a sailor with an alchemical dark-lantern who was signalling 'Permission to dock' in brilliant flashes. But although we

could tell that several of them were civilians, and one a lady, only Jack could see them clearly enough to make out their features. We heard him gasp, and saw him lower his telescope with an expression on his face that was part joy, part shock and part some other emotion which I could not guess.

'It is Sir Richard Burton and Ulla!' he declared.

Now, if you have been following these adventures of mine, you may be able to guess why we were all so surprised by this intelligence. It was only three months since we watched Sir Richard and his Martian wife shipped off to England in tubs of potting compost, having been turned into Venusian Changeling Trees by a spore devised by that black-hearted villain Sir Launcelot Sprigg. Professor Ferny, the director of Kew Gardens, had promised us that he would be able to effect a cure and had sent us several letters assuring us that our friends were doing well. But we had not dared to hope that we would see them restored to their old human forms quite so swiftly. We were delighted to watch them walk down the *Actaeon*'s gangplank and stand upon the mooring platform, looking for all the world their old selves.

Yet there was something more than mere delight in Jack Havock's face. His parents and his brother had been transformed into trees when the wild Changeling Trees of Venus flowered, wiping out the British colonies there, while he was but a babe. I knew what he was thinking as he stared down at Sir Richard and Mrs Burton.

Would Professor Ferny's cure be able to restore Jack's family as well? And how quickly could he reach Venus to try it out?

We hurried down to meet our new guests, and there was much pleasant chatter in the hall as the auto-servants helped them off with their hats and space capes and galoshes. Nor were Sir Richard and Ulla the only agreeable surprise the *Actaeon* had delivered, for along with them came a cheerful, roundish officer named Captain Moonfield, who had helped Myrtle and the Burtons to alert London to the schemings of the white spiders that spring, and with whom we were all jolly glad to renew our acquaintance. And they brought good wishes and Christmas cards from Mr and Mrs Spinnaker, who were spending the season at their new home on Starcross, along with their infant children, Modesty and Decorum, and their dear friend the Moob, with whom they had enjoyed a triumphant reception in the music halls of Farpoo and London.

But they also brought with them a fellow I didn't know: a meek, chinless, dusty-looking cove in a black frock coat, who hugged a large leather document case against his chest and eyed Jack and his crew with some unease. And although I know one should not judge a chap by his outward appearance, I looked at this cove and thought, *He is trouble.*

And what happened later would prove me right, as you shall see.

Anyway, amid much gay talk and merry laughter we made our way through into the drawing room, where Mother clapped her hands and called for more tea, more cakes and extra chairs. But all the time Jack kept his eyes upon Sir Richard and Mrs Burton, noting how well they looked, and how unlike trees, despite a certain green-ness that still haunted their complexions and a faint leafiness about their hair and Sir Richard's beard. And as soon as he had a chance, he said, 'How did he manage it? How did Ferny cure you?'

'Ah,' said Sir Richard. 'It wasn't entirely Ferny's doing.

Rather a long story actually –'

'And not one that should be told in front of just *anybody*,' said the dusty-looking cove, with a meaningful glance at the Sophronias.

'Nonsense, Doctor Blears,' said Sir Richard. 'Jack Havock and his crew are trusted agents of the British Crown. They have saved our bacon twice this year, and I don't doubt that they shall soon do so again! And Jack, of all people, deserves to know the *truth*.'

'I will not have it!' said this Dr Blears. 'I will not have state secrets revealed to these . . . these *persons*. Remember yourself, Sir Richard. You brought me to this place so that we might consult Mr Mum—, about *these*.' And he tapped the leather document case, which he was still holding in front of him like a shield.

'But, Doctor Blears,' said Father, jumping up from his seat, 'unless I mistake your name, you are the Government's Chief of Natural Philosophy. I am not sure why so eminent a person should wish to consult me –'

'What truth?' asked Jack, also standing. 'What secrets?' He glanced at Father and said, 'I'm sorry, Mr Mumby, but if a cure has been found for those spores, I must know about it.'

'Of course, my dear boy,' said Father, somewhat startled by Jack's tone. He had met Jack only as Myrtle's suitor and had never yet seen the grim, dangerous Jack Havock who had fought space battles and stood alone against the whole British Navy until Sir Richard persuaded him to change sides.

Sir Richard had, of course, and he looked warily at the boy and said, 'It's exceeding complicated, Jack.'

'My ma and pa and my brother have been trees on Venus these past twelve years,' said Jack, 'and now it seems there's a cure for their condition. What's complicated about that? All I ask is, what might that cure be and where do I get a hold of it?'

'I warn you, Sir Richard,' said Dr Blears, 'not a word to this space mongrel.'

'Jack is right,' said Mrs Burton. 'If you will not tell him, Richard, then I shall.'

'Sir Richard, control your wife!' demanded Dr Blears.

Sir Richard stared at him a moment, then turned to Jack.

'When Professor Ferny took us back to his laboratory at Kew,' Sir Richard said, 'he sent at once to the Royal Xenological Institute, asking for all their files about the

Changeling Trees. At first they would show him almost nothing, but luckily I have powerful friends, and Ferny persuaded them to make representations to the Institute. Eventually, their efforts bore fruit. Not only does the RXI have some surprisingly detailed files on the trees, they also have a serum which will reverse the effects of Changeling spores. It was devised some years ago, partly as a result of the studies they made of you when you were their guest at Russell Square. For, as you know, Jack, you have a natural immunity to the Changeling's influence.

'Professor Ferny injected the serum into our trunks, and within a few weeks we were restored. We are a little stiff in our joints, perhaps, and sometimes I find myself yearning to curl my toes down into some nice, rich loam, but in every important respect I am myself again, and Ulla is herself.'

Jack's face was a picture. I wish that you could see it, but I doubt that even the great Mr Wyatt could do justice to the mingled look of awe and dawning hope that shone in our friend's eyes.*

'A cure!' he said. 'Then why has it not been used on the Venus colonies? We must hurry there and restore Ma and Pa and Sidney and all the people of New Scunthorpe and Port Victoria –'

'Out of the question!' snapped Dr Blears. 'You see, Sir Richard? I warned you not to speak of this! If rumours get out, there shall be hell to pay. The newspapers will all be demanding serum be sent out to Venus, and it is costly stuff. A hundred guineas for a small bottle! Were we to try to restore all those unfortunates on Venus, why, it would mean an extra penny on the income tax!'

'You should tell Mr Havock the rest, Richard,' said Ulla in a warning voice which I took to mean that if he did not, she would. 'You should tell him *why* the Royal Xenological Institute knows so much about the Changeling Trees.'

Sir Richard looked quite sheepish for a moment, like a schoolboy who has been called to his headmaster's office to explain

* Of course I can, you impudent young pup!
(See right.) — D.W.

some prank. Then he said, 'Jack, the truth is, it was our Government that made those trees what they are. When Sir Joseph Banks brought the first samples back from Venus in the 1770s, the Institute quickly saw their potential. At that stage the Changeling spores had no effect on Earth creatures, so they sent their best xeno-botanists out to Venus to tinker with them. They hoped to breed a tree which would transform human beings. They planned to use it as a weapon against the rebels in America.

'But, as so often happens when we attempt to improve upon Nature, something went awry. The new trees which they had bred got out into the wild somehow, and the result was the Tree Sickness of 1839, in which your parents and so many others were changed.'

Jack looked from Sir Richard's face to that of Dr Blears. 'Is this true?' he demanded.

'It is wild speculation!' retorted that gentleman, who seemed to be trying to conceal his entire person behind that leather case he carried.

'It is outrageous, sir!' declared Father.

'What criminal folly!' cried Mother. 'I remember being quite astonished at the speed with which those trees adapted to work on human beings, but I did not think any sentient creature could be vicious and wicked enough to deliberately have engineered such a development!'

'My dear madam!' said Dr Blears. 'It is natural that a mere woman cannot understand such matters. But I assure you, if you found your home and children threatened by white spiders, or Martian renegades, or the armies of the Tsar, you would soon sing a different tune. "Why does the Government not protect us?" you would cry. "Has it not a duty to investigate every new discovery and see if it may be used as a weapon to defend our homes and our possessions on the other worlds?" Yes, madam; we *do* have such a duty, and if sometimes it goes wrong and results in a few unimportant farmers and fishermen being converted into shrubs, then that is a price that must be paid!'

Having concluded this great speech, the gentleman retreated again behind his document case, like a tortoise into his shell. Jack was looking daggers at him. I believe we all were. I had never dreamed that such unsporting acts were carried out in the name of Britain and her empire, and I had a good mind just then to cancel my subscription to the *Boy's Own Journal* and set up as some sort of anarchist!

And if that was how I felt, you may imagine the emotions which were seething within Jack Havock's bosom.

He had been a sort of anarchist to start with, you may recall, sworn to oppose the might of Britain, and it had only been his encounter with a greater threat in the form of the horrid First Ones which made him join forces with our Government. To discover now that it was that very Government which had orphaned him and turned his family into a small copse or spinney must have been most upsetting.

I saw Myrtle reach out to try to comfort him, but he shoved her away. He was glaring so angrily at Dr Blears that I thought he might at any moment draw out a pistol or stiletto and do that unfortunate gent to death. But at last he collected himself and said in a small, tight voice, 'We are leaving. All aboard that's coming aboard.'

'Now, Jack,' said Sir Richard, trying to stop him as he strode towards the door. 'Be sensible! I shall speak with my friends in Parliament and you may be sure –'

'I am sure of nothing!' said Jack. 'Only this: never again shall I work for you or your country. And somehow I shall get hold of that serum and save those poor folk on Venus who your Doctor Blears thinks so unimportant. And I reckon a lot of them will be hearty men, and maybe they'll want a word with him about how come they've been trees these past twelve years, and *then* we shall see some fun!'

He reached the doorway and turned, hesitating for a moment as his gaze swept past the cringing Blears to fall upon Mother, Father and myself. 'I'm sorry for breaking up your Christmas after you've been so kind, all of you,' he said. 'But I cannot stay. You see that, don't you? I cannot stay.' He looked at Myrtle, and reached out his hand. 'Myrtle,' he said, 'come with me. You truly wish to be an alchemist one day? Then come with me; you can help Ssil in the wedding chamber and learn all that she knows.'

'Jack, I can't!' said Myrtle in a horror-struck whisper. 'You know I can't!'

For a moment more he lingered there, one hand stretched out to her, his face darkening a little with anger.

Then he turned and was gone, striding back to his ship, while his crew hurried after him, some pausing to glare at Dr Blears or wave regretfully at us.

'Happy Christmas!' said Nipper hopelessly, squeezing me gently in his pincers before he left.

'Jack!' cried Myrtle tearfully. 'Oh, make him come back!'

'Captain Moonfield,' ordered Dr Blears, 'that ragged pirate ship is not to leave this house!' (He wanted Jack back too, you see, though not at all for the same reasons as Myrtle.) 'You heard that boy!' he snapped. 'He's a radical! A dangerous revolutionary! Get aboard your ship and stop him! Capture him or blast him from the skies!'

But Captain Moonfield, to his great credit, merely drew himself to attention and said, 'I am sorry, sir, but I can take no such action without written orders from the Admiralty.'

Mother, meanwhile, was hurrying towards the door, dragging Father with her. 'Come, Edward,' I heard her say. 'We cannot let them go off like this . . .'

But Dr Blears barred their way. 'Mr Mumby, I did not come here to waste my time with pirates and their friends. I came to consult you on a matter of some importance, and unless you wish to land yourself in as much trouble as Captain Moonfield here, you will attend to it, sir!'

His long, pale fingers had been busy with the buckles of his document case, and as he stepped in front of my parents he flourished in their faces a photograph. It was not a very good one, for it was all black, except for a pale grey stain in the middle.

Father stared at it, quite perplexed. 'But, my dear sir,' he said, 'what on earth is it intended to show?'

Mother, on the other hand, seemed quite astonished. She forgot all about following Jack Havock and his crew, and stood peering at the photograph. 'Good Heavens!' I heard her whisper.

And outside, the sound of the *Sophronia*'s engines rose in mournful song, and the golden light of her alchemical backwash flickered through a skylight and touched all our faces for a moment as she soared away from Larklight.

Chapter Three

WHEREIN WE LEARN OF A STRANGE PHENOMENON, AND
FATHER HEARS SAD TIDINGS CONCERNING AN OLD
ACQUAINTANCE.

'Oh, Jack!' whispered Myrtle, running to a window
and contorting herself into a most unlikely shape
as she craned to watch the distant light that was
the *Sophronia* dwindle to a pin-point among the other stars,
and then fade altogether. What heart would not be moved
to pity by her grief?

Well, Dr Blears's for one. He was no more concerned about Myrtle than about all those poor colonists turned to trees on Venus.

'Mr Mumby,' he said, 'this photograph was taken by the Astronomer Royal from his observatory on Io a month ago. It has puzzled and confounded all the learned gentlemen who have yet seen it. But when Sir Richard recovered from his sickness he assured me that if we were to come to Larklight and show it to you, you would be able to offer an explanation. Is that so, or have I wasted my time and the tax-payers' money in travelling out to this remote spot?'

'I, ah, do not know what to say,' replied Father. 'Astronomy is not my field, sir. Not my field at all.'

'Indeed, you are mistaken, Blears,' said Sir Richard. 'It was not *Mr* Mumby I told you to consult, but his good lady wife.'

Dr Blears turned to stare at my mother, looking as if he suspected himself the victim of some foolish joke. 'What can a *woman* know of Astronomy, or any other science?' he said.

'More than you might imagine,' replied Mother sweetly and took the photograph from him. 'Pray be seated, sir, and tell me all that you know of this.'

Dr Blears remained standing, watching suspiciously as Mother carried the photograph into the light of an oil lamp which stood upon a nearby table. He said, 'That is an image of the outermost regions of our solar system. The circular smudge near the bottom left-hand corner is Georgium Sidus, which some vulgar people call nowadays Uranus. But that is of no concern to us. What we are interested in is the curious cloud or smear at the centre of the image.'

'A mark upon the plate, perhaps?' asked Mother, looking closely at it. 'Or a piece of dust upon the lens of the Astronomer Royal's telescope?'

Dr Blears shook his head and reached once more into his document case. 'After that first image was made, the observatory's staff took all their instruments apart and cleaned them thoroughly with Morrison's refractor polish. Then more photographs were made, each with the same result. Observe.'

He laid three more photographs beside the first. In all of them the stain showed clear.

'But they are not quite the same,' said Mother. 'In each, the stain is slightly larger.'

'So it is growing!' said Father.

'Either that,' said Sir Richard, 'or . . .'

He did not need to complete his sentence. Mother already understood. 'There is some vast object out there in the gulf which separates our solar system from the other stars,' she said. 'And it is moving closer!'

This is never the sort of thing one likes to hear. Suddenly, despite the fire which burned so merrily in the grate, the room seemed cold, and Myrtle, Father and myself drew a little closer together for comfort.

Mother took up one of Father's magnifying lenses and looked through it at the photograph. I had seldom seen Mother baffled, but when she looked up again there was a look of frank bewilderment upon her face.

'I am sorry, gentlemen, but I cannot say what it might be. I believe my knowledge of everything within the realms of the Sun is sound enough, but this is something else – something from another place entirely.'

'I see,' said Dr Blears, gathering up his pictures and

glancing towards Sir Richard with a look that seemed to say, 'I *told* you a woman would be no help in this.'

'But may I ask,' said Mother suddenly, 'what led the Astronomer Royal to turn his telescope upon Georgium Sidus in the first place?'

'Oh, that,' replied Dr B., somewhat dismissively. 'Some foolish missionary has gone missing out there. A garbled distress message from his ship, the *New Jerusalem*, was picked up by the aetheric telegraph office at the Jupiter station. There was a report that an alchemical flare had been sighted in the portion of space where Georgium Sidus roams, and so the Io Observatory was requested to take a look at the place. No other flare has been seen, however.'

'Great Heavens!' declared Father, startling us all. 'Did you say the *New Jerusalem*? But that is my old friend Cruet's vessel! The Reverend Shipton Cruet, who was up at Oxford with me – I have spoken of him often, Emily. He went on to study Alchemy, before taking Holy Orders . . .'

'I believe Cruet *was* the unfortunate gentleman's name,' said Sir Richard.

'But I thought Shipton had a parish down in Cornwall!'

'I gather he gave that up,' said Sir Richard. 'According to the reports, he set out for Georgium Sidus more than a year ago, saying that the Lord had spoken to him in a dream and was calling him to spread the gospel upon that lonely planet. Alas, he was never heard from again, except for the distress message a few months ago. The only words the Jupiter station was able to pick up were: "*Great danger . . . imperative that –*". Then nothing.'

'Oh, poor Shipton!' said Father.

'It was an ill-advised venture,' declared Dr Blears in a self-satisfied way which made me wish to punch him on the nose.

'It is his little daughter I feel sorry for,' said Ulla. 'She is no older than Art. It was hardly fair of Reverend Cruet to carry her with him into such wild and perilous portions of the aether.'

'Poor Shipton's wife passed away some years ago,' said Father. 'He had no other relations. Perhaps he could not bear to be parted from the child. Oh, I wonder what befell them out there?'

'I expect they were eaten by

monsters, or savages, or fell victim to some hideous alien disease,' said Myrtle, who is always ready to rally round with words of comfort. 'We must pray that their faith in GOD gave them strength, and that the end came quickly.'

'Well, it cannot have come *that* quickly,' I said, 'or they would never have had time to send out a distress message and light a flare.'

'I cannot imagine who he thought would go to their aid, so far outside the bounds of civilised space,' observed Dr Blears.

' "*Great danger . . . imperative that —*" ' said Mother, rehearsing the words of Reverend Shipton's final message to herself. 'Those do not sound to me like phrases from a distress call. Sir Richard, has it occurred to you that perhaps Reverend Cruet was not asking for help, but sending us a warning?'

'Great Scott!' said Captain Moonfield. 'You mean to say, ma'am, that there may be a connection between this space-cloud and the disappearance of the missionary gent?'

'It could be,' Mother mused. 'It could be that his message was intended to warn us of some peril which is fast approaching us across the interstellar gulf. Perhaps its nature has already become apparent upon Georgium Sidus.'

'Ridiculous!' said Dr Blears nervously.

'I know only this,' said Mother, wheeling round to stare at him. 'Thanks to you, sir, and the Pudding Worm, our Christmas here at Larklight has been quite spoiled. So why should we sit about moping when we might be up and doing? If we proceed swiftly to Georgium Sidus to take a proper look at this space-cloud, we may still be home in time for Christmas Day. And we can pick up another pudding along the way, and perhaps rescue Reverend Cruet and his daughter and bring them home to share it with us!'

'Now, steady on!' warned Captain Moonfield. 'I'm as keen to rescue the padre and his girl as anyone, and no one likes Christmas Pudding better than me, but it would take the *Actaeon* months to reach Georgium Sidus. We would be lucky to be home in time for *next* Christmas!'

Mother looked thoughtful. 'Your ship seemed well built,' she observed.

'None better, ma'am. The finest in the fleet. But she cannot zip about the heavens in the way you seem to think.'

'Dear Captain Moonfield!' said Mother. 'Once upon a time I shared with a certain gentleman a few little alchemical recipes of mine which enabled him to change the course of England's history in all manner of ways. I often wonder whether I was right to do so – especially when I hear of the nefarious things your Government has been getting up to.' (Here she paused to shoot Dr Blears a look of such icy disapproval that he hid his face again behind that case of his.) 'But as it is Christmas, and an old friend is in danger, and as that cloud is so very unsettling, I think it may be time to pass on a few more of my secrets. With a little help from me, your chief alchemist should be able to get us to Georgium Sidus and back quite briskly.'

'What is the lady saying?' asked Dr Blears, turning for help to Sir Richard. 'Can she be quite right in the head?'

But Captain Moonfield, who had more faith in Mother, said at once, 'Topping! You're a good sport, Mrs Mumby! I'll go and tell Mr McMurdo you'll be coming aboard!' And he put on his hat and hurried out before Dr Blears could remind him that he would need written orders from the Admiralty before embarking upon a round trip to Georgium Sidus.

'What about me, Mother?' I cried excitedly. 'May I come too?'

'Certainly not, Art,' she said. 'You must stay here with Myrtle and your father.'

'But I'm coming with you, dearest!' protested Father. 'I absolutely insist upon it! Shipton Cruet is my oldest friend,

remember – and anyway, I should love to take a squint at the unknown flora and fauna of Georgian space.'

'And I shall come too!' said Myrtle firmly, much to our surprise. 'I do not intend to be left here all alone like some old maid. I shall show Mr Jack Havock that I am quite as daring and adventurous as he, even though I have somewhat more regard for the conventions of society.'

And so it was, dear reader, that just when we had prepared ourselves for a week of over-eating, parlour games and festive indolence, we found ourselves embarking instead upon a space gunboat bound for the Unknown Perils of an Uncharted Sphere!

Myrtle may say what she likes about our life at Larklight, but it is seldom dull.

Chapter Four

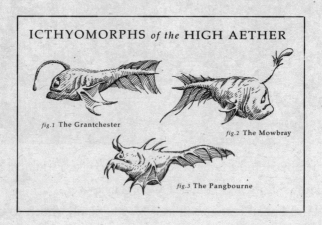

ICTHYOMORPHS *of the* HIGH AETHER

fig.1 The Grantchester

fig.2 The Mowbray

fig.3 The Pangbourne

A DIGRESSION, WHEREIN JACK HAVOCK PASSES A TROUBLED
HOUR ABOARD HIS BRIG, *SOPHRONIA*, AND IS SET UPON THE
RIGHT PATH BY A TRUE FRIEND.

And now I think I must leave off telling you of my
own adventures for a while, because I am sure
you're all agog to learn where Jack Havock had
taken off for, and what had become of him since he
stormed out of Larklight in such a fearful bate.

I am always a bit suspicious of books written in the

Third Person; that is to say, the ones where the author is forever telling us, 'Then Buggins did such-and-such a thing' or 'It seemed to Muggins that . . .' or 'Fuggins felt as if . . .', etc. 'How do *you* know what they did or felt?' is what I always want to ask. But I assure you that what follows is based only on what I heard later from the Sophronias who were there, and it is just as true as everything else in this book.

(Nipper helped me with the soppy bits.)

Jack Havock had no idea where he was bound when he first stormed back aboard the *Sophronia* and shouted to Ssilissa to start the engines. 'What course, Jack?' she asked, but he replied rudely, 'Any course you care for. Just away from here!'

And so, flapping her aether-wings and spewing alchemical fire from all her exhaust-trumpets, the *Sophronia* soared up, up, up until she was high above the Plane of the Ecliptic, where the aether is clear and clean and the passing icthyomorphs wear mild and thoughtful expressions, like country vicars.

'Now what?' asked Mr Munkulus, while the others flew

about fixing small leaks and attending to all the bits of the old ship which had been damaged, spoiled or lost during her breakneck journey.

But Jack gave no reply and issued no orders. He just went up on to the star deck and sat in the thin, chill aether there and watched the unchanging stars. He had never felt so lone and lorn, not even when he was a boy-prisoner in the halls of the RXI. He wanted to set course for Venus and fly straight to his family, but he did not want to go there without the serum that would cure them, and how could he get hold of that? Even in the depths of his anger he still knew that he couldn't assault London and besiege the Institute until they handed the potion over. Against the might of Britain, what would he and his alien crew and their old aether-ship really do? 'How could I have been so stupid?' he asked himself. 'How could I let myself get

snared into working for that Empire of Lies?'

(And while you may think him a jolly poor sport for being so beastly about our empire, you must admit that he had a point: it *had* been dashed rotten of us to turn his family into trees and not let on.)

Meanwhile, below decks, his loyal crew was beginning to fear for him, for they knew that the human form is not designed to breathe the thin aether of those lofty seas for long. And they were wondering, too, what they might do to make him feel a bit more chipper. Now and again Mr Grindle would say, 'Go on, Munkulus, climb up and have a talk with him.' And Mr M. would say, 'Can't you see he wants to be left alone a while?' And then after a bit Mr M. would say, 'Go on, Nipper, you go above and see if you can bring him out of his brown study.' And Nipper would cry, 'But I don't know what to say!' And the Tentacle Twins would trill and twitter and blush mournful shades of lilac and pale blue, and even the tootlings of the hoverhogs seemed to take on a melancholy note.

At last Ssilissa, who had been very quiet and very thoughtful ever since Jack bellowed at her, said, 'Oh, you are all sssuch cowards! Let *me* talk to him!' And she ran to the companion ladder and up on to the star deck and went to where Jack stood all alone, his back to her, gazing out upon the silences of space.

'Jack, we are all wondering what we are to do,' she told him.

'And I'm wondering the very same thing, Ssil,' he agreed. 'I'm wondering if the best thing is not to just turn pirate again and thump that old empire of theirs until they howl. And no more gentleness this time, neither. No more boarding ships and scaring the crew until they give us what we need. From now on we'll kill 'em all and take it. There'll be no quarter given nor asked for. We'll smash their traders and merchantmen out of the aether, and when they send warships after us we'll give them broadside for broadside till they knock us down!'

Ssil said nothing at all to that. She had already noted how Jack had hauled down the British ensign which once flew at the *Sophronia*'s jack mast and had raised his old flag in its place: the three-eyed skull and crossed white bones on a field of black.

'But what of Myrtle?' she said at last. 'Will you ask her to love a pirate and grieve for you when the Government hunt you down at last?'

'She may love whom she pleases,' said Jack. 'Did you not see? I gave her the choice to come with us and she chose to stay. She chose to remain with her father, who is a fellow of the Royal Xenological Institute, and her mother, who has been meddling in the affairs of others since the worlds began and gave the British the means to conquer them all in the first place. Very well. Myrtle has chosen. Let her stay with them. She will not care that I am a pirate again. No one will. No one cares for me at all.'

'Oh, that is not true, Jack!' said Ssil, almost in tears, for had she not loved him very dearly since their earliest acquaintance? '*We* all care about you and would follow you anywhere, into whatever danger!'

Jack hung his head. Her words had touched him, and he knew that he had been unjust in saying what he had. He knew his crew loved him, and knew that he was lucky to have them. And he looked at Ssil standing there, lit by the light of the distant stars, and he began to think that she really was very pretty, as blue lizards go, with her black-in-black eyes a-swim with tears and her head-spines stirring gently in the tides of that high place. And he said gruffly, 'Oh Ssil', and drew her to him, and kissed her.*

For just a moment Ssil returned Jack's kiss. Then she broke free and turned away, and when he tried to come after her she flicked her tail at him, which made him keep his distance and also served as a reminder of just how un-alike they were: he an earthly boy, she a lizard hatched from an unknown egg found embedded in the ice of a far-wandering comet.

* Nipper wrote this bit: don't blame me. If you are a red-blooded British boy you will be squirming with embarrassment by now and may wish to skip to the bottom of page forty-nine at once: I'm sure you'll pick the story up.

'No, Jack!' she said. 'I love you, but it cannot be. You are an Earthlet, and I do not know what I am, or in what distant part of space or remote era of antiquity my race was born. Myrtle Mumby is the one for you. I knew it the first day she came aboard the *Sophronia*. Go back to Larklight, Jack, and make things straight with her. I will steer any course you want, and fight at your side against the whole British Navy if you ask it, but first you must see Myrtle once more. You must not leave her with the memory of your anger.'

She looked lovelier than ever to Jack as she said that, but he knew that she was right. 'Very well,' he said. And he took her hand and squeezed it, and they went back inside together, almost stepping on the eye-stalks of Nipper, who had been watching all this through the half-open hatch.

'Ssil is setting us a course back to Larklight,' he said. 'The rest of you, clear for action. For if HMS *Actaeon* is still there, I mean to take, sink or burn her.'

Now, if this were an Italian opera, that is exactly what would have happened. I mean, the *Sophronia* would have arrived back at Larklight just as we were all setting out aboard the *Actaeon*, and Jack would have blasted her to matchwood, never guessing that Myrtle and yours truly were on board. (Not only that, but Myrtle would have got to sing a tragic aria before she expired – it is almost too horrible to contemplate.)

Luckily for us this is no opera but a True Story, and true stories are never quite as neat as operas. By the time the *Sophronia* came swooping back down to Larklight's mooring platform the *Actaeon* was gone. At first Jack was relieved, thinking that at least he would be able to pour forth his spiritual anguish to Myrtle without having to engage in a messy and inconvenient exchange of cannon fire first. But when he knocked upon the front door, old Raleigh opened it only to tell him that the Mumbys were not at home. And when he pushed past the auto-butler and walked in, crying 'Myrtle!', he found that the house was empty.

But on the hallstand, Mother – unknown to Myrtle or Father or me – had left a little pile of gift-wrapped presents, one for every member of the *Sophronia*'s crew. And propped against them was a note:

Gone to
Georgium Sidus
Back Soon!

Chapter Five

Of Our Voyage to King George's Star and What We
Found There.

If anyone else had written such a note, it would have
been the merest whimsy. Every aethernaut knows that
even at alchemical speeds it would take weeks to reach
Georgian space. But Mother is not one to let such trifling
matters as the Laws of Nature stop her from doing what
she pleases, and whichever combinations of elements she
caused Chief Alchemist McMurdo to burn in the *Actaeon*'s

great alembic worked like an absolute dream. We fairly roared along the Golden Roads, and I believe we touched speeds at which no earthly ship has ever travelled.

Captain Moonfield's crew were very obliging and showed us all over their vessel. I must say, she seemed to me to be a cut above the dear old *Sophronia*. There were no space-damp planks or rusty cannon upon her ordered, whitewashed gun decks, and certainly none of the washing lines and other clutter which make the *Sophronia* look so like a flying curiosity shop. Aboard the *Actaeon* there was a place for everything, and everything was in its place, since the ship was fitted with a gravity generator, which stopped untethered items drifting about in mid-air the way they do aboard the *Sophronia*. The aethernauts in their tarred straw hats and blue uniforms went about their duties as efficiently as automata, but not without a little friendly joshing and the whistling of merry space shanties, for Captain Moonfield ran a happy ship.

Up on the bridge, which was a perfect Aladdin's cave of gleaming brasswork and fitted with all the latest instruments, Captain Moonfield and his officers pored over their charts, breaking off sometimes to listen to the anxious-sounding reports of Mr McMurdo, which issued from time to time from a speaking tube which ran between the bridge and the wedding chamber. 'We're gaeing too fast, Captain!' the ship's alchemist would cry in an agitated manner and a strong Scots accent. 'I dinna ken what this Missus Mumby has poot in mae alembic, but the engines willnae take the strain!' And then we would hear Mother's voice say blithely, 'Courage, Mr McMurdo; we are quite safe, I am almost sure of it.'

Reassured, I peeked round Captain Moonfield at the charts spread out upon the table, weighted down at their corners with compass dividers and other tools of astral navigation. Naturally, the charts were almost entirely blank, for Georgium Sidus swims in that portion of space where No Man Has Gone Before, and all our knowledge of it comes from the astronomers. They have told us that it is a

Mothstorm

bluish-green ocean world with a great number of moons. Beyond it, towards the edge of the Sun's domain, circles another planet: icy Hades with its great companion-moon. There our knowledge ends; there is the outermost limit of the reach of science.*

You may imagine how excited I felt and how pleased Father was at the prospect of travelling into that wilderness and seeing all the unknown forms of life which must inhabit it.

As for Myrtle, I believe she spent the entire journey in her cabin, where she sat gazing from a porthole and confiding her innermost feelings about Jack to her precious diary. But so swiftly did Mother convey us across the

* Oddly enough, one of Mr Wyatt's celebrated cover illustrations for the *Boy's Own Journal* (reprinted on page 294 of *Larklight*) shows the Sun with nine planets, the ninth being a tiny world which he has labelled 'Pluto'. The explanation seems to be that our great illustrator had been at the BEER again and added this ninth world by mistake. But strangely, our astronomers have since detected that a large asteroid or small planet does indeed orbit out in the endless darkness north of Hades. Could it be that in the haze induced by twelve pints of Rugglestone's Best, Mr Wyatt entered into a mystic communion with the forces of the Universe, which enabled him to envision this world, as yet unknown? Perhaps. But whether it be there or no, 'Pluto' is a poor sort of name for a planet and will never catch on.

54

Heavens that she had barely time to fill one volume before we had arrived. I rose from my bunk on the morning of the day after we had left Larklight and found the golden glow of Alchemy already starting to fade outside my porthole and the wild song of the engines subsiding to a harmonious warbling as the vessel slowed.

I dressed quickly, thankful for the Trevithick generators which stopped my breeches drifting up to the ceiling and my collar studs tumbling about, and ran to the bridge. There I found Mother and Father already standing with Captain Moonfield, Dr Blears and a number of the ship's officers at a large picture window. Beyond the glass the glowing caul of alchemical particles which had shrouded and shielded us upon the Golden Roads was fading away. A misshapen, lifeless moon swept past upon our starboard quarter, a shoal of aetheric icthyomorphs flitted out of our path, and there ahead of us waited a large, blue-green sphere, looking for all the world like a marble resting on a sheet of black velvet.

'Georgium Sidus!' said Father, peering at the planet through his spectacles, as though he were already trying to make out the strange flora and fauna which lived beneath its swirling clouds.

'It hasn't changed a bit!' said Mother, which drew her a sharp glance from Dr Blears.

Georgium Sidus! I cannot tell you how privileged I felt to be among the first human beings to set eyes upon that far-flung world! I gazed at it for fully twenty seconds before I started to feel bored.

The truth is, one planet is pretty much like another when you have whirled about the Solar System quite as much as I. Georgium Sidus really did present rather a bland face from where we stood in high orbit around it. No glimpse of its surface features could be seen through those thick, blue-green and ever-swirling vapours. It looked another Jupiter, a gas-world, but cool and cheerless, as if it were a place of eternal fog. What moons we could see were small, rocky and barren, and although the planet boasted a few rings, which it wore at a jaunty angle, they were not jolly rings like those of Saturn, which provide a home to aether turtles, monstrous spiders and other oddities of the type which make a planet interesting. No, these Georgian rings were made only of gas, and rather dank and miserable-looking gas at that, as if a few skeins of the planet's all-enshrouding mist had spilled out into space but lacked the nerve to go any further.

'It looks rather dull,' I complained.

'Dull to your eyes, Art, perhaps,' said Mother. 'But not all eyes are like yours. When I was living as a native of Georgium Sidus one hundred million years ago, I was able to see all sorts of colours which human beings have not even names for. I would break from the surface of the ocean and fling myself into the sky just for the pleasure of looking at those rolling mists, which are woven from so many wonderful shades of blue and lilac, violet and grey, groon and flinge and sprew.'

She spoke softly and to me alone, but I noted that Dr Blears glanced sideways at her and gave other signs that he was listening.

'It is a world of mists,' said Mother wistfully. 'It has no surface, you know; the wet gases of its sky thicken imperceptibly into the wetter ocean, and the liquid ocean thickens similarly into a solid core. It is a place of soft and ceaseless rain, and eternal mist. Not unlike Scotland.'

'And what sort of creatures live there, Emily?' asked Father, greatly interested.

'Well, when I was first there I was a vast, armoured whale,' said Mother. 'And then, later, I tried out life as a sort of mer-person. But that was long ago, and who knows what new forms may have evolved since?'

'Giant moths!' said Father excitedly.

'It is possible, I suppose, though quite unlikely. Why do you say giant moths?'

'Because I see one just there!' cried Father. 'Look!'

Others on the *Actaeon*'s bridge had seen it too by then. There was a soft ripple of exclamations as men pointed out to one another the flashing, silvery wings of the creature which was flying towards us around the curve of Georgium Sidus. Then another ripple, louder, as it passed behind one of those dwarfish moons, and we understood just how big it was.

'Great Scott! It's longer than the ship!'

'What a monster!'

'Magnificent set of antennae! I say, Mr Bradstreet, fetch me my elephant gun.'

And still the space moth kept flit-fluttering towards us, looking quite ghostly in the dim blue light of that alien world.

'Hard-a-starboard, helm,' called Captain Moonfield. 'Wouldn't do to risk a collision this far from a shipyard . . .'

I felt the deck beneath me tilt as the *Actaeon* slid gently out of the creature's path. A moment later Myrtle came up the companionway and joined us at the picture window to see what had caught everyone's attention.

'Oh, how horrible!' she exclaimed, turning pale. At home, she always lives in fear of finding moth holes in her favourite clothes, so the sight of this monstrous specimen was doubly alarming to her; it could have devoured her whole wardrobe at a single gulp. Nor had either of us forgotten the dreadful Potter Moth of the Moon, whose loathsome grubs had once so nearly eaten *us*.

I stared at the moth as it went blundering by. Despite its size, it flew in just the same frantic, aimless, dithering way as Earth moths. Reflections of the *Actaeon*'s running lights glimmered in the great greenhouses of its compound eyes, while antennae which looked like feathers torn from the wings of an angel whisked and batted at the aether ahead of it. And – was I dreaming it? – *tiny, almost human figures were running about upon that vast, furry back, between the ever-beating wings!*

I heard Mother exclaim and knew I was not dreaming,

for she had seen them too! 'What are those things?' she whispered. 'They are not of *my* shaping . . .'

'Gracious!' exclaimed Father. 'It is turning towards us again! Do you think our lights have attracted it?'

'Douse all lights!' shouted Captain Moonfield, and as sailors on the bridge hurried to turn out the lamps above the helm and chart table I heard the order being relayed along the lower decks, like a roll of echoes. Now we all looked like ghosts, illumined only by the bluish radiance of Georgium Sidus which spilled through the windows and stole all the colour from our clothes and faces.

And still the moth came on!

'The brute's trying to ram us!' declared Dr Blears, and for once I agreed with him.

'There are more of them!' shouted Sir Richard. 'Look! There in the rings!'

He was right. The fogs that formed the planet's rings were parting and dozens of the fluttering things were emerging, as if they were forming themselves out of the mist itself. The *Actaeon* swung sharply to port as the first moth swept past, almost brushing our hull with its great dusty wings. On its back one of those flea-like figures leapt up and whirled something about his head and let it fly. I had

'The brute's trying to ram us!' declared Dr Blears, and for once
I agreed with him.

just long enough to see that he wore armour, like some elfin knight out of a fairy tale, and that, although he had two arms and two legs like me, he used a long tail to balance himself. Then the moth was past, and the *Actaeon* was moving again, turning to present a broadside to the swarm that was rushing towards us out of the rings. Bells rang below deck and the sailors' feet pounded on stairways and ladders as they raced to clear the ship for action.

And suddenly that thing that I had seen the moth-rider throw, which must have been tumbling leisurely towards us through the aether, struck our picture window with a startling crack and exploded in a splash of lime-green fire!

All in an instant the order of the bridge was turned to chaos. Wherever I looked there were sharp shards of whirling glass and tongues of that actinic fire. The *Actaeon*'s gravity generators had failed, and those steady shakings and judderings that I could feel were undoubtedly more of the moth-riders' infernal devices slamming into her hull and doing untold damage below decks! The bridge filled with shouted orders and cries of alarm and pain, and the ceiling suddenly tapped me on the shoulder. I looked around me, and saw Myrtle somersaulting past, crying out, 'Oh, *not again*!' and trying to keep her ankles decently veiled as her skirts flapped up over her head.

A hand caught mine. It was Father's, and in another moment he had me off the bridge and down the companionway to the mid-deck. Others were already there, and Mother and Myrtle were swimming behind us, their hair wild and their clothes ballooning in the absence of decent gravity. Voices above were shouting, 'Captain Moonfield! Captain Moonfield!' Then someone slammed the hatch above us shut and things grew jolly quiet, though we could still hear the sounds of alarms and catastrophes going on in other portions of the ship.

'Where is Captain Moonfield?' demanded Ulla Burton.

'He will certainly face a court martial for this!' declared Dr Blears. 'What incompetence! Defeated by a moth!'

'He's gone,' said Mr Cumberbatch, the *Actaeon*'s first officer, his hair sticking up like a boot-brush atop his pale, startled face.

'Gone? What do you mean, sir? Gone where? Gone how?'

'Out into space,' said Mr Cumberbatch. 'We tried to grab him, Midshipman Bradstreet and I, but one whole side of the cabin was blown away and out he went with it.'

'Oh, poor Captain Moonfield!' cried Myrtle. 'But surely we may rescue him? Art is forever being flung into space, and yet he is invariably rescued.'

'We are in no shape to rescue anyone until we have saved ourselves,' said Sir Richard, putting an arm protectively around his wife as another violent lurch shook the stricken vessel. 'That was the great alembic exploding, unless I'm much mistaken. We must abandon ship.'

'Abandon ship!' shouted Dr Blears. 'Outrageous, sir! I will not hear of it! This is a brand-new, Viper-class gun-boat, representing a considerable investment on the part of the tax-payer . . .'

'Pardon me,' said Mother sweetly. 'I am only a civilian, and a mere woman at that, so perhaps I do not fully understand these things, but with poor Captain Moonfield lost is it not Mr Cumberbatch who commands this ship?'

I could barely see Mr Cumberbatch, so great was the shaking and trembling of the ship, but I glimpsed the look of alarm that broke over his honest face as he realised that he was in charge. 'Why, yes . . .' he agreed.

'What do you say, Captain?' asked Sir Richard.

Mr Cumberbatch nodded once or twice, swallowed hard and said, 'Yes – quite right – mean to say – abandon ship! To the lifeboats!'

Dr Blears protested, of course, and vowed that the matter would be raised in Parliament, but his bleatings were quite drowned out by the lusty voices of the sailors relaying Mr Cumberbatch's orders. Mother took Myrtle's hand and then mine, and calling to Father to follow us she kicked off from a bulkhead and started to swim down through the ship to the under-deck, where we had been shown the lifeboats on our tour the day before. We crossed the gun deck, where I saw the heartening sight of great cannon leaping and roaring in clouds of smoke while their tireless crews stood by to clean and load and run them out again, doing their best to keep the moth-riders busy while the rest of us made our escape. But I also saw the guns that had been dismounted and the holes which had been torn in the *Actaeon*'s sides by the terrible explosive devices of our foes. And through those holes I glimpsed the great grey wings of the circling moths . . .

Mother swims as gracefully in zero-BSG as any fish in water and she quickly had us down on the lifeboat deck. It was crowded already with men, some injured, all with smoke-blackened faces: sooty masks out of which their eyes stared white and wide. This being a British ship there was, of course, no panic; but there was a deal of confusion, especially since the place was filling with multi-coloured vapours from the blazing wedding chamber astern. I saw the first mate ordering groups of men into the waiting lifeboats. I saw Mr McMurdo led past in tears by his assistants and heard his doleful tartan voice lamenting,

'Och, mae engines, mae bootiful wee engines!' And somehow, in the crush and darkness and the din, I let Mother's fingers slip from my grasp . . .

That was how I ended up in one lifeboat, with Sir Richard, Ulla and a small midshipman named Tom Bradstreet, while my parents and Myrtle found themselves in quite another.

As soon as I realised my mistake I hastened to put it right. 'No!' I cried, as the sailors outside slammed the hatch shut. 'I'm in the wrong boat!' I protested, hammering on the inch-thick crystal windows as they tugged at the launching levers. 'Stop!'

And then the spring beneath our lifeboat released, and the force of our acceleration squashed me into the upholstery as we were propelled out into space. Ahead of us, one of those vast and awful moths loomed up. I could see every hair upon its hill of a body, and its five riders crouching there with the light of Georgium Sidus silvering their spiky space armour. Then, with a mighty jolt, we crashed into the insect. It crumpled like a paper lantern and we tore clean through it and out the other side, and went tumbling into the blue eye of Georgium Sidus amid a swirl of silver dust.

Chapter Six

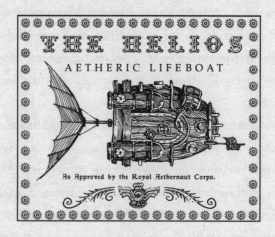

OF SHAPES IN THE FOG AND AN UNEXPECTED MEETING.

You will recall, if you have been following my adventures, the old Daedalus lifeboat in which Myrtle and I once had to make a hasty departure from good old Larklight? Well, these naval lifeboats were quite similar, though rather more *à la mode*; they had a simple steering mechanism, an aetheric distress beacon, and in addition to a copy of the Bible they also carried the *Book of Common Prayer* and the *Collected Poems of Lord Tennyson*.

But despite these innovations our progress towards the surface of Georgium Sidus was just as alarming as the fall of Larklight's old boat on to the dark side of the Moon if not worse. For when we looked back through the isinglass window in the top of the craft we could see the HMS *Actaeon* blazing above us in the depths of a wild swarm of giant moths – a swarm from which a few insects were breaking away to pursue the lifeboats of our shipmates. But none came after us. I think that when we crashed through that brute as we departed, the storm of drifting fragments and the blizzard of dust from its collapsing wings had served to screen us until we were too far away for the moth-riders to give chase.

Naturally I was most concerned for Mother and Father, and even for Myrtle, but it seemed wrong to blub about it; I was certain Mr Bradstreet was just as concerned for his fellow aethernauts, and even Sir Richard and Ulla, while they still had one another, must surely have felt unhappy at the prospect of being shipwrecked on the surface of a world so mysterious and so far from England – a world so alien, indeed, that Mother had said it did not have a surface at all. I looked down with apprehension at the slow dance of the clouds below us and watched as Sir Richard opened the hatch which housed the lifeboat's controls.

Of course there was no room for an alembic on board so small a vessel, and even if there had been we could none of us have performed the chemical wedding. Instead, four brass rockets were bolted to the lifeboat's sides. By firing one at a time, Sir Richard was able to change the angle of our descent and direct our fall towards a point on the planet's northern hemisphere.

'I am taking us down in the region from which the missionary's distress flare was reported to have come,' he said.

We sank into the fog. The winds of Georgium Sidus seized our little boat and shook her furiously, but it was nothing compared to the buffetings I'd endured when I fell with Jack Havock into the wind-race of Jupiter, and I

resolved to endure it without grumbling or being sick. Unfortunately my fellow passengers were less resolute, and the interior of the boat was in a most disagreeable state by the time its plummeting progress slowed and finally ended, with a colossal *SPLAT* and a certain amount of bouncing, as if we had come to rest on some immense trampoline.

When all was still, Mr Bradstreet unscrewed the hatch and out we climbed. Wraiths of mist wavered about us, half concealing the strange shapes of alien vegetation which rose all around. It seemed that our boat had come to rest amid a field of giant green cabbages. Each was about the size of a London hansom cab, though without the horse or driver. Indeed, there was no sign of any animal life in this world of mists; wherever we looked we saw nothing but those silent, towering cabbages. The ground beneath us was

invisible, hidden beneath a dense, rubbery web made from their interwoven roots.

'What a perfectly beastly spot!' I exclaimed. 'I do not even like cabbage!'

'They are more like sprouts,' suggested Ulla. 'How seasonal – for I believe sprouts are a part of your traditional Christmas dinner, are they not?'

'Yes, ma'am, but they are every boy's *least favourite* part,' I told her.

'Then I hope you soon develop a taste for them,' said Sir Richard. 'It may be some weeks before a rescue expedition can reach us, and there seems little else to eat upon this God-forsaken sphere . . .'

'We must find the others,' said Mr Bradstreet in his shrill little voice.

'Judging by the way those moths were hunting down their lifeboats, I think it quite possible that none of our shipmates has reached the surface,' said Ulla.

'Do you mean they may all be dead?' I cried.

'Let us pray that they were just made prisoners,' said Sir Richard. 'But we must not forget that one or more of those insects may have followed us. What weapons do we have?'

We had precious few, as it turned out. Mr Bradstreet

carried a short knife or 'dirk'. Mrs Burton had one of her splendid Martian throwing blades concealed about her person. And I suppose the *Book of Common Prayer* and *Collected Poems of Lord Tennyson* might have been pressed into service as makeshift clubs or missiles (though naturally we could not use the Bible for such a purpose). Otherwise, we were as defenceless as Babes in that unearthly Wood.

Still, like true Britons we did not sit about and mope at our misfortunes, but resolved to begin learning whatever we might about this strange world we had fallen into. Mr Bradstreet was technically in command of our party, for despite being only nine-and-a-half he was the senior naval officer present. He solemnly shared out a ration of ship's biscuit. Then he gladly let the role of leader pass to Sir Richard, who was so much better suited to it, and we set off together into the ever-swirling mist.

'Hallo!' shouted Sir Richard at intervals.

'Hallo!' the rest of us chorused, joining our high voices to his deep and manly one.

But no answer came out of the fog, and the thick, rubbery leaves of the cabbages swallowed any echoes. It seemed to me that there might be no one else living at all in that dismal place.

And then I sensed a movement away to my right. I turned towards it, signalling to the others to follow me, and soon reached the edge of that forest of cabbages. The ground ahead was covered by a thick carpet of fog, whiter and denser than that above it. Again I thought I saw a movement: a figure, faint behind the veils of the mist. 'Hallo!' I called, and stepped towards it.

I realised my mistake at once. What lay beneath that denser fog was not ground, but liquid! I plunged into it and went under with barely a splash, for it was the strangest water I have ever known. When I tried to fight my way to the surface I found that there *was* no surface, just a vague boundary where the water shaded imperceptibly into vapour. I struggled silently, and looked round for my companions – only to find that they were not there!

In that instant, a rush of wild and dreadful imaginings seized me. Sir Richard and the others must have taken a wrong turning in the fog, or failed to notice me branch off at all!

And then strong hands grabbed the collar of my coat and lifted me, propelling me back towards the cabbages. I could see now that these vegetables were not rooted in any soil, but simply grew out of a thick mat of woven roots which must float somehow upon that gaseous ocean. What good fortune, I thought, that our lifeboat had fallen upon such a mat, and not plunged into the water!

I scrambled back on to the safety of the root-mat and turned to thank my rescuer, wondering whether it was Sir Richard or Ulla who had dived into that strange sea to save me. (I was pretty sure that Midshipman Bradstreet would not have had the strength to lift me so easily.)

The figure which loomed over me, however, was not Sir Richard or his wife. Indeed, it was not even human!

From the waist up the thing was roughly man-shaped, but as bony as an Egyptian mummy, with a great keel to its chest like the prow of a boat. It had four arms and four long-fingered hands, one of which clutched a primitive spear while another still had hold of my coat collar. Its head was awful: a finned grey mask with a long slit filled with needles for a mouth and no eyes at all, just two darker patches where its eyes should be, as if membranes of translucent skin had grown across them. It had no nose and no hair either, but from the centre of its high forehead grew a bony rod with a feathery dangling thing upon the end, like the lures with which the deep-sea anglerfish of Earth are wont to attract their prey.

This object twitched and jiggled as the monster leaned

over me, and I felt those eyes-which-were-not-eyes regard me with a curious air, as if it were trying to decide whether or not I would be good to eat.

'Help!' I cried as loudly as I might. The creature jerked away from me at the sound, and to my great relief I heard the running footsteps of Sir Richard and the others, and then their answering shouts. The root-mat trembled under me as they came charging out of the mist.

The creature, alarmed, backed away with an awful swirling movement. From the waist down it was not man-like at all, but more closely resembled an enormous snake or eel. A flick of its powerful tail sent it scooting out into the billows of that fog-sea, where it did not sink from sight as I had done but somehow kept itself afloat, staring back at the rest of us as we crowded along the edge of the root-mat to stare at it.

Ulla drew her throwing blade, but Sir Richard stayed her

hand. 'Don't, dearest! It may be friendly.'

'I can't imagine ever being friends with anything *that* ugly!' said Mr Bradstreet.

The creature came back towards us, parting the thick mists of the fog-sea with quick, muscular movements of its tail. The lure dangling from its head glowed with a faint violet light. It opened its mouth and out came a dreadful noise, like someone dragging a knife over the teeth of a steel comb. It waved its spear and made strange, antic gestures.

'I imagine it thinks we are a threat to it,' said Sir Richard.

'I suppose we *have* invaded its world,' Ulla declared. 'Let us back away slowly so that it may see we mean no harm . . .'

We did as she suggested, but the creature seemed only to grow more agitated, waving its four arms at us and clattering and clicking for all it was worth. Then, quite suddenly, it dived beneath the mist and was lost to our sight.

'Curious fellow,' said Sir Richard.

'A savage brute!' said Mr Bradstreet.

But I was not so sure. Once my initial terror at the creature's horrid phiz and threatening manner had faded, I had begun to remember what Mother had told me of her time on Georgium Sidus so long ago. She had been a sort of mer-person, she had said, and of course I had imagined her like a mermaid in an earthly sailor's story, beautiful and golden-haired and sitting upon a rock with her comb and mirror. But perhaps she had actually been a creature like the one I had just encountered. How strange and unsettling it was to think that once she might have worn an aspect as hideous as that!

'We should get away from this shore before the creature returns with more of his kind,' said Ulla, and her husband agreed. We turned inland and struck out again through that forest of cabbages, wondering how large this mat or island was that we were marooned upon.

We had not gone far when of a sudden there came a rushing noise, and Sir Richard uttered an exclamation, clutched at his neck and fell face downward among the cabbage roots!

We rolled him over. His eyes were closed, his face pale.

'He's dead!' squeaked Mr Bradstreet.

'He is unconscious,' Ulla assured us, though she sounded most awfully afraid. 'Look!'

Sticking from Sir Richard's neck was a tiny dart which appeared to be made from bone. We all began to look about us, alarmed at the thought of some enemy lurking among the mist and vegetables – an enemy with the cunning to make certain that the strongest of our party should be the first to be struck down!

'It's them mermen, I'll be bound!' cried Mr Bradstreet. And as he spoke I thought I saw someone go hurrying across a misty gap between two cabbages not far behind him. Not a merman, but something which ran on two legs, crouching low. Was that the scraping of metal scales I heard? And then, again, that rushing sound, and it was Mr Bradstreet's turn to cry out and spin about and fall.

Ulla had out her throwing blade. She paused a moment, listening, then hurled it into the fog. There was a clang, a shriek, a thud of something falling. The blade came whirling back out of the vapours. Ulla caught it and turned to me with a look of great alarm.

'Art, there may be many of them!'

'We should go back to the shore!' I said.

'But that mer-creature . . .'

'Perhaps his gestures were not as ferocious as we thought, Mrs B. He may have been trying to warn us of the presence of these others. If we can only –'

And then I heard again that rushing sound. Ulla stiffened and let fall her knife and dropped to her knees. 'Go to the waters!' she told me. 'Run . . .' And then her senses left her, and she measured her length at my feet, a bone dart sticking from the nape of her russet neck.

Between the cabbages more man-shapes flickered, closing in on me through the swirlings of the mist, with long, armoured tails a-twitch.

How I wished then that I had been struck down like my companions! Better to be lying insensible among the cabbage roots, I thought, than to be yet conscious and all alone and to have to decide whether to share their fate or try to save myself. But Ulla had told me to run, and so I ran, reasoning that if I could only elude the dart-throwers I might return to tend to my fallen companions at a later time.

I fled as swiftly as I could across that yielding, reverberating carpet of roots, which sprang and bounced beneath my boots like some vast mattress. A hissing cry in the fog behind me told me that my flight had been observed. Another instant and a dart rushed past my left ear with only a quarter-inch to spare. It stuck quivering in the fleshy outer leaves of a great cabbage, which let out a hollow groan and toppled sideways. I scrambled past it and zigzagged through a veritable cabbage jungle, then hid, breathless, and heard my pursuers go racing past me in the mist.

When the sounds had faded I crept from my hiding place, meaning to return to where Sir Richard, Ulla and Mr Bradstreet lay. But when I had walked for more than ten minutes through the fog without happening upon them, I started to realise that I had gone wrong and that in that world of endless murk and identical cabbages I might never find my way back to them.

I was about to give in to despair, when all at once a terrifying shape reared up before me, and I found myself

Mothstorm

confronted by the very being who had saved me earlier in
the gas-sea. I remembered that my own dear mother might
once have been a creature such as this, but I still could not
prevent myself from jumping back and pressing myself
against a cabbage trunk.

'I say,' said a girlish voice. 'There's nothing to be scared
of! I suppose you wouldn't happen to have any chocolate
about you, would you?'

I was startled to hear such high, sweet tones issuing from
that dreadful mouth, which a few minutes earlier had only
seemed able to make grinding, grating, clattering sounds. I
was mystified, too, as to how such a creature might have
learned the Queen's English. But being a well-brought-up
boy, I did not let my surprise show and simply rummaged
about in my pockets till I found a bar of Mr Fry's excellent
chocolate, somewhat melted and misshapen but still
perfectly edible.

This I held out to the mer-person, with the words, 'I'm
pleased to meet you, sir. My name is Art Mumby.'

'Oh, it's not for him!' said the voice. 'Over here!'

I realised that once again I had been deceived by
Georgium Sidus's ceaseless fog. Another figure stood quite
near the merman, but showed so faintly through those

vaporous billows that I had not seen it until then. I went towards it, flapping my hand in front of me to clear the air until I saw the speaker.

She was a girl of about my own age, with freckles and pigtails, wearing a grubby pinafore dress and the remnants of a straw boater.

'Oh, ripping!' cried the girl when she saw the chocolate bar which I was holding out. She took it, broke off a square and ate it with an expression of great relish. 'I say! How utterly divine! I've not had a taste of chocolate for simply months and months. It's one of the things one misses most living out here. Thank you! Charity Cruet.'

'What?' I said, for I was feeling a touch befuddled and did not quite understand that last part.

'My name. Charity Cruet. What's yours?'

'Art Mumby,' I replied.

'No relation of Mr Edward Mumby, of Larklight?'

'He's my father.'

'Gosh! What a coincidence! He's an old friend of my father. Papa is always talking of him . . . He *was*, I mean.'

Of course I had realised by now who this strange girl was. Providence, and Sir Richard's navigation, had brought me to the very spot on Georgium Sidus where Father's missionary friend had been wrecked, and here was his daughter! I said at once, 'Your distress flares were seen by the Astronomer Royal! We came here to rescue you aboard a warship, the HMS *Actaeon*.'

'Thank Heavens!' cried Charity Cruet, clapping her hands together. 'Where is she? Have you lost your companions in the fog?'

'Alas, I have no companions left. We were attacked in orbit by gigantic moths, and the *Actaeon* was destroyed. I landed with three others, but they have been struck down by some jolly unsporting coves who lurked in the mist and shot at us with narcotic darts.'

'Oh, how vexing!' cried the girl. 'Did you not receive my message? I sent it at the same time as I launched the flare: *Great danger threatens. Georgian space in the hands of a Hostile Power. It is imperative that you send a massed fleet.*'

'Only a few words were received,' I explained. 'The meaning was lost. We were not sure if it was a warning or just a distress signal. But who are they, these moth-riders? You say a hostile power . . .'

Before she could answer, the merman let out a clattering cry which sounded like someone kicking a large heap of empty sardine cans down a stone staircase. He pointed with his spear into the mist behind me.

'They are coming back!' cried Charity. 'Quickly! Come with me!'

And so saying, she seized a hold of my hand and, before I could stop her, leapt from the edge of the cabbage island into the sea of mist!

Chapter Seven

IN WHICH I TAKE UP QUEER LODGINGS AND COME TO
LEARN OF THE FATE OF REVEREND CRUET AND HIS MISSION
TO THE OUTER PLANETS.

'Oh!' I cried, as I plunged with Charity Cruet
through that perpetual fog which forms the
surface of the Georgian sea. I remembered all
too well my earlier dip and was certain that we were both
about to drown.

'Take a deep breath!' warned Charity, as the fog

thickened around us into chilly water. I did as she said and kicked out after her as she let go my hand and started to swim. Somewhere nearby in that grey soup which enveloped us I caught a glimpse of the merman driving himself along with powerful movements of his eel-like tail.

Above me I could dimly discern a latticework of sturdy roots and I surmised that we must be beneath the cabbage raft. Then, all at once, there was light ahead of us, and as I looked for its source I crashed against some rubbery, yielding membrane which seemed to be stretched like an invisible wall across my path. I cried out in alarm, and the last air rushed from my lungs and vanished surfacewards in silver bubbles. I floundered, until Charity Cruet's merman took hold of me, used his blade to slash an opening in the membrane and thrust me bodily through it.

I fell on to a wet floor, which wobbled like a jelly. But it could wobble all it liked as far as I was concerned, for there was at least air to breathe. I took a few deep gulps of it before I bothered to say, 'Where are we?'

'Underneath the floating island,' said Charity, wringing out her wet dress. 'Of course, it's not really an island; it's one big plant, and air-bladders like this one help it to stay afloat. There is a whole clump of them down here.'

I glanced nervously behind me, afraid that water must be seeping through the opening which I had entered by. But to my surprise, I saw that there was no longer any opening there! The wall of the bladder had sealed itself shut, leaving only a rough line of scar tissue to show that there had ever been a wound.

'The bladders heal themselves,' said Charity. 'They have to, you see, otherwise they'd just pop like balloons every time a spiny whale-grub went blundering by. They're jolly tough and filled mostly with oxygen, so they make splendid little houses. I usually come in through a trapdoor on the surface so I don't end up so beastly wet, but it's in the middle of the island and the whole place is crawling with moth-riders today.'

'Are they the rulers of this world?' I asked.

'I don't believe they come from this world at all,' replied Charity, pulling off her boots and tipping water out of them. 'There was no sign of them when Daddy and I arrived. But we had barely settled ourselves upon the island and begun to set up our chapel, than all of a sudden the fog was full of wings, and the horrid blighters came and shot Daddy with one of their darts and carried him away.'

'Away to where?' I asked. 'My own friends were treated in the same rough manner. We must find where they are and rescue them!'

'I don't know,' said Charity sadly. 'They took him away on the back of one of those giant moths, I know not where. They would have captured me too, but luckily Mr Zennor rescued me.'

She indicated her strange companion, who was watching us from just outside the bubble. She waved her hands at him, flickering her fingers in a curious way and touching them to her mouth and various other portions of her person. I wondered if her dreadful experiences had made her go a little funny in the head. But Mr Zennor seemed quite unperturbed. His lure flashed brightly, and he turned and swam away.

'Of course, Zennor's not his *real* name,' Charity assured

me. 'His real name is *KrxckKckarrakkkaclkkx akka Xkaggoxka-akx Klllxklplx-atgnsl'xkkanklxlk'abhz nhahmak'k' k'k'k'a-akkamkajrkrkkrkrkrkwkllukk KrxckKckarrakkkacl kkx akka Xkaggoxka-akx Klllxklplx-atgnsl'xkkanklxlk' abhz nhahmak'k'k'k'a-akkamkajrkrkkrkrkrkwkllakk*. But that's a bit of a mouthful, so I call him Zennor, after the place in Cornwall. There are lots of mer-people in Cornwall, or at least there are in the stories. I grew up there. Well, I suppose I'm still growing up, but what I mean is that I used to *live* there. Daddy was the vicar of St Porrock's near Morwenstow until he got his calling. He heard the Voice of GOD, you know, telling him to come out to Georgium Sidus and save souls. I must say, it's a pity the Almighty couldn't have seen his way to mentioning the moth-riders while He was about it, but He moves in Mysterious Ways.'

Charity Cruet was moving in a mysterious way herself while she told me all this. She had put her boots back on and made her way across the bubble to press her hands against the further wall. Then, reaching into a pocket on her frock, she withdrew a penknife, which she opened and used to make a long, curving cut in the skin of the bladder. We stepped through the slit she had made into the next-door bladder as easily as stepping from one room to another.

And this inner bladder was very like a room, for Charity had furnished it with things which she must have salvaged from her father's ship. There was a threadbare carpet on the floor, a cabin trunk, a small bookshelf, a brass bedstead and a portable harmonium. In addition, a tree of pinkish coral served as a hatstand and a huge shell filled with water made a serviceable washbasin.

I peered out through the transparent wall of the bladder, and saw merfolk moving in other bladders all about me. It was as if a great apartment house in London had been built with walls of glass so that you could see into every room. In

one bubble a mer-mother was nursing her mer-children, in another an old mer-crone seemed to be weaving a garment of seaweed stalks upon a coral loom, while in a third a group of mermen were busy at some game involving heaps of shells. Each scene was illuminated by the glowing lures which dangled from the merfolk's brows, so that the bubbles had a cosy, homely feel.

Charity Cruet's bubble, in contrast, was somewhat dark, lit only by a few luminous starfish which were stuck to the walls and by the twilight of the Georgian sky which filtered down through the thick mesh of roots and sprouts above us.

'I'm sorry it's so jolly dingy,' said Charity. 'I can't light so much as a candle, you see, for fear that I'd use up all the air. Would you like some seaweed juice?'

I did not think I would, but Mother and Father brought me up to be polite, and so I accepted the small shell of greenish fluid which Charity handed me and took a sip. And, do you know, it was not half bad? I drank the rest quickly and felt much better for it.

'Seaweed is what we chiefly live on down here,' said Charity. 'I shall ask Mr Zennor to bring us some for our supper.'

'How do you communicate with him?' I asked. 'Have you learned to speak that clickety, clackety language of his?'

'Oh no,' she replied. 'It is far too complicated. But I have taught Mr Zennor and some of his friends the rudiments of Universal Sign Language. It is an invention of Daddy's. Here, I have a pamphlet about it.'

She thrust into my hands a thin soft-bound volume which seemed to consist entirely of drawings of people waving their arms about – touching their noses, pointing to their ears, tapping their elbows and performing other strange contortions. Beside each was another smaller picture, usually showing an object, such as a plate of food, a book, a house or a coin. I gathered that this was a sort of picture dictionary and that if one were to learn it by heart, one would be able to hold simple conversations merely by flapping one's hands about like the people in the drawings.

'Daddy says that it is a great shame that the races of the worlds are divided by our lack of a common language,' explained Charity. 'Several gentlemen have tried to invent one, but theirs were spoken languages, and who wants to give up their own mother tongue in favour of a made-up one? So Daddy decided to devise a sign language. It is not supposed to take the place of speaking, but if everyone were to be taught it, we could all communicate one with another. It would lead to much greater understanding between the nations, and no one should ever have to trouble learning a foreign language.'

I thought this a ripping idea, for, as I've said, Mother had been trying to teach me a little French and Latin, and I had found those verbs and prefixes jolly hard going. (Not only that, but she had suggested that it might be a nice idea to take up Classical Martian next year!) I leafed through Reverend Cruet's pamphlet with growing hope, wondering if I might persuade her to let me learn this Universal Sign Language instead.

'And how many people have learned the signs so far?' I asked.

'Oh, only me, I'm afraid,' said Charity. 'And Mr Zennor, of course. It never really caught on. We have ever so many of these pamphlets aboard our ship. Daddy had twenty thousand printed, anticipating great interest from the school boards and learned institutions. But he only sold four.'

I nodded sympathetically. 'My father published a book called *Some Undescribed Icthyomorphs of the Trans-Lunar Aether* once, and we have whole attics at Larklight simply filled with unsold copies.'

I leafed a little further through the pamphlet but without really seeing it, for suddenly I had been reminded of my own father, and my own family, and dear old Larklight, which I might never see again. I was glad of Charity Cruet's company and the shelter of her curious home, and dashed grateful to the kindly Providence which had brought us together in that lonely place, but I did not think that I could be content to live there for very long, eating seaweed and with none but mermen for company.

'Look here, Charity,' I said. 'What do you think has become of our parents, and my sister, and my other companions?'

'I do not know,' she replied sadly. 'But I cannot imagine we shall see them again in this life.'

'Yet the moth-people took them alive. They must be holding them as prisoners, otherwise they would not have troubled to shoot them with those sleep-inducing darts.'*

'But holding them where?' asked Charity. She took the pamphlet from me and returned it to her bookshelf. 'The

---

* You can probably see where my train of thought was bound, dear reader; after all, I reasoned, this was not the first time I had had a parent or parents snaffled by forces of unearthly evil. I was wondering whether I might not manage something in the Daring Rescue line.

moth-people are not from this world, so they must be from another. From Hades or some still lonelier sphere far out in the darkness at the system's edge, perhaps. And if they have taken our loved ones thither –'

'Then we must go thither too and save them!' I cried manfully. 'Remember, Charity, we are British, and there is nothing that good old British Pluck cannot accomplish!'

Charity looked somewhat doubtful about this. 'Well, for a start,' she said, 'I do not see how it can lift us off this planet. The poor old *New Jerusalem* is a wreck, and even if she were aether-worthy I do not believe that we could fly her. Father was the only alchemist aboard. And even if we *did* get her up into space, she would be brought down again at once by those moths.'

Annoyingly, she was quite right. I found a last square of chocolate in a corner of my pocket and shared it between us, nibbling my half as slowly as I could, for I feared it might be the last that I should ever taste. 'If only we could send a distress signal,' I mused.

'There are some alchemical distress flares left aboard the *New Jerusalem*,' said Charity. 'At least, there are if the moth-people haven't stolen them. But what good would it do to let one off? There is no one to see it.'

'Indeed, you are mistaken!' I cried, and suddenly I was so excited that I had to leap to my feet and pace about the bubble. 'Someone *will* see it! I bet the *Actaeon* got off a distress message of her own before the moth-men wrecked her. More ships will be on their way – a whole squadron, probably. And they'll be ready for trouble this time. We must make sure that they know we're down here! Charity, we simply *must* return to your father's ship and fire off another of those flares!'

I always find that it bucks me up no end to have something to do at times like that. I was all for setting off right away to find the *New Jerusalem* and fetch the flares, but Charity said, 'Oh, no; Mr Zennor will be here shortly with fresh seaweed for our supper, and it is time for my concert.'

I must have looked surprised at that, for she explained at once. 'You don't think I am content to accept these kind mer-people's hospitality and do nothing in return, I hope?

I can't join them on their wild hunts across the floor of the gas-sea or nurse their children, or anything like that. So I play music to them on Daddy's old portable harmonium. They are very musical and most appreciative. Just watch the way that they gather outside the bubble when I start.'

And so saying, she sat herself down at the harmonium, pumped the foot-pedal furiously for a moment or two and then began to play. And sure enough, the merfolk busy in the other bubbles all looked up, and their glowing lures shone pink with pleasure, and it was not long before they were all slithering out of their bubble-homes and coming to cluster outside the walls of ours, gazing with rapt attention at the girl who sat there playing old English hymns.

And I gazed too, in purest wonder. I've often had cause
to speak of my sister's piano playing in these yarns of mine
and to say how utterly beastly it was, so you may have taken
the impression that I am not much of a music-lover. But
Charity Cruet's playing, there in that bubble 'neath the
Georgian waves, struck me with the force of a revelation.
You may find it hard to believe, but I promise you, dear
reader, this is the Gospel Truth:

She was even worse than Myrtle!

I smiled as best as I could, and nodded encouragingly
when she glanced at me over her shoulder, and tried not to
wince each time she hit a wrong note. But I decided one
thing there and then: come what may, I simply *had* to escape
Georgium Sidus!

When the recital was over, and the mer-people had
pantomimed their thanks and swum away, I ventured to
suggest again that we should start for the *New Jerusalem*. I
was quite desperate to know whether there might still be a
flare left aboard the Cruets' ship, or whether the damp or
the moth-people had ruined them all. But Charity cautioned
against it.

'Those moth-men will still be sneaking about,' she
reasoned. 'And it will be night soon, which is when all sorts

of disagreeable Georgian wildlife chooses to emerge. It would be better to wait until morning.' So we dined on the raw fish and seaweed which Mr Zennor brought us, and settled down to sleep.

And while we are slumbering, you would doubtless like to hear what had befallen Mother and Father after our lifeboats tumbled from the Actaeon. *A few of you may even be wondering in a half-hearted way about Myrtle.*

How fortunate, then, that Myrtle has written her own account of the Actaeon*'s defeat and the events which followed, which she has called* A Young Lady's Adventures in Unknown Space – *not the catchiest title, I think you'll agree. But here is a sample of it, so that you may find out how she fared* — A.M.

Chapter Eight

INTERESTING FLORA & FAUNA

Georgian
Tufted Sphagnum

(or
Nibbling
Sporrans)

№ 32

IN WHICH I PRESENT AN INTERESTING PORTION OF MY
SISTER'S DIARY.*

*A Young Lady's Adventures in Unknown Space
by Myrtle Evangeline Mumby (Miss).*

* No, dear reader, I have not simply PINCHED it. Myrtle, being most beastly
envious of my success as an Author, worked it up for publication herself,
meaning it to rival my own account of these adventures. Since no one outside
our own family bought a copy, however, she has grudgingly allowed me to
reprint the good bits here — A.M.

⊂ઠ 1 ⊃ઠ

How am I to express in mere words the terrible series of events which it has been my misfortune to endure? How strange it is to think that back among the orbits of civilised worlds it is the festive season. According to *Crevice's Almanac*, it is already Christmas Day in England. Families there are walking to church thro' the snow or coming home to tables heaped high with good food. Innocent children are exclaiming with delight over presents from their kindly relations* and the gifts which St Nicholas has left in their stockings,† and good Christian men and women everywhere are remembering the birth of

---

* Or, if they are anything like me, they are saying, 'What? Not another pair of socks from Aunt Mumby. Where are the lead soldiers which I requested?' — A.M.

† This is another top-notch Christmas notion from Germany, where aunts and parents are forbidden from choosing presents for their little ones, and the whole business has been farmed out to a jolly, old red-coated fellow named *St Nick* or *Santy Claus*, who goes from house to house on Christmas Eve, dishing out goodies to sleeping children. If you have been well behaved that year, you are allowed to hang up your stocking at the end of your bed and he will fill it with toys and sticks of gingerbread. (But if you've been naughty, a fellow comes down the chimney and punches you on the nose, so it is not all fun.) — A.M.

a baby in that stable in Bethlehem one thousand eight hundred and fifty-one years ago and giving thanks to Almighty GOD for the great goodness of His world . . .

And I am stranded here in the void between the stars, imprisoned, with the dreadful knowledge that that world may be doomed and that those men, women and children may not survive to see another Christmas . . .

Nothing has gone right since the HMS *Actaeon* sailed into the Georgian aether! First there were those awful moths and their dreadful *mahouts* or riders, and the loss of poor, dear Captain Moonfield. And then, among all the alarums and confusion, Art foolishly got into quite the wrong lifeboat, and went off without us. There was nothing to be done but to cram ourselves into another boat and cast ourselves upon the bosom of the aether — and I must say, a thoroughly

wayward, unreliable bosom it has turned out to be!

As we plunged away from the *Actaeon*, I realised for the first time the true size and number of those hateful moths. The whole of space seemed filled with their silvery wings, and along their backs their armoured handlers scurried, hurling more of those fiendish explosive devices at the poor *Actaeon*, which had by then become the merest bonfire! Away on what Jack Havock would call our *port* or *larboard* quarter, I saw one of the lifeboats slam into a moth and tear straight through it like a shell from a howitzer, rending it into pieces and scattering its riders into the void. And although it may be un-Christian of me, I was glad to see them thus brought low, for was it not what they deserved for launching such a treacherous and barbaric attack upon the agents of civilisation?

Yet that was but a single incident in the battle, and wherever else I looked I saw the moths triumphant and their riders casting out great silvery nets which caught the *Actaeon*'s lifeboats and ensnared them, like poor flies in the webs of spiders.

I had barely seen what was happening before there came a cry of alarm from Father, and our own progress was arrested, hurling us about the cramped and gravityless cabin. Our lifeboat hung motionless in space, trapped in one of those nets and at the mercy of an inhuman foe!

It was all so reminiscent of our adventures with the white spiders that I almost fainted. Indeed, I am quite sure I should have done so had not Mother slapped me about the face and said firmly, 'No swooning, Myrtle dear. We shall need all our wits about us if we are to get out of this, and get out of it we must if we are to rescue Art!'

I declare she cares far more for Art than ever she has for me!

Just then there came a deafening thunderclap, a tremendous green flash and a most disagreeable smell. The door of our lifeboat was torn off and there stood one of the brigands who had assaulted us, with several of his accomplices be- hind him. All wore those same spiny metal spacesuits, somewhat in the Gothick taste. Had their suits been

empty and stood in a shop window, I should have asked
Mother to buy a few, for they would look highly
Romantic standing on the landings of Larklight. But here
among the rings of Georgium Sidus they seemed utterly
terrible.

The brigand chief stepped into our lifeboat. I shrieked,
and Father naturally offered to fight, but the thug knocked
him aside with scant regard for sportsmanship, using a kind
of armoured club on the end of his tail. (I had not realised
until then that our assailants had tails. I had thought those
long extensions at their rear ends to be mere whimsy on the
part of their tailor, or their blacksmith, or whoever it was
who ran up those quaint tin suits for them.) Poor Father was
flung back into his seat and lay there groaning, while
Mother and I confronted his attacker.

'Sssurrender!' the brute hissed, dark eyes glinting at us
through the eye-slit of his helmet. 'We are the Sssnilth!'

Muffled though it was, his voice sounded strangely
familiar, and also strangely feminine. He was not a *he* at all,
I realised, but yet another of those shameless Amazons
with whom fate is always throwing me together. And I
thought how deeply wrong it was that a female of any
species should so forget herself as to go rampaging about in

armour and tossing bombs around.

And then, reaching up, the creature pulled off her helmet and shook her head and ran a hand through the long blue spines which served her for hair, and all other thoughts quite vanished from my head – for she was none other than Ssilissa!

☙ 2 ❧

Once more my good breeding almost overcame me, and if there had been any gravity aboard the lifeboat, I am certain I should have dropped insensible to the deck. As it was, however, I was afraid that my skirts might ride up and expose my petticoats, so I mastered myself and exclaimed angrily, 'Oh Ssilissa, you false blue lizard!'

'Sssilence!' she retorted, her black tongue flickering like a snake's. 'Which of you is the Shaper?'

I began to understand then that she was not Ssilissa, but only another member of Ssilissa's race. Her face was broader, her expression fiercer, her head-spines longer and striped with indigo, like serpents. A perfect Medusa she looked, and I stood as if turned to stone while her black-in-black eyes looked me up and down.

'I believe I am the one you are looking for,' said Mother quietly.

The blue creature looked at her. 'You? *You* are the Shaper?' She laughed in the same hissing manner as Ssilissa. 'We were told you were harmlessss, but I had not guessed just how harmlessss. You will come with ussss or we shall kill your companionsss.'

'Oh, that would never do!' said Mother. 'Certainly I shall come with you. But might we close the door? I don't know about you, but I find the aether rather thin out here.'

She was quite right; the aether here was not just thin, but chilly too. I was shivering despite my fur-lined cape, and all three of us were having difficulty breathing. But our cruel captor gave another sibilant laugh. 'We are the Sssnilth. We can breathe thinner stuff than this. We are ssuperior to your creations, little Shaper. You will come with usss.'

So saying, she hissed an instruction to her companions,

who ran out on to the silver mesh of the net which held us and signalled upwards. At once the great moth from which the net hung began to fly towards the rings of Georgium Sidus, apparently following a great crowd of its kind, many of whom carried the lifeboats of our shipmates in similar nets.

'They were clearly expecting us,' said Mother thoughtfully. 'I wonder how they knew that we were coming?' Then she brightened and said, 'At least all the lifeboats are being taken towards the same place. No doubt when we reach it we shall be reunited with Art.'

Ahead of us, ghostly behind the rings of Georgium Sidus, a strange shape hung amid a swarm of the giant moths. I could not make it out at first, veiled as it was by those fluttering, shimmering wings. Then, as we drew closer and the moths thinned, I saw it plain. It was a huge, dark hulk of space-battered metal, shaped in the semblance of some great and evil fish, with bulging window-eyes and iron rudders for fins. Its pugnacious jaws were open wide and the moths were flying into the darkness between them.

'Remarkable!' exclaimed Father. 'Is that thing their home?'

'I think it is a means of transport for them,' said Mother,

watching just as intently. 'Impressive though these moths are, I should not think they can travel at alchemical speeds. The ship is what brought them here.'

'Brought them from where, Mother dear?' I asked. 'For they are Ssilissa's people, aren't they? And I am sure I have heard you say that you had never seen anything quite like Ssilissa on any world of the Sun.'

'That is true,' said Mother. 'Poor Ssilissa. She will be very pleased when she hears we have found her people, but I fear she will be in for a disappointment if they all turn out to be such rascals.' She tapped our captor politely on her armoured shoulder and said, 'Excuse me, but where *do* you come from?'

The blue virago glowered at her. 'We are the Sssnilth,' she

said. 'We come from *there*!'

We were passing through the rings now, a mist of ice particles and aether dust. Ahead of us the Snilth ship blotted out half the sky, but beyond it we could see the star-speckled blackness of deep space, and it was to that that our captor had pointed.

Spread across the face of the heavens was a great cloud of silver and gold. It was the same cloud which we had seen on Dr Blears's photograph back at Larklight, but it was surely far closer now. At first glance it might have seemed enchanting, for it rippled and glittered and shone like fish scales. But although it was still vastly distant and I could not guess what it was made of, some inner voice warned me that this pleasant appearance was false and that the cloud was evil!

'Is that where you are taking us?' asked Father. He sounded both alarmed and stimulated, for he is a man of science, and despite the blow he had received he was eager, of course, to observe that strange phenomenon at first hand. 'But why?'

The moth which was carrying us swerved towards the ship. Its battered iron hull blocked our view, and the cloud was hidden from us. The Snilth leader replaced her helmet as we flew into the darkness between the jaws. 'Your Shaper has been sssummoned,' she said. 'We are taking her to meet God.'

☙ 3 ❧

Naturally, I did not imagine for an instant that GOD really dwelt in that far-away cloud. His ways may be mysterious to us mere mortals, but I feel certain that He would never dream of employing spiny blue termagants. No, this was the Devil's work, and I had no doubt that the deity we were being dragged away to meet would turn out to be a false god, or else some heathen idol. *Presumably*, I thought, *I shall end up as a sacrifice upon some pagan altar.*

The moth which bore our lifeboat let it down with a tremendous thump upon the iron floor of the fish-ship's mouth and soared away to nest with others of its horrid kind upon the walls and ceiling. A great crowd of the Snilth came clustering around to drag us out and herd us, along with the men from other boats, down narrow, winding passages and into a sort of gaol somewhere in the ship's belly, where the *Actaeon*'s crew were being penned altogether. You will be shocked to hear that our captors made no distinction between officers and deckhands, for it seems that all humans are quite alike in the eyes of the Snilth! A score of the blue-skinned villains patrolled on a balcony above us, carrying objects which looked somewhat like bagpipes and keeping careful watch upon the huddled throng below.

Into this mass of captive humanity Mother, Father and myself were thrust. Being quite used to the manners of monstrous aliens, I was disgusted but not surprised to see that the Snilth had provided no separate accommodation for their female prisoners and that there was not anywhere to sit down. However, our brave British aethernauts are gallant even in defeat and shuffled aside to make a space for us near one wall, beneath a sort of great, dim window. Alas, it was only a small space, and that throng of men were packed close all about us so that the smell of tobacco, perspiration and patent hair-oil was almost o'erwhelming.

Not far away from us, among a knot of the *Actaeon*'s officers, I heard Dr Blears's shrill, sniping voice raised up in protest. 'This is intolerable! Intolerable! I am an agent of Her Majesty's Government, and a Gentleman! Am I to be treated like a common sailor?'

I agreed with his sentiments, although I thought he

might have voiced them more diplomatically. Some of the grimy tattooed fellows about him looked quite indignant at being called common sailors. As for the Snilth on the balcony above, they seemed impervious to his complaint. But one of them raised a set of bagpipes and, pointing a pipe at Dr Blears, squeezed the leathery sack from which it projected. There was a rushing noise and Dr Blears yelped in pain, clutched at his neck and crumpled to the floor!

Some of the sailors raised a soft cheer, and one fellow so forgot himself as to mutter, 'That's shut 'im up!' Father pushed his way through the crowd which had gathered about Dr Blears and, kneeling beside him, felt for a pulse and pronounced him alive yet insensible, stupefied by an envenomed dart.

We were wary of the Snilth's bagpipes after that and no one offered any further token of resistance as more and more captives were packed in with us. In vain we sought among the faces of those men for Art, but there was no sign of him. Nor did we see Sir Richard or Mrs Burton. Father asked around the officers and crew, and came back looking grave.

'No one knows what became of them,' he announced. 'Some of the men claim to have seen one of the lifeboats smash against a passing moth and vanish in a cloud of particles. But one fellow reckons that it drove right through the creature and plunged on towards the Georgian cloud-tops.'

'Oh, I saw it happen myself!' I exclaimed, remembering how cheered I felt when I saw that moth destroyed. 'Then, if that were Art's vessel, he may be safe on the planet's surface!'

Mother took my hand. 'We must all sincerely pray that such is the case,' she said. 'If Sir Richard and Ulla are with him, I do not believe he can come to very much harm. Yet as to how we might rescue them, I cannot at this moment imagine.'

By that time the last of the *Actaeon*'s crew had been brought aboard. The iron doors of our dungeon rolled shut with a dolorous clang, and a strange, deep music began to throb through the floor beneath us. It was like no sound I had heard before, and yet I recognised it as being somehow akin to the song of the great alembic that I had heard aboard the *Sophronia* and aboard the *Liberty* during our struggle against the Moobs. It seemed our ship was moving, carrying us away from Georgium Sidus towards who knew what destination.

Soon afterward, Mother drew our attention to the nearby windowpane or porthole. It was beginning to glow from without with a golden light familiar to anyone who has ever travelled the Golden Roads of Alchemical Space.

'The Benign Effulgence!' gasped Father. 'Then these creatures know the secrets of Alchemy.'

'They probably know them better than the Fellows of the Royal College,' Mother said. 'Do you not recall

Ssilissa's natural gift for Alchemy? Just imagine how skilled she would be if she had grown up here among her own kind and her talent had been honed and guided.'

'We certainly seem to be progressing with great rapidity,' I ventured, for I have a natural gift for Alchemy myself, and could sense that we were rushing through space at an immense velocity.

Mother put her arm about my shoulders to steady me, and said, 'Chin up, Myrtle. All will be well.'

But her face was filled with an expression that I had seldom seen on it before, yet knew at once. She was *afraid*. Old and wise and all-knowing as she was, even she had never travelled where we were travelling now, beyond the influence of our own dear sun and into the pitiless night between the stars!

⊱ 4 ⊰

I do not know how long that voyage took. Penned as we were in that uncomfortable and evil-smelling place, it seemed like days, but I am prepared to accept that it may only have been hours. I managed to find enough space to sit down, with my back against the wall beneath that golden window, and there I slept awhile. But it was an uneasy sleep, filled with disagreeable dreams and constantly broken by the groans and grumblings of the wounded, who were being tended by the *Actaeon*'s surgeon in a makeshift sickbay just a little way off.

When I awoke, it was to find that Mother and Father had been joined by Mr Cumberbatch and some other of the ship's officers. They were conversing in low voices and the subject of their discourse was, where might the Snilth be taking us?

'Surely, Mr Mumby, you do not think these brutes have flown here from another star?' asked Mr Cumberbatch. 'I believe there are several planets beyond Georgium Sidus. They must hail from one of them?'

'We have already travelled far beyond those worlds,' said Mother. 'I know them well. One is a water-world, where I am certain no moths could have arisen. The other, which you call Hades, is a small, dark place with a single great moon. Both world and moon are home to forests of greyish lichen and very little else. It is too dark out here at the limits of the Sun's domain for any higher life to thrive.'

'Why, but beetles live in lichen,' said Mr McMurdo. 'And moths are very like beetles, d'ye ken?'

'Oh come, my dear sir,' protested Father. 'Moths are nothing at all like beetles!' (Though personally I cannot see what the difference is, for both moths *and* beetles have abominable manners and a great superfluity of legs.)

Mother, however, was not to be sidetracked down these byways of entomology. 'The Snilth come from another star,' she said firmly. 'I sensed as soon as I set eyes on dear Ssilissa that she was not the progeny of any world I know. I feel it strongly now that I look at others of her kind. There is something about them which unsettles me. They are the children of another Shaper.'

'How on earth can you know such things, madam?' asked Mr Cumberbatch.

'Emily has a profound knowledge of our solar system,' confided Father. 'It may interest you to learn that she is four-and-a-half-thousand-million years old.'

'Though I think you'll agree that I don't look a day over three thousand million,' said Mother sweetly.

'And *I* am not yet quite sixteen,' I hastened to add (for I should not like anyone to gain the impression that *I* was millions of years old).

'Then I hope that with the great wisdom which you must have accumulated you will be able to find us a way out of our predicament, madam,' Mr Cumberbatch said, bowing.

'So do I,' replied Mother. 'But I confess that at present I am quite at a loss. And far from being able to help you out of this trouble, I fear it is my fault that you are here in the first place.'

'Nonsense, Emily!' declared Father. 'What can you mean?'

'You heard what the Snilth who captured us said, Edward,' she replied. 'They were looking for me.'

Just then we felt the ship begin to slow, and a sudden activity among our Snilth gaolers conveyed to us all the impression that our destination was very near. We turned at once to the window, which was darkening again now as the caul of alchemical particles which had surrounded the vessel began to fade. The glass, or whatever it was made from, was coated with dust, for it seemed the Snilth were not just cruel and warlike but bad housekeepers to boot. However, Mother breathed upon the pane and Father rubbed it with his pocket-handkerchief, and soon, between them, they had cleaned a patch through which we might see quite clearly.

But, oh, I almost wish that they had not gone to so much trouble! For would it not have been better to live in ignorance than to see what I saw then? The horror of it will live with me for ever, I am quite sure!

Reader, I implore you, sit down upon a soft chair, take a draft of beef tea or some other invigorating decoction and prepare yourself before you venture to read the next section of my tale, in which I shall describe the dreadful place to which the Snilth had carried us!

03 5 80

How often, over high tea in the drawing room at Larklight, poor Art has bored our visitors perfectly rigid with his account of the Great Storm on Jupiter. Well, at least if I ever return to sensible skies I shall have an anecdote that will trounce his. For the whirlwind into which the Snilth ship was flying was large enough to swallow up a hundred Thunderheads, *and it was made entirely out of moths!*

We were still so far away as yet that they looked no larger than the common moths of Earth. But they were so many that they filled the sky, from top to bottom and side to side: a perfect wall of moths, stretching across the aether ahead of us. And every single moth was flying in the same direction, from left to right, although in places a band of them moved slower or faster than their neighbours, giving the vast swarm a striped appearance. And in one place a sort of gap

appeared, and widened, forming the mouth of
a tube into which our Snilth ship plunged – a
tunnel whose walls and floor and roof were made
from the vast rushing bodies of moths, and their
flapping wings, and their awful feathery feelers!

'It is like a great hurricane!' cried my mother
above the deafening roar of wing beats from outside.
'How ingenious! A tempest of moths! A living tornado,
whirling from star to star across the aether!'

'But it must be travelling at alchemical speeds,'
declared Father. 'How can these insects possibly fly so
fast?'

Mother thought a moment, then replied with a
frown, 'These moths are merely passengers.
They fly endlessly within a bubble or field of
force which must be generated by some
object at the heart of the swarm. An object
capable of moving at immense velocities,
almost like . . .'

And she fell silent, as if she did not
dare to speak her suspicion.

It was dark outside now, for we
were deep inside that swirl of

insects, where even the starlight was blotted out. The aether was thick and silty with the greasy dust that shook from their wings as they battered and blundered one against another. But slowly, as we tore on through the storm's heart, it began to grow light again. Dim silvery beams reached through that tumult of heaving wings and furry bodies, as if some great radiance waited for us on the far side.

'What light is that?' cried Father. 'Surely we cannot have travelled all the way to another sun?'

'Look!' shouted one of the sailors. 'Look there!'

The close-packed moths outside the windows thinned, and were gone. For a moment I thought we had passed clear through that swarm and out the other side. Then I saw that we were actually in the swarm's heart, flying out across a gulf of empty space which lay calm in the centre of that vortex of moths, like the eye of a hurricane.

Far, far away another vast wall of moths whirled from right to left. Closer to us, in the midst of that emptiness, a ball of silver fire blazed like a midget sun, almost too bright to look upon. Around it turned the planets which were home to the Snilth. Tiny, knuckled, bony worlds they were, none as large as Earth's moon, and dark and dry as the clenched fists of dead pharaohs.

'It is a tiny solar system!' exclaimed Father.

'But it is not!' said Mother. 'That sun is not a real sun and those little worlds are not real planets! Look!'

The Snilth ship slowed and slid through a tight passage between a pair of the little worlds, and we saw that they were made not of rock and water, but of moth-stuff. Moth wings and moth bones and the dry, papery carcasses of long-dead moths had been bundled together with silvery thread and hung in orbit round that gimcrack sun. And over the surfaces of those worlds Snilth farmers crept, harvesting crops of blue-grey mushrooms from fields of moth dust. And out of holes and windows in the walls of the worlds Snilth faces peered to watch us pass, and we

peered back and saw in the shadowy galleries within whole families of Snilth, old ones whose spines had fallen out and infants whose tails had not yet grown, and large, blue, speckled eggs from which the baby Snilthlets must hatch. The eggs were tended by smaller, paler, less spiny versions of the Snilth who had captured us. I imagined that they must be slaves or some type of servant class, but Father (who has an eye for such things) said, 'Those must be the males! Look, my dears! In this strange place the natural order is reversed; the male Snilth keep house and tend to the needs of their children, while their women-folk are the fighters and doers.'

'How deeply improper!' I cried.

'I don't know,' said Mother, with a smile. 'It is not so very unlike Larklight.' (I suppose that was one of her jokes. I shall never understand them.)

And still our gaol-ship kept moving, gathering speed again and showing no sign of putting in at any of those pocket-planets. We flew over one where Snilth were tending rows of furry white moth-pupae and huge maggots were truffling for food, lifting their horrid faceless heads towards us as we went rushing by. We passed another where dead moths were being rendered down into broth and meat and piles of bone and wing, much as whales are treated on the Earth. In the chasms between the worlds flew other ships like ours, and harnessed moths carrying captured comets and asteroids towards still other planetoids, where smoke belched from the chimney pots of manufactories.

And then, ahead of us, close to that pocket-sized sun and half hidden in its radiance, we saw another world, still smaller than the rest. So small, indeed, that it was not a world at all, but just a house. A house like Larklight, hanging there in silver sunlight – except, unlike Larklight, it was not built of bricks and stone and mortar, but all of moth-bits, and with proportions that obeyed no earthly geometry.

And then our Snilth guards came shoving roughly through the crowd of prisoners, and the one who had treated us so rudely when she came aboard our lifeboat strode ahead of them, using her tail to knock down any man who did not step out of her path briskly enough. I looked studiously at the floor, hoping not to attract her attention, but it was me whom she had come to find – me, and Father and Mother too.

'You will come with usss,' she hissed. 'The Mothmaker is waiting.'

Chapter Nine

PREBENDARY MORTLAKE'S

'The Baptist's Bastion'

PORTABLE PULPIT EMPORIUM

In Which Your Hero Explores the Wreck of the SS
New Jerusalem and Experiments with an Ingenious
Yet Alarming System of Powered Flight.

W ell, that's all jolly interesting and spectacular, I'm
sure, but no doubt many of you are wearying of
Myrtle's company by now and are asking
yourselves in hushed and trembling voices what has become
of Art on Georgium Sidus, and how will he fare in his quest
to reach Charity Cruet's abandoned ship and there secure

one of her father's aetheric distress flares?

So I shall tell you, and we may return to Myrtle's account later, if we can find nothing better to occupy us.

I must have been quite exhausted by all my adventures of the previous day, for I slept as sound as any log, and when I woke I could not think, for a moment, where I was, until I looked out through the wall of Charity's bubble-home and saw a gigantic three-eyed fish go swimming by.

Soon after breakfast Charity's friend and protector, Mr Zennor, arrived, paddling up outside in a sort of underwater boat called a squoracle and letting himself in by slicing open the old wounds in the walls of the vestibule-bubble of Charity's little nest. He and Charity conversed a

long while in the Universal Sign Language, and I detected that she was telling him what we planned to do and that he was cautioning us to stay hidden, lest there were more moth-people abroad. But Charity won him round at last, and we set off, with Mr Zennor accompanying us for the first part of the way. I am pleased to say that we did not swim out through the gas-sea, but went by a much more convenient route through a whole series of neighbouring bladders, whose inhabitants greeted us with clickings and clatterings and cheerful sign-language 'good mornings'.*

At last we reached a central bladder, which seemed to

---

* The mer-people of Georgium Sidus are well known now, so I shall not trouble to describe the features of their undersea town – the luminous starfish which serve them for lamps, the water-filled bladders which they use as nurseries for their tadpole babies, the charming gardens of seaweed and shells. Nor is there space here to record the glimpses which I had through the bladder-floors of merman hunting parties down in the deeps beneath me, chasing luminescent sea-slugs across the ocean floor – that boundary below which the gas is so compressed that it becomes a solid, and where all manner of strange creatures creep about. But Mr Wyatt has essayed a few pictures to give a general impression of what I saw. Should you wish to know more I can recommend Professor Eden Griffith's *Descent into the Gas-Sea: A Compendium of Georgian Haunts and Habits* (published by Cutlet & Shortstop of 12 Clerkenwell Lane, London).

serve the merfolk as a type of marketplace, judging by the heaps of shells and baskets of fat Georgian lug-worms which lay about, though this was early morning and there were few merchants or shoppers present yet. In the centre of that great sphere a root-like structure hung down almost to the floor, and at its foot we parted from Mr Zennor with many kind farewells on either side, expressed through the medium of mime.

Then, feeling rather like that chap in the fairy tale climbing up his beanstalk, I followed Charity up the root and pushed my way out after her through a sort of rubbery trapdoor on to the upper surface of the floating island, emerging in the shadow of the largest cabbage I had yet seen.*

For a short time we lingered there beneath the shadows of the great plant's rubbery leaves, listening intently for any sound which might suggest the presence of moth-men out

---

* Now that I have read Professor Griffith's book I know that those cabbages were really Georgian sea sprouts (*Brassica aquatica*) and that the one I was looking at was the king sprout, the original plant from which that whole island of roots, buoyancy sacs and lesser sprouts had grown. There are now believed to be many thousands of such sprout colonies adrift upon the gas-sea. Several of the older ones are the size of small continents.

in the swirling mist. We heard nothing but the wap and waft of the gas-sea beneath the fibrous mat of roots we sat upon, and so, quietly and ever watchful, we set forth. Charity knew where we were going, and despite the mist she threaded her way with great confidence through that maze of towering vegetables, until I saw ahead of us a grey shape which turned out to be the good ship *New Jerusalem*.

My admiration for Charity's father increased no end, for I could tell at once that he must have had courage and an enormous faith if he had been ready to set out across uncharted aether seas in such a grotty old tub. She looked very like one of the little puttering pleasure ships which carry day trippers from Margate up on excursions into near-Earth orbit, except that she had been fitted with some spare water-tanks and cargo containers, all bearing the words, *LONDON MISSIONARY SOCIETY*.

She lay keeled over on her beam ends, which I think was a result of the moth-men's cowardly attack on her. Half crushed beneath her I could see the remains of a makeshift chapel which Rev. Cruet must have built against her side like a lean-to when she was resting upright. Chairs lay smashed and scattered on the rooty ground, and some kind of Georgian snail was creeping across the mouldings on the front of a patent portable pulpit.* Bright prints of Bible scenes blew about among the cabbages. Nothing else moved in that dreary place except for Charity and myself, who approached the wreckage carefully, half expecting lurking moth-men to leap out upon us, wielding their blowpipes.

You may have noticed by now that Charity is not the sort of girl who's forever reminding a fellow to brush his hair or fretting about getting smuts upon her bonnet. Not, to be blunt, a *Myrtle-ish* sort of girl. Quite the contrary; she has as much pluck as any chap. She scrambled up through a shot-hole into that poor old ship's interior as nimbly as you please, and then reached back to help me climb after her.

There were no moth-men waiting in there, thank

---

* There are so many portable pulpits on the market these days that it was hard to be certain, but I believe this one was a Campion Preach-Easy ('The Revivalist's Friend').

Heavens, though everything was awfully torn and tumbled where they had gone rampaging about. The wallpaper and furniture were sadly scorched and shattered, presumably by the same sort of fireballs which had been flung at the *Actaeon.*

Yet when we reached the flare locker and undid the catch, we found that its contents had not been disturbed. There were three flares and they looked just like outsize firework rockets, although a note from the Lord Chief Alchemist printed on their labels assured us that they were infinitely more powerful. Light the blue touch-paper and stand extremely well back and one of these beauties would soar a hundred miles into the aether and burst with the brilliance of a small sun.

'Well, they should do the trick!' I said, reading the instructions.

'Let's not linger here, then,' said Charity. 'I'd lay a hundred to one that there are moth-men about still, and the sooner we are safe under the cabbage-mat again the happier I shall be.'

Personally I should have liked to stay awhile and explore the wreck. I don't know about you, but I always find there is something about a wrecked ship that seems to *demand* exploring. But Charity was growing nervous, and I thought that perhaps it caused her pain to see her home laid waste in that untidy fashion and that it might bring back melancholy thoughts of her lost father. So she took one flare and I took the other two and we found our way back to the hole we'd climbed in by and jumped down on to the cabbage roots.

But no sooner had we reached the ground than Charity turned to me with a look of great alarm, signalling that I should be silent.* I understood at once, for I too had heard something. Out there in the endless fog, hissing voices were calling to one another, and they were drawing closer!

It was easy to guess what had occurred. Despite our caution we must have made some sound which had alerted a passing moth-man patrol, and they were coming to investigate!

We hurried round the *New Jerusalem*'s bows – but there were voices on that side of the ship too! We were surrounded, and it would not be long before our enemies were upon us!

'We must run for it!' I whispered urgently.

---

* The signal for 'be quiet' in Cruet's Universal Sign Language is a raised forefinger waved to and fro in front of the mouth. It is a great improvement on Myrtle's signal for the same thing, which involves throwing some books at my head.

'We cannot!' Charity whispered back. 'The moth-men will outrun us easily, and their darts will strike us down!'

'Then at least let me fire off a flare before they take us,' I pleaded, rummaging in my pocket for a packet of lucifers, 'so that people may know we were here . . .' And then, of a sudden, I had one of those Brilliant Ideas which come to me from time to time and have so often saved my bacon in sticky moments like this one.

There was no time to explain, so I took Charity by the hand and led her back around the ship to where the remnants of her father's chapel lay scattered. The snakey voices we had heard were closer, but we could not yet see their owners. Quickly, I propelled Charity up the steps of her father's portable pulpit and set to work. Like all good pulpits, this one came with a variety of Gothick arches and clustering vines and leaves. Pulling some string from another of my pockets, I quickly lashed my two flares to these handy decorations, one on each side of the pulpit, and struck a lucifer to light the touch-papers. The paper was reluctant to light at first, after its long exposure to the Georgian damp, and when I peeked around the pulpit and saw the grey forms of armoured moth-men appearing through the mist a few yards away, I thought for a moment that we were done for. But first one paper and then the next burst into sputtering sparks, and I hared up the pulpit steps to join Charity, who was still clutching her own flare.

'Cling on tight!' I warned her.

'Why?' she asked. 'What have you done?'

The moth-men must have heard us. There was a hissy cry, and one of their darts dinged off the pulpit rail close to my hand. It didn't matter; a second later the first flare fired, and the pulpit began to whirl dizzyingly about on the spot. A half-second after that the other flare lit, and the force of both combined was enough to lift us off the ground and send us soaring through the mist, startled moth-men diving from our path. Charity screamed, clinging to the rail. I clambered upright and gripped the sides of the lectern. It was shaped in the form of an eagle, and it wore a cheerful expression, as if it were pleased to have taken flight at last.

For we were airborne, propelled by those clever flares! If I had lashed them on vertically, I daresay we might have shot all the way up into space, but as it was we flew horizontally, low over the undulating root mass of the floating island. Cabbages flicked past on either side of us. Once one loomed ahead, but almost before I could begin to feel alarm we had smashed through it and were racing on

amid a storm of juice and sauerkraut. Looking back, I saw the stricken vegetable collapse, with a pulpit-shaped hole drilled clean through it . . .

And I saw something else too. Up in the foggy air a great shape was moving, tearing the vapours with beats of its enormous wings. One of the giant moths was pursuing us, and on its back crouched armoured moth-men, readying things that looked like bagpipes – yet I was sure they were not going to all that trouble simply to give us a rousing tune. Sure enough, an instant later, darts began to rain about us, clanging and sparking from the flying pulpit's ironwork.

I rummaged in a locker under the lectern and found several prayer books and a copy of Mr Wesley's *Hymns, Earthly and Otherwise*. These I hurled at our pursuers and I believe I hit one, for I saw him plummet from the moth's back. But the moth came on, and I had no more projectiles.

'A light!' cried Charity, and I looked round at her and saw that she was holding the remaining flare ready, aiming it at the moth.

I was loath to waste our last flare in this way, and yet I could see no other hope of escape. I remembered my victory over the dread sky-squid in the Jovian wind-race the previous spring, and the way my sister had exploded a pre-historic Martian starfish a few months before. There is something decidedly invigorating about blowing up gigantic alien monsters and it seemed unsporting not to let Charity have a go. So I fumbled a match out and lit the touch-paper of her flare, which she had wedged into a gap between the pulpit and the rail at such an angle that it pointed towards the pursuing insect. The touch-paper smouldered, sparkled, and with a swoosh of alchemical flame which singed our clothes and took our eyebrows off, the flare went soaring skyward.

But the pulpit chose that moment to buck, almost

throwing us off, and the flare missed the moth entirely and shot up into the clouds, where its light was quickly lost.

A dart snagged in the sleeve of my Norfolk jacket, but happily did not penetrate far enough to pierce my skin. Thank Heavens for good, thick tweed!

'Art!' cried Charity, above the rushing of the air past the pulpit. 'The other flares! Will they not soon explode?'

I had to concede that her point was a good one. The flares which powered our flight were meant to soar quickly for a hundred miles, but we must already have covered a large part of that distance, and soon they would detonate. I felt that it would be unwise to be aboard the pulpit when they did so.

I seized hold of Charity's hand again and together we scrambled to the top of the pulpit stairs – and jumped. We had long since left the floating island behind; only the swirling surface of the gas-sea lay below. We plunged into it and sank deep, while darts

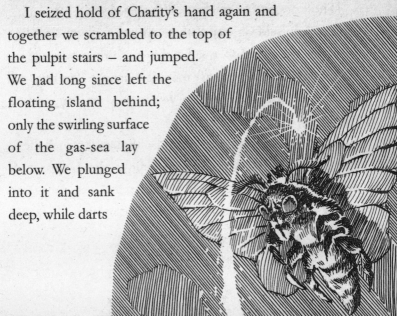

whizzed through the waters all around us, leaving trails of bubbles. Even before we regained the surface a dazzling light broke overhead, telling us that the flares attached to the pulpit had gone off.

We rose, spluttering, into that brightness, treading water in the gassy sea while the brilliance slowly faded. Of the moth there was no sign, and, remembering the habits of earthly moths, I hoped that it might have been drawn to that flame and burned up. But after a minute or so, when the flares had fallen into the sea and their light had gone out, we heard the sweep of great wings and knew that it was still up there, flying to and fro in search of us. And then, from another quarter of the sky, more wing beats sounded . . .

'There are two of the brutes!' I gasped.

'Oh Art,' said Charity. 'I think we must resign ourselves to captivity. If we do not let the moth-men take us, we shall surely drown. At least there is a chance that they will cast us into the same prison where they are keeping our parents.'

I saw the sense in what she said, although it pained me to admit it, since no true Briton enjoys the prospect of surrender to a foreign foe. It seemed that I was to have no choice in the matter anyway; already the moth was drawing nearer, and after another half-minute its horrid form became apparent, descending through the vaporous billows a few hundred yards to my left.

And then, a few hundred yards to my right, the second moth appeared – and, vague and ghostly though it was through all that fog, I sensed that there was something odd about it. I think the riders of the first moth sensed it, too – I heard them hissing to each other, and no darts came whirling down to knock out Charity or myself.

The second moth's wings beat more steadily and mechanically than the first, and sounded heavier, squeaking and clunking as they heaved up and down. Instead of fur, its great, rounded body was covered in oaken planks and sheets of copper, held in place by big square-headed nails. It was an aether-ship! And what was that line of square ports which opened so suddenly along its flank?

'Duck!' I told Charity.

'Ooh, where?' she asked, for she was a keen ornithologist, and she looked about eagerly for this specimen of Georgian bird life. As she was looking there came a resounding crash, and the mist on our right flared red and gold with cannon fire. Grape- and chain-shot went howling above our heads, and the giant moth crumpled like

a circus tent with all its strings cut and collapsed into the gas-sea, throwing up waves which almost overwhelmed Charity and me. But by then the ship which had rescued us was edging nearer, and ropes were hanging down from her open hatches.

I am sure you have already guessed what ship she was. I know I had. '*Sophronia* ahoy!' I shouted, cupping my hands around my mouth as I washed up and down in the waves. '*Sophronia! Sophronia!*' And she came lower, until she was riding like an ordinary ship upon the billows of the sea, and her main hatch opened and there stood Jack Havock, a piratical silhouette against the yellow light from the cabin!

Chapter Ten

Of Cocoa and a Captive.

'Art?' cried Jack. 'Can that be you?'

'It can and is,' said I, striking out for the *Sophronia*, and looking back to make sure that Charity was following.

'And is that Myrtle with you?' asked Jack, squinting at her through the fog as he reached down to help us aboard.

'No,' I replied, 'this is Miss Charity Cruet, whose father was a missionary here before those moth-riding ruffians made off with him. They have captured Myrtle too, I believe, as well as Father, Mother, Doctor Blears, the Burtons and the whole ship's company of HMS *Actaeon*. Oh Heavens, Jack, but I am glad to see you!'

I sat dripping beside him in the open hatchway while Nipper and the Tentacle Twins hauled Charity aboard. If Charity was alarmed at meeting a giant land-crab and two man-sized anemones, she did not let it show, being made (as I believe I've mentioned) out of Sterner Stuff than certain girls I know.

'But how on earth did you manage it?' I asked, as my mind ran on and I contemplated the sheer unlikeliness of Jack's appearance there. 'How did you come to Georgium Sidus so swiftly?'

'Oh, that was ssssimple,' laughed Ssilissa, joining the other Sophronias who were clustering about us. But we almost had to do without her explanation, for at the sound of her hissing voice Charity Cruet looked up, gave a cry of horror and, snatching Jack's sword from his belt, swung it at Ssilissa with all her might!

Luckily, all Charity's might was no match for Mr Munkulus, who caught her wrists in two of his powerful hands and used a third to wrench the cutlass from her grasp.

'Steady, young miss,' he rumbled.

'But she is one of *them*!' cried Charity, much alarmed. 'Art, we're betrayed! These people are in league with the moth-riders!'

'No, no,' I assured her. 'They are my friends. This is Ssilissa, the *Sophronia*'s alchemist, and as brave and true a blue lizard as one could ask to meet . . .'

'But hold hard,' said Jack. 'Are you telling us that those moth-jockeys look like Ssil?'

'I do not know,' I said. 'I never saw one yet without his armour.'

'Well, I have,' said Charity, still glaring most suspiciously at Ssil. 'And they are the very image of your friend here!'

Ssil pushed past us and stood in the hatchway, gazing out into the fog. 'Then there are more like me on this world . . . More like me, and we have drowned them!'

I feared she was right, for only a few fragments of the smashed moth remained, mere flotsam on the bosom of the gas-sea, amid a greasy slick of silver dust. No doubt those riders in their spiny armour had sunk like stones, and good riddance – but I could not help feeling sorry for Ssil, who had sought so long after her own kind.

'There are plenty more,' I said consolingly. 'They are *on* this world, but not *of* it. We don't know where they come from, but there were hundreds of them up in orbit when the *Actaeon* arrived. Did you not encounter them yourselves?'

Jack shook his head. 'We saw the wreck of the *Actaeon* adrift among those lumpish moons,' he said. 'But no sign of life.'

'How *did* you come here, Jack?' I asked.

''Twas your mother's doing, Art,' he replied. 'She left a note at Larklight, telling us where you had gone. And presents too: a Christmas cake for Grindle, a chart for me and a keg of some rare element for Ssil that made *Sophronia* fly faster than I believed a ship *could* fly. She was almost wrenched apart.'

'Mother did the same for HMS *Actaeon*,' I said sadly. 'But we had no sooner reached the planet than a squadron of those monstrous moths attacked us, and battered her most dreadfully.'

Jack nodded sombrely, as if he were seeing again the

wreck that hung in orbit. 'She's a rare old mess, all right. When we saw her we feared – well, we feared the worst. Yet when we boarded her we found her empty. A ghost ship, coated with silvery dust . . .'

'The dust of moth wings!' I explained.

Jack nodded. 'A dozen dead moths tumbled about her in the aether, and we saw fragments which told of the fall of many others. We thought they were mere monsters of space; we had no idea that they had had riders and that there was intelligence behind the attack upon your ship. But we saw that the lifeboat holds were empty, and then, when your flare came up through the clouds –'

'Charity's flare!' I cried. 'She fired it at the moth, but it missed.'

'A good thing it did,' said Mr Munkulus. 'Or we should not have known where to start looking.'

'And then those other flares went off in all this fog and showed us where to *finish* looking,' added Mr Grindle. 'And we homed in upon 'em and found that great insect flapping about, so we ran out the guns and fired off a broadside.'

I shook my head, puzzled by it all. 'There were legions of those moths in orbit yesterday,' I said. 'Where have they all gone?'

'Back to their own mothy world, I suppose,' said Nipper.

'And taken their prisoners with them!' I said. 'None of the other lifeboats made it to the surface. The moth-men threw nets and snared them all. And then they took Sir Richard and Ulla and Mr Bradstreet, who were aboard my boat, just like they took poor Charity's papa . . . Oh Jack, we must find out where they have gone, and follow them there, and fetch our people out!'

'Jack!' said Ssilissa suddenly, from the hatchway. 'Listen!'

We all listened, and from outside we heard a faint, hissing cry. At once we crowded to the hatch, Jack and Grindle reaching for their pistols. Ssilissa stared a moment into the fog, then pointed. A little way off an armoured figure clung to a shard of moth wing. Its helmet was off and, as we saw it, it raised its blue head again and let out that cry.

'She is alive!' said Ssil.

'How do you know it is a she?' asked Nipper.

'I don't know, Nip; I can feel it sssomehow. Oh, she needs help!'

'Well, she ain't getting none, the treacherous lepidopterist!' growled Mr Grindle.

'Now, now, Grindle,' chided Munkulus. 'That there is a shipwrecked mariner and deserving of our help, no matter what or who she is. That is one of the rules of the aether.'

The shipwrecked moth-rider hissed again. Ssil turned to Jack. Her face had turned palest lilac and her dark eyes brimmed with tears of pity. 'Jack, please help her!'

Jack looked grim. 'We don't know these creatures, nor what they may be capable of. What do you say, Miss Cruet?'

Charity looked nervously at the shape in the fog, and for a moment I thought she would tell Jack to fly away and leave the moth-rider to her fate. But then she said, 'Of course we must save her. It would be most un-Christian to let her drown.'

'Then jump to it,' said Jack, and the Tentacle Twins fetched a lifebelt on a long rope, which they hurled towards the moth-rider on her flotsam raft. Three times they threw it out, and three times it fell short and had to be dragged back and thrown again. But on the fourth attempt it

dropped upon the piece of wing, and the moth-rider looked warily at it, as if she suspected it was some strange weapon and we were trying to hasten her end.

'Clap on, dearie!' shouted the Sophronias. 'Grab a hold!' They illustrated their words with gestures which were nothing like as precise as those in Reverend Cruet's pamphlet, but which seemed to make their message clear all the same. The moth-rider seized hold of the lifebelt, Yarg and Squidley hauled hard upon the line and a minute later we were all leaning out of the hatch to help her aboard. And I must say I was pleased to see her safe, despite the fact that she and her friends had been shooting their darts at us a quarter-hour before.

But Jack knew better than to let his heart rule his head, or to expect gratitude from that rescued foe. 'Bind her good and tight, Mr Grindle,' he said. 'If she is anything like our Ssil, she will be nimble and clever and devilish strong.'

The creature on the floor looked up fearfully at us and gave a sort of snarl as Grindle looped a rope about her wrists and tied it in a series of firm knots. Then she saw Ssilissa and her expression changed; she flushed purple, her spines bristled upright on her bony blue head and she began to hiss words that none of us could understand.

'What is she saying?' I asked Ssil.

'How would I know, Art? It is in no language I have ever heard. And yet I can feel her dimly in my mind . . . Her race . . . *my* race . . . we are called the Snelth . . . no, the *Snilth*. She thinks I am a traitor; she wonders what I am doing here with you. She thinks I have betrayed the Mothmaker . . .'

'Who?' asked Jack. 'Who's the Mothmaker?'

Ssilissa shook her head, looking confused and distracted. 'I do not know . . . Oh Jack, someone . . . something . . . wonderful and terrible . . . and She is coming . . . ! The Snilth who came to this world were just an advance guard. Many more are coming, and the Mothmaker comes with them!'

Everyone stared at Ssil and looked from her to her armoured twin and wondered what it could all mean, until Jack said, 'Enough of this. Fire up the alembic, Ssil. We're bound for high orbit.'

'What about our prisoner here?' asked Mr Munkulus.

'Why, shut her in a spare cabin and see if you make any sense of her hissing and spitting. I want to know who these blue devils are, and what they want, and where they are holding Myrtle and Mr and Mrs Mumby. And then perhaps we shall go after them and teach them what happens to creatures who make prisoners of our friends.'

'Aye aye, Jack,' the Sophronias mumbled, hurrying to their stations while Yarg and Squidley heaved the hatch to, blotting out that foggy Georgian morning. But Ssilissa still lingered, staring after our prisoner as Mr Munkulus and Nipper pushed her firmly towards the spare cabin.

Jack looked worriedly at Ssil. He never normally had to ask her twice to do a thing; usually she was a step ahead of him, ready to obey his orders before even he knew what they would be. But she seemed quite distracted now, and washes of colour chased across her strange blue face, turning it lilac, mauve and many other similar shades which only the French have bothered to think up names for.

'The engines, Ssil,' said Jack.

'Of course – I mean, aye aye, Jack . . .'

But Jack and I stood watching her as she hurried aft into the wedding chamber.

I believe we were both wondering the same thing. If it came to a fight with the moth-riders, would Ssilissa side with us or with them?

While Jack took the wheel and guided the ship spaceward through the soggy clouds, Nipper took charge of Charity and me. Hot chocolate, warmed on the galley stove, was poured into mugs and handed to us with instructions to 'drink up quick, afore we lose gravity'. For despite Jack's radical notions he is a great traditionalist and still hasn't fitted a gravity generator aboard that old ship of his.

I took Nip's advice and gulped my cocoa quick, but Charity, less used to space travel than I, sipped hers gently and still had half a mugful when we broke from the planet's gravity. It went wobbling out of her mug like a glistening chocolate balloon. I swam after it, hoping to trap it in my own mug and show her what an old hand I am at aether-faring, but before I could reach it Jack came drifting by, his telescope in his hand and a look of worried perplexity upon his face.

'Art,' he said, 'come and give me your opinion upon this.'

'Upon what?' I said.

'There is a sort of cloud or stain upon the aether. It was hidden from us by the planet's face when we arrived, but now there is no missing it . . .'

'Oh, that,' I said, taking the telescope and boosting myself to the nearest porthole. What with all the excitement of moths and mermen which Georgium Sidus had offered us, I had quite forgot the mystery cloud, but now I recalled it. 'That is what brought us out here in the first place. It is an anomalous spatial phenomenon.' But just when I was thinking myself very clever for trotting out all those long words, I peeked out through that porthole, and almost squeaked with fright.

That cloud, which had been a merest smudge on Dr Blears's photographs, looked vast and threatening from here, blotting out the stars and dwarfing Georgium Sidus's tiny moons, which showed black against its glittering, shimmering pallor. I wondered why I had not noticed it when I first entered Georgian space. Had the *Actaeon*, too, been on the wrong side of the planet? *Or had it grown immeasurably during the time that I had been upon Georgium Sidus?*

'Reckon that has something to do with our mothy chums?' asked Jack.

I nodded. 'Do you think that is where we will find Mother and Father and Myrtle?' I asked. 'Do you think that is where we must go?'

Jack shrugged (it is horribly difficult to shrug convincingly in zero BSG, but Jack is an old hand at such manoeuvres). 'Don't see much point in going to meet it,' he said. 'For from what I see, that thing is coming to us, and coming at a fair old speed too.'

'Oh Rowlocks and Ratlines!' exclaimed Mr Grindle from somewhere below us. I thought at first that it was the horrid prospect of that vast approaching cloud which had driven him to use such colourful language, but when I looked I saw that he did not even have his telescope out. He had been into the galley to begin preparing our dinner, and now he had emerged again, still in his grease-stained cook's apron, and was doing what appeared to be a savage war dance on the planking just outside the door.

Jack shut up his telescope and jumped down. 'What is it, Grindle?' he asked.

Grindle made a few last savage stamps, squashing flat what appeared to be some raisins. He swiped another from mid-air and said, ''Tis those pesky Pudding Worms again, Jack! The cake Mrs Mumby gave us must have been infested with them while it was still at Larklight! The little beggars have scoffed all that was in the galley too!'

Jack uttered an oath which would have made Myrtle faint away had she been there to hear. Indeed, I almost fainted myself. Where *did* he learn such words, I wondered?

'So we have no provisions left?' asked Mr Munkulus, drifting by with a worried expression.

'Not unless you fancy pudding-beetle for breakfast, dinner and tea,' retorted Grindle. 'There's a few boxes of ship's biscuits left, but all else is quite ruined. I hadn't planned a long voyage, see – thought we'd be tied up snug at Larklight for a week or two, with never a need for salt beef or salmagundi.'

Jack shook his head. 'This ain't so good. There's unknown dangers coming, and whether we stand and face 'em or run before 'em, we shall need a good full larder.'

'Oh, sir!' cried Charity Cruet, putting up her hand. 'If you please, sir! We could catch some fish. There are shoals of great, vast icthyomorphs cruising all about this planet and its moons. My father called them Georgian gulpers, and declared they were the fattest space fish that he ever did see. Might we not lay in a few of them?'

Jack looked thoughtful for a moment, but I could see that my friend's quick thinking pleased him. 'Very well, miss,' he said. 'You and Art can go aloft with line and tackle, while the rest of you make the ship ready to fight or flee before that cloud arrives.'

And so it was that, by the light of that immense, ominous, approaching cloud, Charity Cruet and I went space-fishing.

Chapter Eleven

In Which, with Our Pocket Handkerchiefs at the Ready, We Return to Myrtle's Account and Learn of a Tragic Event within the Storm of Moths.

A Young Lady's Adventures in Unknown Space (Continued).

 C₃ 6 ₰

It never ceases to astonish me that our English fashions in interior design have yet to be adopted by the residents of other spheres. You would think that a Martian, having once seen one of our lovely homes with all its carpets, wallpapers and panelling, would begin to feel dissatisfied and even peeved with his own miserable dwelling place, which is made like a wasp's nest out of paper and spittle. You might imagine that the people of Io, having once been exposed to our superior architecture, would knock down their warrens of blue mud and start putting up some nice townhouses in their place. But no; Martians and Ionians alike cling to their old ways, and we have hard work ahead of us if ever we are to persuade them to change.

Which is why it seemed very wonderful to me when the Snilth forced me after my parents through the door of that strange moth-built house in the heart of the maelstrom of moths and I found it to be decorated as prettily as any villa one could hope to find in Hampstead or Kensington. It is true that at first glance it seemed no more than a nasty, dusty den of moth wings and moth bones, bound together with strands of their silvery thread. But as the door swung shut

behind us I realised that my
eyes had been playing tricks
on me, and that I actually
stood in a very pleasant
hall, with a great sweep of
banistered stairs rising to a
landing high above, and
long windows through
whose lattices of stained
glass the silver light of the
pocket-sun outside slanted
sweetly. The mounted

hunting trophies on the wall above the hallstand were the
heads of creatures I had never seen or heard of before, but
is that not often the case in houses on other worlds? And I
was almost certain that one of the paintings on the stairway
was the work of Sir Edwin Landseer . . .

'Be careful, my dears,' said Mother softly. 'All here is not
as it appears.'

Father did not seem to hear her. He was looking about
him with an expression of great admiration. 'My word!' he
cried. 'What a superb display! I have never seen such an
extensive collection of aetheric icthyomorphs, all quite

unknown to science! No doubt they were collected in the void between the stars . . .'

I began to fear that the strain of our capture had disordered his intellects, and I looked questioningly at Mother, for the only specimen I could see was a stuffed pike in a case above the fireplace. But Mother said, 'Edward, I believe the owner of this house is working on your mind to make you see what she wishes you to.'

'But how can you know that our host is a lady?' wondered Father.

'Because only a Shaper could have contrived all this,' said Mother, 'and all Shapers are female.'

'Bravo, my dear!' called a voice from above us – a pleasant, educated, English voice; the last thing I had expected to hear in that far-flung quarter of space. We looked up, and there on the elegant staircase stood a gentleman in grubby tweeds, scuffed leather gaiters and a clerical collar. 'Your guess is quite correct!'

'Shipton!' cried Father delightedly.

'Eddie!' replied the other, with a look of great affection, and came hurrying down to meet Father at the foot of the stairs, where they shook hands in a most hearty manner.

'My dears,' said Father happily, 'this is Shipton Cruet!'

And, turning back, he asked his friend, 'Shipton, my dear fellow, how came you here?'

'The Snilth brought me,' replied that Reverend gentlemen, in a way that made it sound as though he felt most grateful to the Snilth for having done so. 'They picked me up on Georgium Sidus. Did you stop there on your way out, I wonder? It is a horrid planet – interesting flora and fauna, of course, but damp and dull and drear. I only went there because I thought I had heard the voice of God calling me to go and preach to the Georgians. Can you imagine anything more absurd? Of course, the Snilth were soon able to set me right; it was not God's voice I'd heard, but Hers.'

'Whose?' asked Father.

'Her. The Shaper who created and still rules this wonderful little universe of lepidopterae. She began to send out Her thoughts as She drew near our solar system, hoping that there might be one or two who would sense them and come to meet Her. But it seems I was the only one who did. At least, the only one who had access to an aether-ship. I was walking on the clifftop near St Porrock's one evening when I heard it clear as a bell: "Come to Georgium Sidus, Shipton; come and serve me!" Naturally, I thought it was the Lord speaking; my mind was terribly limited in those days, hedged about by primitive superstitions. She's explained it all to me. She's made me understand that there is no God; all our earthly legends of gods and angels are simply reflections of the Truth. It is the Shapers who guide and govern life all over the Universe.'

'I don't know about "govern",' said Mother, frowning slightly. 'I would not even go so far as "guide". We merely do our little best to set things moving.'

But the Reverend Cruet did not appear to be listening. 'In return,' he said, 'I have taught Her English – alas, I could not persuade Her to learn my Universal Sign Language – and told Her a little of the history and customs of our empire. She was most attentive. Most attentive. She really is a rather wonderful person, you know . . .'

'But tell me, Shipton,' Father said, 'what of little Charity? Is she here with you?'

'Eh?' said his friend, looking puzzled. 'Who?'

'Charity, old chap. Your daughter. Pretty little girl, about so high. Blue eyes. Pigtails.'

Shipton Cruet shook his head. 'No. No, I'm sorry, Eddie,

I have no idea who you mean. But to return to the Mothmaker –'

'Who is this Mothmaker?' asked Father.

'*I* am the Mothmaker!' called another voice. It had a clear, bell-like, musical tone, not at all like the reptilian hissing of the Snilth. I sensed a movement on the landing at the head of that elegant staircase and looked up.

What did I see? Even now I am not sure. At first I thought some vast and odious shape was stirring there, a slithering darkness pricked by many eyes. But before I could cry out or faint away, or do any of the other things that well-brought-up young ladies are supposed to when confronted by a monster, my vision cleared, and I saw that a tall and graceful lady was walking down the stairs towards us. Her hands were outstretched in greeting, and the vast skirts of her gorgeous dress, which were made of some fine, dark fabric patterned with golden eyes like the tail of a peacock, whispered down the stair carpet. Her face was pale, ageless and beautiful, and her eyes were as dark and wise as Mother's. She might almost have been Mother's sister.

'Welcome to Mothstorm, my dears,' she said warmly. 'I am so pleased that you could come to meet me!'

❦ 7 ❦

She smiled so kindly at us all as she reached the stairs' foot that it would have been easy to forget that we were not guests but captives, who had not come to her strange house willingly but had been dragged there in a prison-ship by her friends the Snilth.

'So this is the girl,' she said when she came to me, and she looked deep into my face. How strange and musical her voice was – as if an invisible choir were chanting all her words along with her in a great variety of cadences and melodies. 'But where is the other child? Dear Shipton told me you had two.'

'Art was lost when your soldiers attacked our aether-ship,' said Mother.

'Lost? How careless!' said our hostess, and for a moment the invisible choir took on a less agreeable sound – a discord of minor notes. 'But it is no matter. My moth-patrols will find him. He may already be on his way to join us.' She peered at me again. 'Quite fascinating! And did you really *give birth* to this child? You actually grew her inside your own body? How *deliciously* primitive!' She stared at Mother for a moment, then laughed. 'What fun we are going to have!'

Mother smiled sweetly at her the way you might at a foreigner or someone not quite in their right mind. 'And what has brought you to my sun, Mothmaker, across all the leagues of interstellar space?' she asked. 'I assume it is not merely a social call? Our kind do not usually seek each other out.'

'Our kind are not even supposed to go on living once they have helped to form a planetary system about their chosen star,' replied the Mothmaker. 'Are we not meant to Cease To Be as soon as the first life begins to creep and crawl across the faces of the worlds which we have shaped? And yet here we are.'

Mother inclined her head, allowing the point. 'Once I had shaped my worlds,' she explained, 'I found that I did not wish to die. So much life was stirring on all my planets! It all looked so *interesting*. I decided that I would live and walk a while in the gardens I had made.'

'And no doubt you thought that you were the only Shaper who had ever done such a thing,' the Mothmaker said. 'I, too, chose to linger and enjoy those worlds which *I* had shaped. Seven worlds in orbit around a silver sun. Beautiful worlds they were. Why should I fade away and leave them at the mercy of fate? So I stayed and steered those little creeping creatures to intelligence, and showed them my power, and let them worship me!'

'Then that is where we must differ,' said Mother. 'I have watched my creatures, and cared for them, and even taken on their forms, but I have never asked to be worshipped.'

'*I* worship you, dearest,' said Father shyly.

'Why, thank you, Edward!' replied Mother with a smile and quickly kissed him.

The Mothmaker made a disagreeable noise, like a pig snorting, and her invisible choir snorted with her. (It sounded like someone sneezing inside a diving bell.) 'You are fond of your beasts, I see. Well, so was I. It was amusing to watch them fight and bicker. It was delightful to raise one up as a tyrant over the rest, and then throw them down again. I revelled in their wars. I showed them the secrets of space flight and let each world battle against its neighbours. The faces of the worlds I'd shaped shone bright with their blood!'

I glanced at Reverend Cruet, expecting him to show some sign of disapproval at these un-Christian sentiments, but he simply stood watching her with a simpering smile upon his face. It was clear that the Mothmaker had him under some spell or mesmeric influence.

'Oh, my creatures kept me entertained for aeons!' she went on, smiling happily at her memories of all that blood-letting and chaos. 'But then a dreadful thing occurred. My silver sun failed. Some instability deep within it caused it to split asunder. It exploded, and all my pretty worlds were roasted and stripped bare!

'I just had time to save a few of my Snilth – they had always been my favourites, for they are so fierce and such a pretty blue – and I set out across the aether to find a new home for them. In the outskirts of my system lived a breed of giant space moths, and a few had escaped the explosion of their star. I bred more moths, even bigger and stronger. I formed them into the swarm that surrounds us. I used the engines of my Shaper vessel to forge a home there where my Snilth might live during our long voyage across the night. And I set a course towards the nearest solar system.'

'Which is this one, I suppose,' said Mother.

'Oh no. Not at first. Mothstorm has been whirling across the Universe for longer than you think. Our voyage has taken us a million million years. We have passed a dozen stars, but none has suited me; one was too hot, one was too cold, one was just the wrong shade of yellow. Most had never felt the hand of a Shaper at all and were home only to nasty spiders and other creatures of empty space. Some had been shaped, but the races which thrived there were too few or too stupid to make good slaves. So my Snilth took what they wanted from the worlds of those suns and on we whirled, seeking another. Until I saw a golden sun, with a teeming sea of worlds and moons around it. There, I thought, my Snilth will find a home.'

'And I am sure that they will be most welcome,' said Mother. 'There is plenty of room for them here among the outer planets. But I am afraid they shall have to mend their warlike ways, and I am at a loss to know what we shall do with all these moths.'

'You misunderstand me,' said the Mothmaker.

She still spoke sweetly, but the choir that sung her words beneath the surface of her voice had changed: they sounded shrill and angry, more screeching than singing. Her skirts seemed to stir and shift in some ghost-wind that I could not feel, and for an instant I thought they were not skirts at all but some oily, shadowy substance filled with cold gold eyes!

※ 8 ※

'You misunderstand me, Mrs Emily Mumby. I did not bring my creatures here in search of charity. I am here to take your worlds from you. They will become the worlds of the Snilth, and all the creatures who live on them shall be the slaves of the Snilth. From across the universe I sent forth the power of my mind. Your creations are not as susceptible to the power of my thoughts as those of my own Snilth and I could sense them only dimly, yet I was able to probe a few of them and I soon learned of some primitive primates who possessed devices which could only have been made by Shaper science. I guessed at once that you were still among them. I sought and sought for you, but could not trace you – until I happened upon the mind of this idiot priest. Among his thoughts I found the image of your Shaper vessel, which he knew as Larklight, the ancestral home of his dear friend's wife. I knew who she must be, this Mrs Emily Mumby. So I lured the fool Cruet to me in the hope that you would follow him and meet me here upon the outer edge of your system. For before I venture any closer to your sun, I have decided to make you a proposal. Will you join me, so that we may rule as gods together? Or do you mean to try to stop me?'

Mother spread her hands. 'How can I stop you? I have no powers to match yours. I gave them up when I chose to become human. The vehicle which brought me here has become a simple home, draughty but much loved. The machines which shaped my worlds have been destroyed. Unlike you, I do not simply manipulate the thoughts of others to give me the outward appearance of a human woman. All that I am is contained within this body of flesh and blood and bone. When it dies, so will I.'

'Then that is why I cannot see your real self!' said the Mothmaker, almost to herself. She circled us and her skirts rustled in a way that was somehow quite exquisitely repellent. She opened her mouth too wide and laughed in a manner I thought most unladylike. 'You fool!' she said, and her choir went on laughing as she spoke. 'You could have been a god, and yet you have chosen to become one of these brief, limited creatures! You are as powerless as them! I shall kill you, Mrs Emily Mumby, and I shall enslave these creatures that you love.'

Mother simply shrugged. 'You shall do as you wish, I daresay,' she said. 'For you are horribly powerful. But someone will stop you. Sooner or later, someone will grow tired of your tyranny. Perhaps it will be a human being, or an Ionian, or another from the worlds of my sun. Or perhaps your own Snilth will overthrow you.'

'They tried it once,' sniggered the Mothmaker. 'A queen rose up among them who dared to challenge me and tried to turn them against me. That was fifty thousand of your years ago, but my vengeance was so terrible that it still lives in their legends. Let them try again! I shall destroy them as easily as I destroy you.'

Mother reached out and took my hand and squeezed it hard for a moment, and let it go. I saw her do the same to Father. Then she stepped forward, and the Mothmaker took a step back despite herself.

'All I know is this,' said Mother. 'A god who does not understand suffering or love is worth very little, and how else can we learn to suffer and to love except by living as mortal creatures live?'

I thought her sentiments very beautiful indeed and well suited to that Christmas season, when we recall how one far mightier than any Shaper chose to be born a human baby in a manger. But our hostess only laughed and laughed, and as she laughed so she seemed to grow. A vast and inky shadow swelled around her, speckled with drifting motes of golden light, and her own shape blurred and spread and smudged till she and the shadow were one, an immense cloud of darkness and fire!

'Well, isn't this nice?' observed Reverend Cruet, beaming at us all.

'You wish to learn to suffer?' the Mothmaker demanded, with an unearthly laugh. Long tentacles of shade reached out and wrapped about Mother and pinioned her and lifted her from the floor. '*I* shall teach you how to suffer!'

Oh, gentle reader, I can hardly bring myself to write these next lines. My eyes grow misty as I set the pen to the page; my hand trembles and I get ink all over my cuffs. I close my eyes and I can still see quite clearly in my mind's eye the way the Mothmaker lifted my mother up, her myriad eyes glittering with chilly laughter, and how Father ran forward to try to defend Mother and was flung aside by a blow from one of those shadow-tentacles. The elegant hallway was fading from my sight, as if the Mothmaker no longer deemed it worth deluding us with her glamours. I saw her house now as I believe it truly was: not carpeted or furnished at all, but ancient and foul and full of dust and webs, its walls and stairways built from Snilth bones and the desiccated carcasses of moths!

Mother, struggling in the merciless embrace of the Mothmaker's tentacles, looked down at me and said, 'The Tin Moon, Myrtle! *You must go to the Tin Moon . . .*'

And then, as easily as a heartless boy might kill a butterfly, the Mothmaker crushed her. I heard her cry and the dreadful sound as her neck was snapped, and I saw the shadow-tentacles release her and watched helpless as her poor broken body fell upon the floor in front of me, stone dead!

And then I saw nothing more for a while, for merciful darkness overwhelmed my senses and I fell down beside her in a swoon.

Chapter Twelve

INTERESTING FLORA & FAUNA

Georgian
Gulper

№ 2

WHEREIN CHARITY AND I GO FISHING AND MAKE A MOST
SURPRISING CATCH.

I
t is strange to look back with the benefit of hindsight
and recall how happy I was that afternoon. I stood with
Charity upon the *Sophronia*'s star deck, casting our lines
out into the dark in hope of catching some of the great
icthyomorphs which came scooting past us, and thought
that truly this was the life for a British boy. Even the sight
of that ominous cloud smeared across the northern sky

could not dampen my spirits. Yet how soggy they would have been had I known that within that cloud my own dear mother had just been slain and that her murderer was plotting the overthrow of us all!

'Got one!' cried Charity at last, as her groaning rod bent almost double. I clipped my own rod into a brass contraption which had been screwed to the star-deck handrail for the purpose and ran to help her. Luckily we had both put on magnetic space galoshes, which clung like limpets to the iron angling-plates in the deck, for else we should certainly have been hauled clean off the ship.

Charity had caught an absolute whopper! I could see the starlight slinking along its scaly flanks as it thrashed to and fro in the dark off the larboard beam: an ugly-looking brute, whose wide mouth looked quite capable of swallowing us both! We wrestled with it for a few moments, attempting to reel it in, but it was too strong for us. Had the rod not been made of best Venusian bamboo it should certainly have snapped in half. When the angling-plate which Charity was

177

stood on started to be wrenched free of the *Sophronia*'s planking by the force of the fish's struggles I decided that, just this once, safety and speed were more important than good sportsmanship, and I drew a pocket blunderbuss from my fishing bag and shot the blighter dead.

Even then it proved no easy feat to drag the huge carcass alongside, but we called below for help and within a few moments were joined by Nipper and Grindle, who helped us heave it on to the star deck and lash it down with ropes. Grindle had his kitchen cleaver stuck through his cummerbund and set about butchering the fish there and then so that we could have it safely stored before the *Sophronia* moved off. Its severed head and still-twitching tail went tumbling away into the void, where they were set upon by shoals of smaller icthyomorphs. But as Grindle brought his cleaver down upon the dead fish's belly, a strange cry seemed to issue from within it. Grindle jumped back, much alarmed, as from the cut that he had made a human hand extended. It formed itself into a fist, which shook violently at us.

'I say!' complained a muffled voice. 'Watch what you're doing! You nearly had my eye out!'

Nipper quickly used his pincers to widen the cut, and in

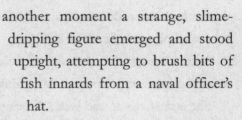

another moment a strange, slime-dripping figure emerged and stood upright, attempting to brush bits of fish innards from a naval officer's hat.

'Good Lord!' it said. 'Master Mumby? Heavens, but I'm glad to see you. I don't mind telling you it was jolly stuffy inside there!'

'Captain Moonfield!' I cried, overjoyed at this happy turn of events.

And indeed, it was he. Charity and I led him down inside and helped him to change out of his sodden uniform, while Grindle and Nipper went on butchering the fish. In the main cabin, under the wary gaze of Jack Havock, the good captain told us how he had been hurled from the bridge of HMS *Actaeon* by the moth-riders' bombs, and had plummeted through space until he was swallowed like a minnow by that passing Georgian gulper. (So you see how the Pudding Worm which had caused so much trouble at Larklight turned out quite providential in the end, for if its offspring hadn't eaten all the *Sophronia*'s provisions we should never have thought to go fishing, and poor Captain M.

should have been doomed to circle Georgium Sidus in an icthyomorphous belly till he died.)

'And what of the *Actaeon*?' he asked worriedly, as he struggled into a spare pair of Mr Munkulus's trousers.

'She is destroyed,' said Jack. 'We saw her wreck in orbit as we arrived.'

'Great Scott! And my men?'

'Captives, I think,' I said. 'The moth-riders herded them up and carried them away. They have my mother and father too. And the Burtons and Doctor Blears. Oh, and Myrtle.'

Captain Moonfield shook his head. 'This is a dark day. What do you think their aim is, these moth-rider johnnies?'

'I know what mine would be were I as strong and as clever as them,' said Jack. 'And that would be to smash your empire utterly and scour it from the Heavens.'

'Righto,' said Captain Moonfield. 'I detect, young Havock, that you're still feeling a tad peeved about that Changeling Tree business?'

Jack did not answer, but swam himself to a porthole and put his telescope to his eye again.

'You see,' the captain went on, 'I was rather hoping that you might carry me back to civilised space, so I can raise the alarm about these lepidopterous bounders.'

'Oh, I'll do that,' Jack said, as he looked out into the unending night. 'But I'll ask a reward for my services. Enough of the antidote to bring my family and the rest of the Venus colony back to human form. Do you think the British Government will think that a fair price for my saving their empire once again?'

Captain Moonfield said, 'If it were down to me, you know, you'd have your antidote straightway, without needing to perform any service in return. You're a brave lad, Jack Havock, and we should do whatever we can to put right the wrongs we've done you. That's what I shall tell my superiors.'

'That sounds fair enough, Jack, doesn't it?' I asked.

But Jack did not seem to be listening. He lowered the telescope slightly, gulped and put it back to his eye. An instant later he was turning from the window, kicking his way up to the steering platform and snatching his speaking trumpet from its hook. 'All hands!' he bellowed. 'Nipper, get that hatchway closed! Ssil, stoke up the alembic!'

'But half the fish is still outside, Jack,' Nipper protested, as he reluctantly bolted the star-deck hatch.

'Then it shall stay there!' Jack vowed, taking the *Sophronia*'s wheel in both hands and spinning it so that the old ship turned her bows towards the far-off Sun. 'We'll wait no longer here. That cloud is coming fast, and I can see now what it is made of.'

'And what is that?' asked Captain Moonfield, clapping hold of a huge chunk of Georgian gulper that hung amidships and carrying it towards the galley.

Jack Havock shook his head, as if he still could not quite credit what his spyglass had shown him. '*Moths*,' he said grimly. 'It is a million million God-Almighty *moths*.'

And as he spoke, the whole ship shook. Charity shrieked, tipped head-over-heels, and I too was caught all unawares and flung against a bulkhead. A greenish light flared through the portholes. I clawed my way to one and saw a great shape go swooping past us, vast wings black as a scrap-book silhouette against the ice blue of Georgium Sidus. 'The moths!' I shouted. 'They are upon us!'

'Oh Lord!' cried Charity.

'Ssil! Full ahead!' bellowed Jack.

And the alembic in Ssil's wedding chamber swelled with a song I'd never heard, and all the *Sophronia*'s aged planking groaned and creaked and crooned as Mother's magic swept the ship away from that moth-haunted planet and threaded her like a needle through the sighing, silken, shimmering stuff of Alchemical Space.

'That cloud is coming fast, and I can see now what it is made of.'

Chapter Thirteen

ON MYRTLE'S CAPTIVITY IN MOTHSTORM AND HER
OBSERVATIONS OF THE SNILTH.

*A Young Lady's Adventures in Unknown Space
(Further Continued).*

CS 9 SO

O
h, would that I had never woken from that swoon but had joined poor Mother in the sleep of Death! Yet wake I did, eventually, and found myself a prisoner, laid all alone upon the floor of a horrid chamber made of moth wings and moth bones and skeins of silken thread. Where was Father? Where was poor deluded Reverend Cruet? Where were all the officers and men of HMS *Actaeon*? Had they too been murdered by the beastly Mothmaker?

I did not know. My memories all ended with the sight of poor dear Mother cast down dead upon the floor at that creature's feet. I could only fear the worst.

It will not surprise you to hear that I wept bitter tears, abandoned there in that noisome oubliette. I did not even run to check the doors and walls for chinks and weaknesses and possible escape routes. What had I to escape to, motherless as I was, and perhaps an orphan, trapped inside that storm of moths, upon the fringes of a solar system which must soon fall utterly under the dominion of an insane demigod?

It was all too vexing for words.

After a time – I do not know how long – a hatch or doorway opened in the mothy wall and one of my blue gaolers entered, bearing a tray of what I took to be food. At first I turned my head away and was inclined to be haughty, but then I recalled Ssilissa and how good and kind she was, despite her silly infatuation with J.H. *These Snilth are God's creatures too,* I thought, *and it would be well for me to be civil to them, at least.* So I dried my eyes upon my handkerchief and looked at the one who stood over me.

I noticed at once that this Snilth was less spiny-looking than the rest and wore no armour, only a papery sort of shift. Its tail did not end in a bony club like Ssilissa's, nor in an arrangement of spikes and spines like those of other Snilth, but simply tapered to a point.* Indeed, this creature looked less ferocious in every way than other Snilth I had

---

* Tails are important to the Snilth. Only the tails of females carry spikes and clubs, and the number of the spikes and shape of the clubs are used to distinguish between the various Snilthish clans and families, which have names like Forktail, Threespike, Fisttail, etc. — A.M.

encountered, and it was watching me with unexpected sympathy.

'Your eyes are leaking,' it said. 'Are you ill?'

'I am bereft!' I replied. 'I am weeping for my mother, who was killed by your horrid bully of a Mothmaker.'

The Snilth hissed softly. It might have been angry at me for those unkind words about its goddess, but I chose to interpret the sound as a sigh of sympathy.

'And what has become of my father?' I sobbed. 'And all those other gentlemen?'

The Snilth glanced over its shoulder at the doorway, and then crouched down beside me, curling the tip of its tail across its blue feet. 'The other males are all unharmed,' it said. 'They have been carried to the moth-moon of Snil-ritha, there to toil as slaves. But the Mothmaker ordered you be held here in Mothstorm.'

'Why?' I asked.

'Because your mother was a Shaper,' said the Snilth. 'And because you are a female, and therefore more dangerous.'

'Whatever do you mean?' I cried. In my grief I had quite forgotten Father's theory about the strange reversal of the natural order among these creatures, and this slur against the gentler sex nettled me. 'I am a lady, and not the least bit dangerous.'

'But . . .' said the Snilth, and stopped. It touched both its ears (which I think was its way of showing puzzlement, rather as you or I might scratch our heads). 'Among the Snilth,' it said, 'it is the females who fight, and build, and plan, and make wars. It is the job of males like me to mind the eggs, and prepare the food, and keep the nest clean. Small wonder that your race is weak and easily conquered if you send mere males to fight for you!'

'But among my people,' I explained, 'the gentlemen are quite the stronger of the two sexes. They do all the soldiering and exploring and build up great businesses, while we ladies content ourselves with the domestic realm: needlework, watercolours, playing the pianoforte, etc.'

The Snilth looked amazed. Could it be that our earthly arrangements seemed as shocking to him as the Amazonian Snilth ladies and their meek menfolk were to me? Hoping that I had not offended him, I strove to change the subject.

'You speak surprisingly good English,' I commented. But alas, in my eagerness I spoke too loudly! There was a clash of armoured feet outside my door and a bitter, hissing torrent of commands, and our conversation was at an end.

The poor he-Snilth leapt to his feet and scurried away, pausing to glance back regretfully at me before he left my cell and closed the door behind him.

Alone again, I settled into my previous position on the floor, disdaining the bowl of bluish gruel my gaoler had left me. But although I wept many more tears, until my hankies were quite soggy and needed to be wrung out, there was a spark of hope now in the darkness of my soul; I felt that even here, in the house of the Mothmaker, I had a friend.

☙ 10 ❧

After that, whenever Alsssor (for that was his name) brought food in to me, he stopped a little while and found some excuse to talk. Strange and unearthly though he was, I became quite glad of his company, and the sight of his blue face always cheered me when it peeked at me around the corner of the door.

He seemed intrigued by the topsy-turvy world I told him of, where males toiled while females cared for them, and asked me a great many questions. I found it most pleasant to recall the little ways of earthly life: how gentlemen would open doors for ladies, and pull up chairs for them at dinner,

and walk on the outside of the pavements to save them
from being splashed by passing carriages.

In return, he taught me a little of the history of the
Snilth. Most of it was dull and bloody, since they had done
nothing for millions of years but whirl through space amid
their herds of moths, stripping bare any world which lay in
their path. But when I asked him whether no Snilth had ever
thought to question this brigandly behaviour, he grew
thoughtful and lowered his voice still further, and told me
the awful story of Zssthss Hammertail, a Snilth war-leader
in the olden days who had grown so powerful and so
popular that at last she tried to challenge the Mothmaker.

I guessed at once that this
was the rebellion of which
the Mothmaker herself had
spoken, so of course I did
not expect a happy ending to
the tale. But I was still
shocked at the cruelty of the
Mothmaker's revenge, which
was still remembered by the
Snilth thousands of years
later. All brave Queen

Zssthss's followers had been rounded up, and the queen and her clan had been put to death in a very dreadful manner.

'In *what* manner?' I asked.

Alsssor turned a greyish colour and said, 'It is too horrible to speak of. All her followersss . . . the whole Hammertail clan, right down to her poor little eggsss. Since then, not one of us Snilth has ever dared to even think of disobeying the Mothmaker's commands.'

೦೩ 11 ೮೦

Not long after that, I heard a great commotion of orders and jangling of armour somewhere outside, and the door of the cell opened to reveal not just Alsssor, but a female Snilth who was carrying the insensible form of Mrs Burton!

I cried out in surprise and leapt to my feet as the Snilth warrior dumped poor Ulla on the ground and stood back. 'How came she here?' I asked. 'Do you have her husband too? And Art? Was Art with them?'

Alsssor spoke in his own sibilant language to the she-Snilth, who lifted her visor to reply. She had a rather sweet face, with fine cheekbones and a small blue mouth. When she had spoken, Alsssor turned to me and said, 'This red-skinned female was taken along with a hairy-faced male and a young male hatchling.'

I guessed at once that the 'hairy-faced' must mean Sir Richard Burton, who persists in wearing the most peculiar beard. And as for the hatchling . . . 'Was he named Art?' I asked, overjoyed at the thought that my brother might be alive, yet wondering how I should break to him the bleak intelligence that we were motherless once more.

'I do not know. They were found on the water-world you call Uranus.'

'*I* do not call it Uranus,' I retorted. 'It would not be ladylike. Georgium Sidus is the name which well-bred people apply to that sphere.'

Alsssor seemed to be explaining my words to his armoured companion. She walked all round me, sniffing in a rather impertinent manner and reaching down to lift up the hem of my dress and rub the fabric between her blue fingers. All the time she and Alsssor kept up a hissy, slithery talk, which I presumed was about me. After a little of this the warrior reached out and brushed Alsssor's chest with her tail, then turned on her heel and stalked out of the cell.

'What was all that about?' I asked.

Alsssor blushed deep mauve. 'That is Ssoozzs Forktail. She has asked me to marry her. We shall mate as soon as she has money enough to furnish a nest for us.'

I blanched a little at his use of the 'm' word. (Not 'money'. The other one.) 'How quaint!' I replied. 'Where I come from, it is the gentleman who must ask the lady and provide a home and all the furnishings to go in it.'

'That is what I was telling Ssoozzs,' said Alsssor.

And he smiled, I thought, rather mysteriously.

12

There was no time just then to ponder Alsssor's words, for he had not long been gone when Mrs Burton sat bolt upright, clutched at her neck and cried loudly, 'Richard!'

She seemed quite discomposed, the poor dear, to learn that she was no longer upon Georgium Sidus, and that, indeed, whole leagues of space separated her from that squelchy and unprepossessing orb.

'The moth-riders must have kept me unconscious while I was flown here,' she said, springing up and beginning to check the walls and door of our prison for chinks, weaknesses, etc. 'But what have they done with Richard?'

'The Snilth are enthusiasts for women's suffrage, rational dress and other such reversals of the natural order,' I said (and I said it meaningfully, since Ulla Burton was herself somewhat of an enthusiast for the so-called Rights of Women. I hoped the Snilth might serve as an example to her of just where such unfeminine behaviour may lead if one lets it get out of hand!). 'The gentlemen are all imprisoned in one of their ramshackle satellites, but since we females are thought to be superior we are housed here, beneath the Mothmaker's house. The Mothmaker is another Shaper, like my mother, only a great deal more powerful and not nearly so well mannered. It is she who controls this odd rabble.'

Ulla looked at me. 'And where is your mother, Myrtle?' she asked. 'Is she held here too? Surely she will find a way out of this?'

I began to sob and told her all that had befallen us, while she held me in her arms and said, 'There, there.' Being a Martian, she offered a somewhat bony shoulder for me to cry on, but it was good to have a shoulder of any kind after all those hours and days alone.

'Do you think it possible that she is not really dead?' Mrs Burton asked. 'After all, she was thought dead before, and then your brother found her among the spider webs.'

'This time is quite different,' I said, shaking my head sadly. 'This time I *saw* her killed. And she has said often and often that when her mortal body died, that would be the end of her life in this world.'

'And are you sure she spoke the truth?' asked Ulla. 'If I had all her power and wisdom, I am sure I should never entirely give it up. Surely there is some hope?'

I dried my eyes and considered this. 'She did say something rather mysterious before she . . . before she . . .'

'Go on.'

'She told me that I must go to the Tin Moon. Why do

you think she said that?'

Mrs Burton shook her head. 'I cannot imagine. The Tin Moon orbits the planet Mercury, I believe. I seem to recall that it is a bleak and lifeless object. But if your mother said that you must go there, it would be foolish not to do as she asked. I am sure she had some reason.'

There was sense in what Ulla said, and I confess that she made me feel almost hopeful, until I recalled that I was at quite the other end of the Solar System from the planet Mercury, and a prisoner to boot.

'And what of Art?' I asked, drying my eyes. 'Alsssor – the Snilth who guards me – said that a young boy was captured with you on Georgium Sidus . . .'

'That was Midshipman Bradstreet,' explained Ulla. 'I saw him fall. If the Snilth brought only one boy back, it must be him. Which means that Art is still free! Oh, I pray he may find some way to rouse the Empire and let them know what this Mothmaker is planning!'

I agreed, but privately I held little hope. Art is so much better at getting into trouble than out of it that I feared he had almost certainly been drowned or eaten by now, and even if he had not, his chances of communicating with the wider Empire must be vanishingly slight.

∞ 13 ∞

A night passed, during which the Mothmaker's house turned away from the home-made sun which hung outside it, and the silvery light which had poured in dimly through our prison's moth-wing walls faded and was replaced by velvet darkness. I slept but fitfully, curled on the unyielding floor beside Ulla. Mr David Wyatt seems to have rather a soft spot for Mrs Burton and always portrays her looking very exotic and alluring, so perhaps it will shock you to learn

THE RECUMBENT MARTIAN ∿
D. A. WYATT

that she snores like a carthorse? It was almost a relief when the silvery sun returned and I could rise and stretch my stiff limbs and look forward to the arrival of Alsssor with our breakfasts. (The blue gruel, I had discovered, was a form of Snilthish porridge and really quite palatable.)

But when Alsssor arrived he brought no porridge with him, only two armoured female Snilth, who dragged Ulla and myself from the cell and started to haul us along the winding, dusty corridors of the house. Alsssor ran behind them, and I looked back and asked him plaintively what was happening, and whither we were being taken.

'The Mothmaker has called for you!' he said. 'I do not know why . . .'

Mere instants later we were thrust into a huge room, one wall of which was taken up by a surface of shiny darkness, like a pool of oil stood up on end or the blue-black shell of an enormous mussel. In front of this weird wall stood our foe, with Reverend Cruet at her side. The Mothmaker was once again in human form, her haughty face so distressingly like Mother's. 'Do not be fooled by her cunning disguise!' I warned Ulla. 'She is really a sort of smoky jellyfish, with ever such a lot of eyes.'

'And what about her friend, the clerical gent?'

'Oh, that is Reverend Cruet; he is a real person, but quite under the Mothmaker's control.'

'Silence!' commanded the Mothmaker. She was not speaking to me but to our two Snilth guards, who had been whispering behind us in their hissy voices.

The Mothmaker waved one pale hand, and the strange wall behind her flared with light. It was, I realised, some form of magic-lantern screen, and upon it was projected a picture of our sun and its various worlds.

'Mothstorm is travelling into the heart of your system,' she said. 'I wish to learn more of your mother's planets before I make them my own. Shipton has told me much, but you shall tell me more. Already we have passed the outer worlds – dingy, primitive little places, barely worth troubling with. The next is this . . .' And as she spoke, the picture on the screen changed to show a sulphurous yellow gas-planet girdled by fine bands of rings.

'The planet Saturn,' said Shipton Cruet triumphantly.

'Indeed,' Ulla agreed, but uneasily, as if she feared that even that might be too much information to give to the Mothmaker.

'It looks pretty when you see it like that,' I observed, 'but it is a horrid place. Those rings are infested by gigantic spiders.'

'First Ones,' said the Mothmaker. 'A formidable enemy. Very well; we shall pass by your *Saturn* for the time being and speed on to the next world . . .'

Behind her head, like a poisoned halo the banded disc of Jupiter appeared.

'This planet has many moons,' she observed. 'And there is life on all of them. Will the inhabitants attempt to fight me?'

'Never, dear lady!' said Reverend Cruet loyally. 'Not once they realise how charming you are!'

'Of course they will!' said Ulla fiercely. 'The Jovian moons are under the protection of Great Britain, and when they see your insect fleet approaching they will launch every ship they have, and . . .'

'Wonderful!' said the Mothmaker, with immense self-satisfaction. 'Jupiter shall be the place where I begin my conquest. You will tell me all you know of the ships that guard it, their bases, their numbers and the weapons with which they are armed.'

'I do not know any such thing!' I declared, quite truthfully, for I think it is unladylike to stuff one's head with facts and figures.

'I don't believe you do, dear,' said the Mothmaker gently, smiling at me. 'You are as innocent of military matters as Shipton Cruet. But this other creature, this red-skinned thing . . .'

'I shall tell you nothing,' said Ulla grimly. As an intelligence agent she had doubtless stuffed *her* pretty head brimful of facts and figures, but she was far too brave to betray what she knew to the Mothmaker.

The Mothmaker looked at her, and her smile faded. 'Oh, but I believe you will,' she said. And all at once she was back in her true form, and a tentacle of shadow lashed out and gripped Ulla tight, and other, lesser tentacles seemed to reach inside her head and go feeling about in her brain. And the Mothmaker laughed and said, 'So *Io* is their chief harbour – a squadron under the command of Admiral Chunderknowle – twelve ironclads – two dozen sloops of war – a scattering of gunboats – so few! So few! Why, this Jupiter will be even easier to take than I had hoped! I shall use it as a base from which to launch my onslaught on the central planets. How stupid it was of my sister to build such rich worlds and then to let mere fools and weaklings gain dominion over them!'

And her cackles pursued us along the corridors of Mothstorm as our guards dragged us back to the cell, like the maniac laughter of Snow White's step-mama in the pantomime.

I did not see what was so funny, of course. Nor did Ulla; it must be a quite horrible experience to have someone raking about inside your brain. She fell in a faint as soon as we reached the cells, and I asked the guards for water. One of them brought it, and then stood over me while I lifted Ulla's head and let her take small sips.

'Isss it true?' this Snilthess asked.

Ulla started to recover. I laid her down and turned to face the armoured termagant. 'Is *what* true?'

'That in *your* world the males

look after the females. They hold doorss open for you and provide for you? You are not expected to fight for a mate and are permitted to play with your hatchlingsss?'

'We do not use the "m" word in polite circles,' I replied. 'Not "male", the other one. And nor do I have any "hatchlings". But yes. You have been talking to Alsssor, I collect?'

'Talk to a male?' spat the guard. 'Why should I stoop to do that?' And she turned, and she and her comrade went clanking out.

Before I could construe the reasons behind her strange question, I felt a horrid yawning sensation in my stomach. Ulla felt it too, and moaned.

'Oh, whatever is that?' she whispered.

'We are changing direction,' I replied. I was not sure how I knew this, and yet I did. It was something to do with my talent for Alchemy, I think. In my mind's eye I saw the whole vast hurricane of moths and all the worlds and ships which hung within it changing course. And I knew that we would soon go swirling across the orbit of Saturn, and on towards the distant beacon that was Jupiter!

Chapter Fourteen

OUR VOYAGE TO THE MOONS OF JUPITER, WHERE THE CITY
OF SPOOLI PREPARES ITSELF FOR BATTLE!

O n and on the *Sophronia* soared, swooping across
the pastures of the Sun to where great Jupiter
hung amid its crowd of moons: the furthest
outpost of Britain's power and the first place where we
could hope to find help. A day and a night was all it took to
get there, thanks to the secrets which Mother had shared
with Ssilissa. On the way (when we were not busy repairing

the poor *Sophronia*, which was in constant danger of being shaken apart at that tremendous speed) we busied ourselves in making ready for war. Guns were cleaned and oiled, cutlasses sharpened, gunport hinges scoured of rust, and Charity and I, armed with hammers and chisels, set about chipping imperfections from the cannonballs, so that they would fly straight and true when we sailed into battle against the moths.

And behind us, as if it were chasing us, that unearthly cloud of insects seemed to grow larger and larger as it crossed the orbit of Georgium Sidus and then of Saturn, following us towards borders of British Space!

'Your mother knew something, Art,' said Jack, as I stood with him at a stern-port, taking turns to gaze through his telescope at the cloud, which held a horrid sort of fascination for us all. 'She sensed that cloud meant danger,' he went on. 'Why else would she have shared her Shaper potions with Ssilissa? I suppose she has never said anything to you about this Mothmaker?'

I shook my head. 'She has never mentioned any such person.' I thought back to the moment when I first saw the moths, from the bridge of HMS *Actaeon*. Mother had been beside me then, and I well remembered her surprise. 'She said the moths were not of *her* shaping . . .'

'Whose, then?' asked Jack. 'Is that what this Mothmaker is? Another Shaper?'

'Oh, I do hope not!' I exclaimed. 'For I do not see how even the British Empire could hope to fight such immeasurable power!'

Jack patted me firmly on the shoulder, which made me feel jolly manly and soldier-like, but set me spinning like a windmill in the absence of gravity. 'Don't tell the others,' he said grimly, as I struggled to right myself. 'If only we had a way to speak to that prisoner, we might learn something useful. But I won't send Ssil to question her. She's busy in the wedding chamber, and besides, it wouldn't be right to make her gaoler over one of her own kind.'

Charity, who had been listening to all this, now raised her hand. (She always did this when she wished to speak to Jack, as if the *Sophronia* were a schoolroom and Jack the teacher.) 'By your leave, sir,' she said, 'I may have a way to communicate with the prisoner.' And out from a pocket of the vast space trousers she wore, she drew a crumpled copy of her father's pamphlet on the Universal Sign Language.

'What is this?' asked Jack, frowning as he turned the pages. Then, 'Yes; yes, I see . . .' He glanced behind him to

make sure his ship was running
smoothly. The Tentacle Twins had
the helm; Grindle was in the galley
frying up steaks of Georgian
gulper, with Nipper helping him;
Mr Munkulus stood amidships,
ready to do anything that was
needed; the mysterious particles
of Alchemical Space whispered
against the speeding hull. Jack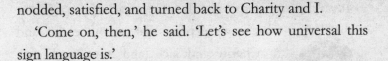
nodded, satisfied, and turned back to Charity and I.

'Come on, then,' he said. 'Let's see how universal this
sign language is.'

The Snilth floated sorrowfully in a spare cabin. She had
been fetched out of her wet armour and now wore a set of
Ssil's old clothes. She had been tied with stout cords and the
sorts of knots that only aethernauts and sailors know to a
ring-bolt on the bulkhead. She looked up and hissed at us as
we came in, and bared all her needle-teeth.

'Now, now,' said Jack, 'that's no way to show your
gratitude. "Thank you, Captain Havock, for saving me from

a watery death." That's what you should be saying.'

The Snilth watched him as he spoke. I thought there was something like understanding in those black, black eyes, but I knew there could not be. How could a creature from another star have understood the Queen's English?

Then began the greatest test of Rev. Cruet's Universal Sign Language. We showed our prisoner the pamphlet and untied her hands. Then, while Jack lounged against the cabin door with a pistol trained upon her, Charity and I engaged her in conversation.

It was heavy going at first. It took at least fifteen minutes for us to explain that we were Art and Charity and Jack (and how her lizardy mouth and hissing voice mangled those names when she spoke them!). It took fifteen more before we learned that she was called Thsssss Sixspike (which Charity said sounded more like a gas-leak than a name, and I agreed). And after that we found ourselves at a bit of a loss. The sign language is very useful for asking someone if they are hungry, or sleepy, or ill, or for discussing the weather, or talking about pieces of furniture. It is not so useful if you wish to say something like, 'Who exactly is this Mothmaker, what does she want and how do we defeat her?' We could find no sign for 'Mothmaker' at all and had to make do with saying, 'Who is the Fabricator of Flying Insects?'

I think that after an hour of fruitless hand-waving even Charity was willing to admit that Rev. Cruet's brainchild needed a little more work before it could truthfully be called universal. Or, indeed, a language.

All we really learned was this: that Miss Thsssss hated and despised us, that she revered the Fabricator of Flying Insects and that she expected our kind and the worlds we lived upon would soon be laid waste, flattened or possibly spread with butter (the signs for all three things being the same in Rev. Cruet's universal language).

'Well, I do not like the sound of that,' said Mr Munkulus a little later, when the captive was safely tied up again and the crew sat eating gulper steak around the cabin table.

'Me neither,' agreed Nipper. 'I do not want to be

flattened or laid waste.'

'Even to be buttered would be most disagreeable,' added Charity, 'if it were done against one's will.'

'I don't believe that blue baggage and her Mothmaker mean to butter us,' said Mr Grindle. 'You should have seen the look in her eye when we was tying her. She'll kill us all if she can. I say the best thing to do with her is —'

I imagine he was about to suggest that we throw our prisoner into space, since he likes to cultivate a bloodthirsty image and is forever saying things like that. But he trailed off in mid-sentence, for at that moment Ssilissa came out of the wedding chamber to collect her dinner, which she would take back aft with her and eat beside her alembic. Had she heard what we were talking about? I felt sure of it. There was a wary, suspicious look upon her face and her spines were all a-quiver.

'Then we must make sure Miss Thsssss don't get the chance to make trouble,' said Jack, watching Ssil as he spoke. 'We'll hand her over to the British authorities as soon as we reach Jovian space.'

'Oh no, Jack!' cried Ssilissa, almost dropping the covered bowl which she had just picked up. 'No, please! You know what they will do with her! They'll quessstion her, torture her perhapsss, and then, if she ssstill lives, they will take her to . . .'

'The Institute,' said Nipper.

Yarg and Squidley's twin mops of tentacles crackled with angry pea-green light as they too recalled the time they had spent penned and studied in the halls of the Royal Xenological Institute. No matter how dangerous our Snilthish prisoner seemed, they would not deliver her to that fate!

'Promissse me, Jack,' said Ssilissa softly. 'She ssseems unfriendly, I know, but she is the only other creature of my race I have ever ssseen, and I cannot bear to think of her in that place!'

'I reckon you'll be meeting a lot more like her pretty soon,' said Grindle darkly.

'Fair enough,' said Jack. 'We'll keep her aboard until we think of what to do with her. But we'll keep her well guarded. Yarg, Squidley – keep watch on her.'

When I awoke next morning we had slowed; Alchemical Space no longer soughed and whispered outside the curved wall of my cabin, and when I lifted the tarpaulin curtain aside to look out of the window I saw that the light of the Golden Roads had faded and the *Sophronia* was coasting in towards Jupiter. The giant world lay ahead, barred with its candy stripes of cloud, looking like some titanic boiled sweet adrift upon the blackness of the aether. Io, the most important of its many moons, was out of sight behind it somewhere, so rather than waste time steering the *Sophronia* through the gravitational tide-rips and shoals of system-ships which clog the Jovian aether, Jack set us down at the aether docks of Spooli, which is the chief city on the ocean-moon of Ganymede. Harbour officers came aboard at once, very angry at us for appearing so suddenly and unannounced, and for docking at an empty pergola without permission. But Jack greeted them with piratical insolence and said, 'Better send word to Io. That cloud astern of us may herald the ruination of your empire.'

'Some breed of beastly alien moths,' agreed Captain Moonfield, standing squarely beside the young pirate. 'And if we don't stop them they'll take these worlds for their own, and then head on to Earth.'

The harbour officers looked at one another and turned pale. They might have scoffed at such a warning if it had come only from Jack and his crew of ne'er-do-well

Jack set us down at the aether docks of Spooli.

unearthlies, but Captain Moonfield was so clearly an officer and a gentleman that they could not doubt him for a moment, but hastened off to the aetheric telegraphy office at once.

Within a quarter-hour the whole of Spooli was buzzing with the news, and we quickly found ourselves besieged by sailors and harbour folk of every race and species, demanding to know if it were true that giant moths were coming to attack us. Jack stood at the gangplank and told them all we knew, and it was not long before the Spooliites were arming themselves with whatever they could find and preparing to defend their fair city to the last being.

One memory comes back to me very clear out of the busy days and nights which followed. It is eventide, a few days after our arrival. All that can be done to prepare the *Sophronia* for the coming storm has been done, and I am strolling along Spooli's broad seafront, watching the light of Jupiter fade from the shining levels of the sea. Charity is with me, and Mr Munkulus, and we are all licking water-ices and feeling fairly content, for we know the *Sophronia* is in fighting trim, and we have been much reassured by the way the Army and Navy have been preparing to defend the Jovian system against the fast-approaching moths.

Soon after our arrival, Captain Moonfield left us and travelled round to Io, where he conveyed our news to Admiral Chunderknowle, the old officer who commanded the British squadron there. The Jupiter station was regarded among naval gentlemen as rather a dull posting, as there was never any trouble on the moons of Jove. So Admiral Chunderknowle and his staff were quite pleased when they heard Captain Moonfield's account of the loss of the *Actaeon* and realised that there was a *real* enemy in the offing. I think they looked upon the Snilth and their moths as a sort of Christmas present.

And, of course, he was very careful to let the admiral know that the warning had been brought by Jack Havock and his piratical crew, and to suggest that a certain serum held by the RXI might be a suitable reward.

There was one piece of information, though, which Captain Moonfield did not share. True to his promise, Jack had kept secret the fact that we had one of those enemies locked up in his ship and that he was still trying, through the medium of sign language, to prise from her any useful intelligence she might have about the mysterious

Mothmaker and her schemes. But since Miss Thsssss would tell him precisely nothing, that was perhaps no great loss, and if they had known of her, I do not think it would have altered the actions which the authorities were making. Indeed, I am convinced that they were doing everything which could be done.

As we stroll along the promenade that evening, we see everywhere the preparations for war. Sand-bagged gun emplacements are being constructed, and soldiers are

wheeling quick-firing cannon and phlogiston agitators into position on the rooftops of the taller buildings. Over the sea come sweeping squadron after squadron of warships, while at lower altitudes fly the slow-moving system-ships of Jovian merchants, on whose outer decks we see Ionians and anemones and Nipperish land-crabs and all sorts of Grindle-like goblins from the minor moons, waving ancient muskets and ancestral broadswords. The art of war is long forgotten among Jupiter's moons, but word of the coming of the moths has roused even those peaceable beings to anger. It is both thrilling and frightening to reflect that it is we who have set all this in motion!

Admiral Chunderknowle's flagship, the thousand-gun HMS *Unflappable*, with Captain Moonfield on board as an advisor, has lately arrived from Io and hangs in the sky offshore like a military moon, casting a deep shadow across the western headland of Spooli Bay. From launching cannon near the docks, pressure-ships take flight, ripping out of the fragrant Ganymedian atmosphere with dull booms and soaring towards Jupiter, where they will plunge into the wind-race to take the news to Thunderhead and ask for his advice and blessing on the coming struggle.

And yet, despite it all, the busy life of Spooli goes on. Fair Ganymede is a water-world and Spooli is a water-city, where elegant canals curve between the buildings.* Whole districts of shops and houses lie underwater for the

* You may sometimes have heard Spooli referred to as the 'Venice of Space'. But since it has been there for ten thousand years, it would be more accurate to call Venice the 'Spooli of Earth', don't you think?

convenience of the amphibious natives. Ever and again, as we cross the spindly bridges which that world's low gravity allows to be built in the most fantastic and delicate shapes, we look down and see streets beneath us where hundreds of anemone-folk are going about their business: a forest of gently waving tentacles, pulsing with multicoloured light. It is a lovely place, and I vow there and then that I shall return with Mother and Father as soon as this business with the moths has been sorted out and the moons of Jove are all at peace again.*

And as our portion of Ganymede turns its back on Jupiter for the night, and the twilight deepens, we see people gathering on the promenades to gaze wonderingly at the sky and at that splodge of ugly light which marks the approach of our enemy. And I look up at the British flag which flaps from a flagpole on the promenade, and despite all the ships and troops I have seen I wonder if it will fly there much longer, or if our empire shall soon be swept

---

* Of course we should have to find some way of losing Myrtle, for nothing is more likely to spoil a holiday than to have her drizzling on about the prices of everything and complaining that her delicate constitution has been upset by all the funny foreign food. It is a great pity that someone does not open a sort of boarding kennel for older sisters.

away and become one with Athens and Rome and the ancient empire of the Martians?

We walked back towards the *Sophronia*, through a harbour crowded with soldiers, and part-time soldiers, and plump merchants playing at being soldiers. There was a sense of confidence and almost gaiety in the evening air. 'We'll swat a few moths for you!' shouted cheerful redcoats, puffing out their scarlet chests and squaring their shoulders to impress the onlookers as they marched by.

A shipload of Threls was disembarking at No. 6 pergola, and among them, proudly bearing their knitted battle-flag, I recognised Sergeant Tartuffe. 'Sophronias!' he shouted when he saw us. 'The news has reached Threl, and we came as fast as we could to add our strength to yours! Our needles are with you!' And the Threls about him raised their gleaming crochet hooks and knitting

needles with a lusty war cry that I'm sure would have made the blood of a giant space moth run cold had there been any present to hear it.*

But we could not stop to chat to the Threls, for official-looking gentlemen were intent on hurrying them off to some mustering-point on the far side of the harbour, so we contented ourselves with waving and wishing them luck, and went on our way. Cranes offloaded shiny new artillery pieces from military transports, and passenger steamers crammed with ladies and children and their servants took off for Mars or Earth, where they would be safe when battle came. How happy I was that I was not being packed off like a parcel out of harm's way! I was eager to see those moth-riders taught a lesson after the way they had used us

* You will recall, I'm sure, how the Threls have laboured throughout their history to knit a lovely cosy coverlet for their asteroid home. Thanks to the wool which we had caused to be sent to them after their bravery during the Starcross affair, they had completed nearly the whole northern hemisphere and were busy decorating it with some pretty pom-poms. So you may imagine what alarm the space moths' arrival caused on Threl! Indeed, their prophets in ancient times had foretold just such a catastrophe. So it was small wonder that Sergeant Tartuffe and all other able-bodied Threls had cast off their knitting, picked up their war-needles and taken a train to Modesty Junction and then a ship to Spooli. They were a small army, both in number and in height, but their hearts were stout.

at Georgium Sidus!

We were close to the *Sophronia*'s berth when we were startled by a cheerful hail. 'What ho! Sophronias!'

We looked round and there, riding on a splendid tricycle-o'-war, sat another old friend from Starcross, Colonel Quivering (Ret'd). I had forgotten that he lived on Ganymede, where the gentle gravity and balmy airs were good for his lumbago. He was resplendent now in his regimental colours, and pedalling at the head of a column made up of elderly gentlemen of various species, some armed with dusty hunting rifles and elephant guns, others with golf clubs or broomsticks with knives lashed to the ends. 'The Verdant Meadows Retirement Colony Militia is at your service,' cried Colonel Quivering, standing up on his pedals and saluting smartly while his followers stumbled to a halt behind him. 'I hear it was you who raised the alarm about these invaders, Art. What is that they're called? Noths?'

Poor Colonel Q. He was a little hard of hearing, as were most of his troops, and they had ventured out to do battle with only the vaguest notion of what it was that they were battling against. I quickly set him straight and watched his cheery face grow stern and solemn as he began to understand the scale of the menace we faced. The other old gentlemen, who were not quite accustomed to military discipline, clustered around us to hear what we were saying. 'What's that?' they asked, cupping their hands behind their ancient ears or unfolding collapsible hearing trumpets. 'Moths?'

'I thought you said Goths!' declared a retired government clerk.

'Well, *moths* should not prove any great problem . . .' laughed an aged Hindoo merchant, who wore moustaches of such majestic size that even in Ganymede's soft gravity they required small helium balloons attached to the ends to hold them up.

'I don't know what all the fuss is about!' cried a superannuated aethernaut.

'Young people today panic so easily!' agreed an elderly Ionian. 'Now when *I* was a larva . . .'

As loudly as I could, I explained to them about the moth-men's explosive projectiles and the colossal size of the insects upon which they rode into battle. Several looked as if they might be regretting having joined Colonel Quivering's brave militia and might be thinking up some excuse to scurry away. But before any of them could say anything, we were interrupted by a shout from the *Sophronia*'s open hatchway.

'Help! Help!'

We looked up to see Nipper standing there, waving his pincers at us. A cutlass had been thrust clean through his shell and clear blood trickled down his legs. His eye-stalks drooped; his eight knees buckled. 'Help!' he gasped again and tumbled down the gangplank in a tangle of armoured limbs to land, unmoving, on the cobbles before us!

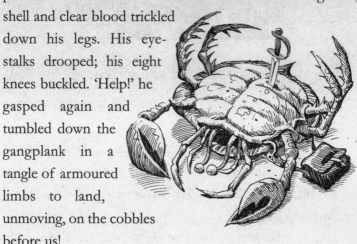

Chapter Fifteen

COOK'S EXCURSIONS

VISIT SPOOLI

THE VENICE OF JUPITER!

OF BATTLES BOTH SMALL AND GREAT.

'Nipper!' I cried.

He was alive, thank Heavens, and a medical gent from Colonel Q.'s company bent over him at once and said, 'He'll live. Some of you chaps help me staunch the bleeding.'

'The rest of you, aboard that ship!' bellowed Colonel Q., rising to the occasion. 'Charge!'

The charge of the Verdant Meadows Retirement Colony

Militia was a leisurely affair, for many of the gentlemen were in bath chairs and most of the others needed their walking sticks to help them climb the steep slope of the gangplank. Charity, Mr Munkulus and myself were well ahead of them and reached the top before they were halfway up. Mr Munkulus led the way with all four cutlasses drawn, and Charity and I peered between his arms into the cabin.

It had been shipshape when we left it: tidied and swept and cleared for battle. Now it was a chaos of burst lockers and upturned chairs, and in the middle of it stood our ungrateful prisoner, Miss Thsssss, a hatchet in one hand and a belaying pin in the other. The rest of the *Sophronia*'s crew stood round her, keeping out of reach of that flashing hatchet blade. Grindle, cursing inventively, trained a revolver on her. I wondered why he had not simply shot her down – and then saw the reason. Jack lay pinned beneath one of the creature's armoured feet. If Grindle's shot did not kill her outright, she would have time to bury that hatchet in Jack's skull before he could fire again!

I guessed at once what had occurred. Jack must have been questioning our prisoner, hoping to gain some extra scrap of knowledge about the moths and their masters, and

she had taken the chance to escape
and arm herself with some of the
arsenal of weapons which stood
ready in racks around the cabin.

'Sssurrender!' Miss Thsssss
hissed, glaring round at us.
'Sssurrender, or I shall kill
your little captain!'

'Golly!' exclaimed Charity.
'She speaks English!'

The Snilth laughed. 'Of
course. We Sssnilth learn
ssswiftly; the Mothmaker made uss that way sso that we
could more easily conquer and enssslave you lesser racesss!
I began to learn your language the insstant you brought me
aboard thisss reeking ——* of an aether-ship.'

'Then why didn't you say so?' Jack asked groggily. 'Why
did you make me muck about with all that silly sign
language?'

'It is not silly!' cried Charity indignantly, but no one
listened.

* I know where she learned *that* word – from naughty Mr Grindle.

'Because it meant that you had to free my handsss to let me make the ssigns,' Miss Thsssss said. 'I waited for my moment, and now the ship is mine! We shall take it to meet the Mothmaker and join in the conquessst of this sssun and all its worldsss!'

'All of them?' said Colonel Quivering, who had arrived, panting, at the top of the gangplank. 'I say! That's a bit greedy, don't you think?'

Miss Thsssss ignored him. 'Come, sssister!' she said, and I realised that she was talking to Ssilissa, who stood in the doorway of her wedding chamber, looking on, the only one of the Sophronias who had not snatched up a weapon when she saw her captain's plight.

'Don't listen to her, Ssilissa!' said Jack, who was rewarded with a fierce kick.

'Ignore her, Ssil,' said Mr Munkulus, taking a step towards our blue friend, but Ssilissa waved him angrily away.

'Can you not sssee what you are?' the other Snilth insisted, sensing that she had Ssil's sympathy. 'You are like me! We are the children of the Mothmaker! How can you let these inferior creaturesss keep you as their pet? How can you sside with them in the ssstruggle? Help me and I shall take you into the presence of the Mothmaker!'

Ssilissa turned a colour I had never seen her before: a pale blue-white, like moonlit snow. She did not move.

'Join me!' Miss Thsssss entreated her. 'Will you betray your own ssspecies for the sssake of these doomed creaturess?'

Slowly, gingerly, Ssilissa walked towards her fellow Snilth. Her head twitched from side to side, birdlike, as she studied Miss Thsssss's strange, familiar face.

'Can you imagine how I have longed to sssee a face like yours?' she asked gently. 'Can you imagine how I have always dreamed of meeting sssomeone elssse like me? It has been my dearessst wish, ssince I was jussst a hatchling. But if I have to choose between you and my friendsss, I choose my friendsss. These are the people who care for me, Miss Thsssss. I have lived among them all my life, ever ssince my egg was found frozen in the ice of a wandering comet in orbit about this sun.'

This intelligence had a most surprising effect on Miss Thsssss. She drew back, staring at Ssil. She hissed and flickered her black tongue like a viper. 'You lie . . .' she said, and then a jumble of spitty phrases in her own language. 'It cannot be . . .' she hissed. 'Show me your tail!'

Ssilissa looked bewildered by this request, but Jack, from

his position on the deck beneath the Snilth's foot, said, 'Do as she asks, Ssil!' So she shrugged her tail out from beneath her skirts and raised it in front of Miss Thsssss, so that Miss Thsssss could see the bony club upon its end, quite different from the six little spikes on her own tail.

The Snilth prisoner's eyes widened and she let out a sort of sigh. Then, to our great astonishment, she flung aside the hatchet and belaying pin ('Ow!' cried Mr Grindle, as the latter landed on his toe), got down off Jack and crouched before Ssilissa, bowing her head and spreading her hands in a gesture of submission.

'Forgive me!' she said. 'I did not know!'

'Didn't know what?' asked Jack, sitting up and rubbing his head.

But there was no time to enquire further, for just then, from outside the ship came a great loud boom, and then another. Preoccupied as we had been with the battle inside the *Sophronia*, we had missed the beginning of the greater conflict in the skies above Spooli!

While Yarg and Squidley dragged the Snilth prisoner back to her quarters, the rest of us turned to the open hatchway. Nipper, already much recovered, was limping swiftly up the gangplank, pointing with his pincers to something in the sky above the city. High above, a flower of black smoke stained the sunset. Higher still, something blazed and glittered.

'A ship is coming off the Golden Roadsss,' said Ssilissa. 'And look, another! And another!'

Pulses of light danced silently across the sky. High over the shoulder of Ganymede, warships were letting fly with broadsides of cannon fire. The pale beams of Rokeby-Pinkerton phlogiston agitators blenched the stars.

'But the Snilth don't have ships, do they?' asked Jack. 'They just ride moths, I thought . . .'

As if to prove him wrong, something came swooping

down out of the heavens, low over the sea, rushing towards Spooli like a storm wind. It was a ship, and yet it was like no ship ever seen before in the realms of the Sun. It was built in the form of a huge fish. Behind the windows of its eyes scuttled the tiny, armoured shapes of its Snilth crew, and from turrets and gun-emplacements on its back, banks of guns shot green explosions at the British warships which pursued it, hammering it with cannon fire. And as it came howling over Spooli's rooftops, its broad mouth hinged open and it spewed out a cloud of moths!

'An advance force!' cried Colonel Quivering. 'A surprise attack! Oh, the sneaky blighters!'

'Take us up!' shouted Jack, and at once Mr Munkulus started heaving up the gangplank, trapping Colonel Quivering and half his venerable army inside the ship. Ssilissa ran into the wedding chamber, Jack took the wheel and Grindle, Nipper and the Tentacle Twins leapt to their stations at the ship's guns.

'Miss Cruet,' I cried, as the engines howled and the *Sophronia* shot upwards into the noisy sky, 'can you fire a cannon?'

'Well, it is not something I have ever done,' said Charity, 'but I am sure it cannot be all that difficult . . .'

I snatched a ramrod from a rack and threw it to her, and then, as we broke gravity, picked up a canister of grape-shot in either hand. Together we flew to the nearest gun, ready to play our part in the defence of all that is Good and Decent!

Now, if you read an account of a battle, it is usually all very clear and easy to understand. You will learn how General So-and-so deployed his troops upon this ridge, while Marshal Such-and-such placed his cannon upon that hillock. There may even be maps, with little coloured squares to represent each regiment and arrows to show you where one advanced and another retreated. But when you are actually *inside* a battle, caught up in the rattling, rushing machinery of it, it is not at all like that. So please bear in mind while you read this account of the Battle of Jupiter (as it has come to be called) that most of the time I had no idea where I was, nor what was happening.

What became clear afterwards was this. That fiendish Mothmaker, hoping to catch us with our long johns down, had sent a dozen or more of those fish-shaped ships speeding ahead of her moth-cloud to breach the defences of the Jovian moons. Fourteen of them had appeared in the aether around Ganymede and from each there poured out a monstrous regiment of moths.

All I knew, as I clung to my cannon in the *Sophronia*'s main cabin, was that there was a whole lot of shaking going on, and that great balls of fire were bursting ever and anon in the void about us, causing the entire ship to shake, rattle and roll in a most alarming fashion!

Shouting over the din of the engines, I instructed Charity Cruet in the use of the space cannon, and together we loaded it and waited for something to fire it at. There was an isinglass porthole above the gunport, and through it we saw shells and grenades burst brightly in the inky dark, and once a ship a-fire, with sailors crowding into her life rafts and the Union Jack flapping sadly at her stern as she turned over and over, spilling splinters and smouldering debris. The *Sophronia* cut through that spreading cloud, with flotsam rattling upon her hull, and plunged straight into a mass of flapping wings!

'Fire!' I shouted.

'Dear me, where?' yelped Charity, and then, 'Oh, you mean the cannon!' With that she tugged the firing lanyard and somersaulted aside as the great gun leapt back at her with a ship-shuddering boom. The smoke was quickly left astern and I peered out and saw a vast moth coming into pieces where our shot had torn through it, and its armoured riders cartwheeling into space. Quick as a flash I picked up a second canister and stuffed it into the cannon's breech. But before we could fire again there was a shrieking crash from close outside, and acid green light shone in at us through countless gashes in the planking. Our gun was thrown backwards, breaking the ropes which held it to the deck, and went tumbling free across the cabin.

'Lash it! Lash it down!' bellowed Jack from his place at the wheel.

'Eh? What's that?' shouted Colonel Quivering's wrinkled

space marines, fitting hearing
trumpets into hairy ears
and frantically spinning
the wheels of their bath
chairs as they pirouetted
in mid-air, tugged this way
and that by the wind as air
spilled from the shot-holes in
the cabin walls. The tumbling
cannon batted Colonel Quivering aside and slammed
against the door of a cabin, smashing it into splinters which
twirled gracefully in every direction.

'Are battles always like this?' asked Charity, drifting past
me. 'I had no idea!'

Outside, a hundred ships did battle with a thousand
moths along a broad, curving front which stretched clean
around Ganymede's northern hemisphere and away
towards the flanks of Jupiter. Who was winning? I could
not say. I peeked from a porthole, but wherever I looked I
saw mere confusion. Ships were blazing or drifting
rudderless or vanishing into great thunderstorms of smoke
and flame as they fired broadside after broadside at each
other. Moths were flying into dust or fluttering wounded in

hopeless, dizzy circles or swooping about in squadrons shaped like arrowheads, their riders flinging bombs far faster than the British tars could fire their cannon.

A rusty old Ionian system-ship went flapping by, with knitted banners unfurling proudly in the winds of space and the Threl Expeditionary Force clustered on its star deck and fo'c'sle, hurling insults and sharpened crochet hooks at any moth which dared to flutter near.

A passenger liner, caught up somehow in the battle, tore past us, with schoolboys in scholars' caps and Eton collars leaning from the stern-rail to defend their mothers and sisters from the Snilth with catapults and pea-shooters.

And even in those bits of space where no ship fought or flew there were lifeboats tumbling, and huge sections wrenched from exploded ships twirling slowly, and bombs and rockets trailing streamers of smoke, and struggling Snilth clinging desperately to torn-off moth wings.

Looking back, it is strange to think that what I saw was only a skirmish, an outlying part of the great battle which was raging in the aether all around Jupiter. The great, striped face of the gas-world formed a backdrop to our struggle, and it was not long before even the Jovian cloud-tops were showing the marks of war, speckled with sooty black stains where burning ships and bits of ships had plummeted into the swirling atmosphere. I remember wondering what Thunderhead would make of it when he found some of that wreckage falling past him, or *through* him. And I wondered if it would matter to him whether the rest of the Solar System was taken over by the Snilth and their moths.

The *Sophronia* shook herself and her old timbers thrummed as Ssilissa brought the reactions in her alembic back under control. Shot-tattered space wings beat at the aether, righting us, while Mr Munkulus, bellowing through a speaking trumpet, encouraged Colonel Quivering's aged troopers in their efforts to stop the holes in our hull with tarpaulin patches and catch a hold of that dismounted cannon, which still twirled and bounced above our heads.

'Huzzah!' I cried, as we plunged into a great struggling mass of moths and British cruisers, and the cabin filled again with the stench of powder smoke and the booming of the great guns. A piece of shattered bulkhead struck me as I spoke, whirled me about and slung me head-over-tip towards the bows. As I righted myself, I found myself face to face with Ssilissa.

'Ssil?' I gasped, surprised, for she was the last person I should have expected to meet at that end of the ship. If she was here, then who was it working such miracles in the wedding chamber?

She raised one blue finger and waved it to and fro in front of her mouth in the universal sign for 'Be Quiet!'

And then I realised. It was not Ssil at all, but that other Snilth, whom I had forgotten in all the rumbustiousness of battle. That blast which had done so much damage must have smashed the bulkhead she was bound to and freed her! 'Miss Thsssss!' I cried – and she seized me and flung me aside, springing past me with an easy grace, like one well used to zero BSG.

I turned to try to follow her, but she had set me whirling like a top and there was, for the moment, nothing I could snatch a hold of to steady myself. Through the smoky air of the cabin I saw her soar up to the ceiling and go scuttling across it, lizardy-quick and quite unnoticed by the rest of the crew, who were all busy with the guns or at the helm. 'Watch out!' I shouted – or at least I started to shout it, but just then the rogue cannon, rebounding from a beam amidships, came hurtling towards me, crashed into me (which set me spinning in a new direction) and plunged out through the planking near the bows, leaving a large and ugly hole.

The air swilled out, the winds of space swirled in and I lost sight of the escaped Snilth for a moment. I was going to shout out again and warn the others she was loose, but I decided not to. She could have killed me if she had wanted to, but she had chosen not to, and so it seemed unfair to give her up. Let her escape, I thought, and return to her own people, whose ships and moths were all about us. And I forgot her and began snatching up a few spare shards and slabs of planking to wedge them across the hole.

Charity came to my aid and between us we managed to make a serviceable repair – but no sooner had we finished than the sound of the *Sophronia*'s engines faltered and died, and we felt the old ship slow and wallow, adrift upon the aether.

'Ssilissa!' I gasped.

Kicking off from the makeshift patch I had just made, I swam the whole length of the ship in one swallow-like swoop. Jack and the Tentacle Twins were already on their way to the wedding chamber to see what was amiss, and we arrived together at the door, which stood wide open. The Twins gave little trills of worry, flickering grey and lilac. Jack said, 'Ssil?'

She was gone. The emergency hatch in the outer hull stood open and I closed it sharply to stop the floating pots and vials which filled the air all flying out and being lost in space. But I could not help thinking as I did it that it would not much matter if they did fly out. For Ssil was gone, and without her what use were all her alchemical powders and potions to us? There was not one of us who could work the great alembic in whose heart the alchemical fires which powered the *Sophronia* were dying down to ruddy embers.

'It was Miss Thsssss,' I said, feeling very ashamed of myself for having let her escape. 'I tried to warn you . . .'

'It ain't your fault, Art,' said Jack. 'What we must do is find her.'

We ran up on to the star deck, half hoping to see Ssil and her Snilthish captor a-swim in space behind us. But it was impossible to see anything much in the fug of gun smoke which enveloped us. All about us bits of broken moth drifted aimlessly, and now and then a living moth whirled by. Far off, beyond the smoke, a steady hammering of gun fire and the regular stabbing flash of cannons showed us where the battle still went on, but the *Sophronia* was drifting away from it.

Yarg and Squidley gave shrill twitters of alarm and flashed indigo for danger. Their meaning was clear. The *Sophronia* had been caught in the gravitational tides of Jupiter and was being drawn slowly, helplessly towards the giant planet!

'D— it!' said Jack, striking his fist against the star-deck rail. 'We shall never find her now. Why did Thsssss take her? I thought she had come around; I thought she liked Ssil. It was all a ruse, I suppose. Throw us off our guard and then grab poor Ssil and carry her off. She's aboard a moth by now, or in the belly of one of those great ships . . .'

One of those great ships passed us as he spoke, cutting through the smoke above, battered and listing, its engines making a dismal moan. When it had passed we began to hear bursts of loud huzzah-ing coming from the shadowy ships which hung about in the smoke. 'They're going!' a distant voice shouted. 'We've won, lads! We've seen them off!'

The *Sophronia* turned lazily about, drifting sideways out of the smoke-bank and into the lambent light of Jupiter. And the feeling of victory that had started to swell in my breast at the sound of those lusty British huzzahs seemed suddenly to turn to ash.

The defeated remnants of the Snilth fleet were high above us, dwindling quickly as they fled towards the Mothstorm. But from the Mothstorm a fresh fleet, even larger than the first, was curving down towards us: a veritable horde of huge moths and still huger ships flapping across the flotsam-strewn and smoky aether. Very fast they came, and on the moths' backs their armoured riders could be seen fitting bombs into their slings and beginning to whirl them about their heads, ready to hurl at the *Sophronia* as soon as they were in range!

Behind us, as the smoke thinned, the crews of other ships saw this new threat too. Their cheering ceased and I heard yells of alarm and the shouted orders of the officers. Battered as we were, how could we hope to hold firm against another onslaught? I clung to the star-deck rail and watched, and knew that the battle was lost and the Sun was setting at last upon the British Empire!

Or so I thought . . . But just then, the narrowing gap

which separated us from these fresh moth-riders was filled by a bright rushing swirl of — what? Smoke, I thought at first, imagining that the Snilth's bombs had struck us and I was seeing flame-lit vapour venting from our wedding chamber. But the ship did not tremble or shake or fly into pieces. And now, before my eyes, the vapour was curling over, falling away from the *Sophronia* towards the Snilth and clenching itself like a great smoky fist upon those dreadful moths!

'It is a storm!' cried Charity delightedly. 'It is lots of storms! "O clouds unfold!"'

Out of the haze of Jupiter's stormy airs, great plumes of cloud were boiling up, for all the world like fists punching out into space. Wherever a Snilthish fish-ship or a concentration of their moths flew, one of these vaporous limbs reached out and seized them and dragged them back into the impossible pressures of the wind-race.

'The storms!' I shouted, opening the hatch to share the good news of our deliverance with those below. 'The storms of Jupiter are coming to our aid!'

'Good old Thunderhead!' yelled Jack, and I gasped as I recognised the great storm himself: a pillar of cloud shot through with lightnings and swathed with lesser storms, towering into space. He reached out cyclonic limbs and seized the fleeing remnants of the new Snilth fleet in half a dozen vaporous hands.

And was it only my imagining, or did that tower of cloud turn then towards the *Sophronia*? And did the top part of it seem to bow towards us? And did the thunder, booming through the gulfs of space, seem to rumble, '*My regards to your mother, Shaper's child!*' before, folding in upon itself, it went rushing back down into the wind-race, leaving the aether smeared and speckled with the dust of crushed moths?

I cannot be sure. I think those things happened, but no one else aboard the *Sophronia* noticed them, for they were all too busy scrambling up through holes and hatches on to the star deck and gazing out across the battlefield from which our enemies had been so abruptly swept. A few wisps of cloud blew past us: remnants of some small storm which had strayed too far from Jupiter's embrace and disintegrated in the wilds of space. The dust of dead moths drifted all about, filling the aether with undulating silvery veils through which shoals of icthyomorphs darted, nibbling at larger moth fragments.

'Good old Thunderhead!' I exclaimed, quite touched by the great storm's heroic action.

'And all those smaller storms too,' said Colonel Quivering. 'Friends of his, I suppose. Dashed brave. Deserve a medal, every single one of 'em. But where would you pin it on?'

'Not for nothing did my people worship him in years gone by,' said Mr Munkulus, pulling off his cap and bowing towards the mighty storm, which could be seen swirling once more in its customary place upon Jupiter's flank, a little more ragged than before and speckled with dark blots, but still magnificent.

'But all those poor Snilth,' said Charity. 'What will become of them?'

'The armoured minxes will be squashed flat as old tin cans down in the pressure-deeps,' said Mr Grindle with a heartless grin, 'and serves 'em right!'

'Not necessarily, Grindle,' said Mr M., still gazing up thoughtfully at Thunderhead. 'Thunderhead has his own ways and his own reasons. Maybe he'll keep those poor misguided creatures safe down in the wind-race and let them stay there till they see the error of their ways.'

'Who cares what happens to them!' I said gaily. 'It is over! We have won!'

'Oh no we haven't, Art,' said Mr Munkulus. 'We've won one battle, thanks to Thunderhead, and been granted a little more time, that's all.'

'And we've lost Ssil,' said Jack. He was staring aloft, where the surviving ships from the Snilth's first attack had shrunk to a cluster of speeding stars, bright against the speckled immensity of the Mothstorm. Somewhere in there, if she still lived at all, Ssilissa was a prisoner. Without her the *Sophronia* was powerless. And despite our victory, the Mothstorm was still approaching, and I did not believe that even Thunderhead could help us fight it!

Chapter Sixteen

Myrtle Tells More of Her Adventures in the
Mothmaker's Lair: of Curious Allies, Touching
Reunions and a Desperate Flight.

*A Young Lady's Adventures
in Unknown Space
(Continued Once Again).*

ᘔ 14 ᘓ

For how long was I incarcerated within that filthy, Snilthy gaol? I cannot say; the turning of the silver sun bore no relation to the passage of earthly days and nights. Indeed, in Mothstorm, day and night seemed to have no set duration, but to happen entirely at the whim of the Mothmaker. However, I believe I suffered there for at least a week, with only Ulla Burton for company and nothing to look forward to but the visits of the gentle Alsssor.

And then, quite suddenly, my captivity came to an end in a way which I shall now set down for you.

I woke one morning, in the usual silvery twilight of the cell, to find that I was being shaken. No well-brought-up young lady takes kindly to being roused in such a manner. 'Really, Mrs Burton,' I complained, before I had even opened my eyes. You may imagine my displeasure when I *did* open them and realised that the person doing the shaking was not Ulla, but Alsssor!

'Unhand me!' I cried, starting up at once and thinking that if my blue friend thought his recent kindness towards me gave him the right to go about shaking me, then he was very much mistaken!

But Alsssor, instead of apologising, merely set a finger to his mouth to hush me and then stooped to waken Mrs Burton in the same familiar way!

'You are to be moved,' he whispered, when she too was conscious. 'Come with me quickly.'

We did as he said. In the narrow passageway outside the cell, two armoured she-Snilth were waiting, carrying those horrid bagpipe-weapons. One, I was almost sure, was Alsssor's betrothed, Miss Ssoozzs. The other I did not know, and yet she seemed more kindly disposed towards me than many of the Snilth I had encountered. Was that a curtsey that she tried to bob, as Mrs Burton and I stepped out into the passage? Or was she simply adjusting her armour?

There was no time to wonder, or even to curtsey back — alas, points of etiquette must so often be cast aside when one is having an Adventure. With great haste, and with many urgent signals for us to remain silent, Alsssor and his lady friends hurried us along the winding passageways beneath Mothstorm, until we passed out through a bony arch on to a sort of quay, from where we looked out again over the Mothmaker's strange domain. Its walls of moths were whirling faster now than ever, and strange eddies flowed through the swarm, in the midst of which little pools of darkness would now and then appear. Since I am unused (thank Heavens!) to looking at a sky made out of insects, it took me a few moments to understand that those darknesses were holes through which I was catching glimpses of open space, before the moths around them adjusted their flight to close them off.

It was foolish, I know, as those fleeting holes were very far away and whole worlds of Snilth hung between them and myself, but they gave me hope. For the first time since I entered Mothstorm I began to wonder if escape might be possible after all!

Now Alsssor and his companions were hastening us across the quay to its edge, where a horrid moth, larger than many elephants, sat with its wings folded and its nasty feelers twitching and flicking. A ladder made of moth bones

led up on to its furry back, and I realised that Alsssor intended me to climb it.

'Oh no!' I declared, stamping my foot. 'I am most certainly not taking a ride aboard that horrid creature!'

Alsssor looked meek, for he had been brought up to fear feminine anger. But Miss Ssoozzs said sharply, 'Miss Mumby, do you not undersssstand that we are your friendsss, and trying to sssave you from the Mothmaker?'

'Don't be such a stubborn little prig, Myrtle!' Ulla admonished me (most unfairly!). And between them they coaxed me up on to the insect's back, where its rider, a male, sat holding the long reins with which he would control its flight. We had barely time to settle ourselves and to take a firm grip upon the monster's coarse red hair, before it flapped its wings and bore us away across the gulf. I looked back and watched the Mothmaker's ugly house dwindling behind us, until my view of it was blotted out by one of her gimcrack wordlets.

'The Mothmaker is busy with Her war,' explained Alsssor then. 'A great battle is raging, and She is watching and planning. She will not notice our essscape.'

'I take it that you are not friends of the Mothmaker, then?' asked Mrs Burton. 'Is there a rebel movement in this universe of moths? How many are you?'

'We are not many,' said Ssoozzs, while her fiancé explained what had been said to the moth-mahout, who spoke no English. (Indeed, I was startled to hear Ssoozzs speak it – I was sure she had spoken only Snilth when she first came to my cell.) 'We are few, and fearful,' she confided, 'and the Mothmaker is very sstrong. But Misss Mumby has brought hope to usss and made usss understand the way ahead.'

'Miss *Mumby* has?' said Ulla. And I am pleased to say that she looked a little vexed that it should be I and not her to whom these brave blue rebels looked for their example!

'We women of Sssnilth are tired of having to fight and be fierce and trample the corpssses of Her enemiesss under our iron-shod heels,' said Ssoozzs. 'Thankss to Misss

Mumby we can now imagine a better life.'

'We want to wear pretty dresssses, not thiss ugly armour!' agreed the other she-Snilth, blushing a fetching shade of turquoise.

'We want to be looked after for a change,' said Ssooozzs. 'We would like our menfolk to take care of us, to open doors for us and be bold and brave for our sakes . . .' And she shyly laid her head upon the shoulder of Alsssor, who put his arms about her in a most protective and gentlemanly manner!

'Oh dear G-d!' groaned Ulla Burton. (Though I cannot think why. Surely she should have been *pleased* to see that these Snilthish viragos had understood the error of their ways?)

 C§ 15 ю

We flew onward, and our Snilth companions fell quiet, looking up at a strange object which hung in the sky close by. A spiky, spiny star, the colour of dirty ivory, it dangled in orbit around the silver sun like some gigantic, unappealing Christmas-decoration. It was quite unlike the other little wordlets of the Snilth, since no one appeared to live upon it.

'What is that?' asked Mrs Burton bluntly.

Alsssor would only hiss, as if the spiky planetoid was a thing of which he dared not speak. But his fiancée, turning pale grey with emotion, whispered, 'It is made of *bonesss*. It is a world made from the boness of Queen Zssthss Hammertail and all those who joined her in her rebellion againsst the Mothmaker.'

'But that was millennia ago!' I cried, remembering the sorry tale Alsssor had told me about that doomed Snilth heroine and looking again at the thing, aghast at the sheer number of skeletons it must contain. 'Why have they not crumbled into dust?'

'The Mothmaker preserves them,' said Ssoozzs, 'as a reminder to usss all of what will happen to usss if we dare to disssobey her.' And it was no wonder that she looked so solemn, for was she not disobeying that cruel tyrant even now, by flitting us away from Mothstorm? 'All of Zssthss's family and all her followerss were killed and lie in that world of boness.'

'The Mothmaker seems to enjoy her little operatic flourishes,' Ulla observed.

I shuddered as the shadow of the bone-planet swept over us, and the moth yawed violently, forcing me to cling with great concentration to its fur while Alsssor exclaimed, 'Here we are! Thisss is the prison-planetoid of Snil-ritha. Many friendss are waiting for you here.'

∞ 16 ∞

I had been so intent upon our conversation that I had not noticed how far our moth had borne us. It was fluttering towards the face of one of those moth-built planets, and in a few more moments it had fluttered right inside through a ragged opening in the world's surface. I found myself looking at a most peculiar sort of town, in which all sorts of platforms and walkways were jumbled about on top of each other to make a great many floors of galleries. It was a little like looking into a doll's house with its front taken off, except that most dolls' houses are not made out of bits of moth and the dolls are not busy slaving away among vast

heaps of blue-white moths'
eggs.

I was tempted to faint at
the sight of all those slimy
spheres, some of which
were wriggling, and others
hatching to let out horrible
blunt-headed maggots as
large as hansom cabs. But I
restrained myself, for many
of the slaves who were busily
pouring glutinous liquids
over the eggs and carrying
the new hatchlings away on
litters up the winding
stairways to the surface, were
my former companions from
HMS *Actaeon*. And the Snilth
who stood guard over them,
upon seeing our moth
approach, flung aside their
whips and bagpipe-guns and
came hastening to meet us at

a landing quay, where several small fish-shaped ships were tethered. The moth found a perch between them, and I heard our welcoming committee hissing to one another, 'It'sss her! She'sss come!'

Could it be that they meant *me*? Was it possible that all these Snilth were would-be ladies, like Ssoozzs? I barely dared to hope it might be true. And yet, as the moth settled on the quay and our mahout lowered the boarding ladder, every one of those armoured she-devils sketched a clumsy curtsey!

I went down the ladder, slapped the dust of the moth's wings from my skirts as best I could, and stood before them. They surged forward to greet me with an eagerness that was almost alarming. And almost every one of them seemed to speak English!

'Welcome, Misss Mumby!' said one.

'We've heard ssso much about you,' said another, who was balancing a stack of books upon her spiny head, doubtless with a view to improving her posture.

'Will you share with usss the ssecrets of embroidery?' asked others.

'And dressssmaking?'

'And water-colouring?'

'Will you teach usss to be as ladylike as you, Misss Mumby?'*

I confess I felt a little overwhelmed. *Surely*, I thought, *they ask too much of me!* It would take someone far more accomplished than I to turn this gang of spiny sauria into ladies.

And yet, whispered a little voice inside of me, perhaps this was the destiny for which GOD had carried me here? Perhaps, if I could bring civilisation and good manners to these savage children of the Mothmaker, then dear Mother's fate might not have been in vain. So I said, 'You are most kind, every one of you, and I shall teach you all that I can.'

* It has always seemed very strange and wonderful to me that these warlike women of the Snilth were so taken with Myrtle. We now know that ideas can spread among Snilthkind in much the same way that germs spread among us. No doubt the Mothmaker had shaped them thus in order that they should be easier to rule. It explains why they were all so quick at picking up our lingo. (And jolly useful it would be if *we* could learn like that, I must say. There would be no more slaving over Latin verbs; I should simply get a schoolmaster to sneeze on me – and *iacta alea est*.) But this infectious learning was also the Snilth's Achilles' heel, for Myrtle's silly notions seem to have been particularly virulent. Having never been exposed to such novel ideas as crinolines and swooning, their minds had no defence against them, and the new fad passed among them like a summer cold — A.M.

At that they set up a great hissing and flapping of tails, which I suppose was their way of applauding. I was about to point out that this display of emotion was hardly lady-like, but I was distracted. For behind the crowd of armoured she-Snilth and the meek males who had joined with them upon the quay, I now beheld the ragged forms of sailors and officers from the *Actaeon*, making their way down from the lofty galleries where they had been put to work. The crowd of Snilth parted to let a few of them through. One of them was Sir Richard Burton, and beside him walked my own dear father!

❦ 17 ❧

'Oh Papa!' I cried and ran to him, though I restrained myself from hugging him, since he was very much befouled with slime and moth dust and I should have feared for my dress. But Ulla hugged Sir Richard and then hugged Father, and I believe she would even have spared a hug for Dr Blears, who stood scowling behind them, except that that gentleman cringed away from her.

'Well, Miss Mumby,' he said, looking me up and down in a nasty, sneering sort of way. 'I hope you can see now that I

was right to be suspicious of your friend Jack Havock. For are these savages not the very image of the wench who practises Alchemy aboard that ship of his? No doubt she was an agent of the Mothmaker, sent ahead to soften up our empire from within, and Havock is her willing accomplice!'

'Oh, what stuff!' I declared and went so far as to stamp my foot. (I would never have dared speak to a gentleman in such a fashion before, no matter how provoking he was – what has happened to me this year? I wonder.)

Just then, I was interrupted by a horrid, hissing voice which seemed to come from all about us. I presume the Mothmaker had installed some form of speaking trumpet in the fabric of this world she had made, and that what we were hearing was her voice, booming commands at us from her distant house. I squeaked and covered up my ears, and yet I could still hear it. Around me, several of the Snilth ladies copied my actions, and one or two had a go at swooning, though they were not yet very good at it, and the equally inexperienced males who tried to catch them were knocked down by their weighty, armoured forms.

'She is ordering more shipss into battle!' cried Ssoozzs, taking my hand and speaking with great earnestness. 'The firsst fleet which she sssent out has been defeated by the Children of the Yellow Sun. Now a sssecond is to be disspatched! We are to join it!'

'We shall not go!' declared one of her friends.

'We cannot!' hissed a third. 'It would be mossst unladylike!'

'But you must!' declared Mrs Burton forcefully. 'For think: if you disobey her order, she will learn of your rebellion and it will be crushed before it can spread any further!'

Some of our Snilth friends, seeming to agree with Ulla, turned towards the ships which waited empty at the quay and made as if to start up their boarding ramps. Others, who had travelled further down the road which leads to good manners, hung back and looked wistfully towards their meek little Snilth males, as if hoping that they might protect them. But suddenly, from amid the ragged band of British tars assembled on the ramps and stairs behind the quay, the voice of Mr Cumberbatch shouted lustily, 'Here's the chance we've waited for! Up and at 'em, lads!'

The sailors rushed forward in a tattered, howling wave which caught the Snilth quite by surprise. One or two, it is true, snatched up their bagpipes and pumped darts into the oncoming ranks, but most simply dithered. 'Oh, surely you would not strike a lady,' I heard Ssoozzs cry, as Dr Blears brandished his fist at her. But I am afraid he would and he did; poor Ssoozzs fell before him, and so did Alsssor, struck down as he stepped nobly forward to defend her.

'But they are on our side!' I cried, thinking it a very poor show that our sailors should set such an example to creatures who seemed honestly desirous of learning gentleness. But I got no reply; instead, I was snatched up by two sailors as if I were a parcel, and the last sight my Snilth pupils had of me must have been my boots kicking in a perfect froth of crinolines as I was carried aboard the fish-ship.

'Leave me!' I remember crying, as I struggled against their burly, tattooed arms. 'My place is with those good Snilth!'

'No, Myrtle!' said Father. He was running at my side, and indeed it seemed that it was he who was responsible for ordering those tars to abduct me. 'Your place is with me, and with GOD's help we may together find Art. Then we must carry out your mother's instruction.'

'Mother?' I cried.

'We both heard what she said as she perished, Myrtle,' said Father, instructing the sailor men to set me down in some out-of-the-way corner of the Snilthish vessel. 'She told you to go to the Tin Moon.'

'Yes,' I agreed, struggling to rise. 'But why?'

Father gently restrained me. 'It is one of the oldest and strangest objects known to man. We know that it is artificial, but who built it and what its purpose was, no one has ever understood. I have been thinking a great deal about it while we were captives in this dreadful place, and I wonder if perhaps it may not be something to do with your mother. I think that we shall learn some secret there that will help us to defeat the Mothmaker. And perhaps we may find some clue as to what has become of Emily herself – for I refuse to believe that someone as strong and as wise as she can be truly dead.'

I strove again to rise, but by then the ship was moving. Mr McMurdo, complaining loudly about the strangeness of the Snilth's Alchemy, had nevertheless contrived to start the alembic working, and with Mr Cumberbatch at the helm the fish turned cumbrously about and flew into the silver skies outside Snil-ritha. I ran with Father to a window and looked out. Many other ships were also crossing the emptiness at the heart of Mothstorm, and at first, when I saw them, I thought that they had been sent to stop us. But the Mothmaker, it seemed, knew nothing of our leaving. These were warships, soaring out in squadrons through holes that opened for them in the moth walls.

I looked back then and saw Mothstorm, the house, hanging in the void beyond us, and I fancied that it turned our way, as if it were a great misshapen head and its windows were the Mothmaker's many eyes.

'Poor Reverend Cruet!' I said, cowering. 'We are leaving him behind at *her* mercy!'

'Alas,' said Father, 'would that there were some way we could bring him with us. But he would never have come. The Mothmaker has turned his wits; her hold upon him is too strong.'

'And Alsssor and Ssoozzs and their friends,' I whispered. 'Will *they* be all right? How will they fare without me to teach them manners?'

'They must fend for themselves,' said Father. 'And we must fend for ourselves and somehow find our way to Mercury and the Tin Moon.'

Then Mr McMurdo did something inventive to the ship's alembic, and the engines fairly howled, driving us at full speed towards the torrent of moths which walled in that world of the silver sun.

Chapter Seventeen

FOND REUNIONS UPON THE FIELD OF BATTLE, A VOYAGE TO
MERCURY IS PROPOSED AND A GENTLEMAN OF OUR
ACQUAINTANCE RECEIVES A KICK UP THE FUNDAMENT,
WHICH HE THOROUGHLY DESERVES.

H aving admired the view awhile, Jack recalled that
the *Sophronia* was powerless and being drawn into
Jupiter's crushing gravitational embrace. He yelled
through his speaking trumpet at the nearby ships, until that
armed merchantman with our friends the Threls aboard

heard him and came swooping to our rescue. The Threls flung out strong, knitted tow-ropes, and soon we were being dragged across the battlefield to the region where the British fleet was regrouping in the orbit of Querp.*

Even though we were up-wind of Querp, a certain cheesy whiff hung in the aether, but there was so much to

---

* Querp is an odd little moon with an interesting history. Back in the 1780s, when our first expeditions to Jovian space were being prepared, a gentleman named Lord Appledore made a foolish wager with his friend the Duke of Stairbrass, that somewhere in Jupiter's orbit there would be found a moon made entirely out of green cheese. In the years that followed, he watched with growing concern as first one and then another of Jupiter's moons was explored and found to be made of ordinary rock. At last, fearing that the bet would soon be lost and that the sum he must forfeit would bankrupt him, he resorted to a most underhand ruse. He hired some Ionian dairymaids to *build* him a moon out of their finest cheese and caused it to be towed out and abandoned in a close orbit around Jupiter. Then, taking out full-page advertisements in *The Times* and other journals of note, he announced that he had been proven right; no one could deny that there was a moon made of green cheese in orbit around Jupiter.

Sadly, the expense of this operation broke Lord Appledore just as completely as paying his wager would have, and he died miserably in a debtor's prison. But his cheese-moon remains in orbit, growing riper and mouldier with each passing year and tainting the aether for miles down-wind with its distinctive pong. Named Querp by the Jovians, it is now officially recognised as the smallest and smelliest heavenly body in British Space.

look at as we plunged among that shoal of tattered ships that I scarcely noticed it. I was jolly glad to see the many lifeboats being towed in by space tugs, bearing the crews of ships which had been lost during the battle. Aetheric rowing boats were pulling to and fro among the swirls of floating debris, magnanimously rescuing moth-wrecked Snilth. But none of them were Ssilissa or Miss Thsssss, and we had to assume that either they had both perished in the open aether, or that Miss Thsssss had managed to drag her prisoner aboard a passing moth and escape back to the Mothstorm with the rest of the first Snilth fleet.

So there was an air of melancholy aboard the *Sophronia*, and indeed there seemed little sense of triumph in the fleet: no huzzahs ringing from ship to ship or bunting decking the yardarms. For all eyes were turned towards that ugly stain which besmirched the aether: the horrid immensity of the Mothstorm! I think every one of us believed that the insects in that swarm would soon be descending again upon the Jovian aether to complete the conquest that their advance guard had begun.

'How can it move so fast?' asked Charity, watching wide-eyed as the cloud drew nearer.

'Something within it must be moving at alchemical speeds,' said Jack, who had left his place at the helm to come and stand with us upon the star deck. 'Some great engine within that cloud is carrying them along with it. They'll be upon us within the hour.'

'Perhaps Thunderhead will save us again?' suggested Grindle hopefully.

Mr Munkulus shook his head. 'The Snilth have learned to keep out of his reach. As long as they keep well away from Jupiter, he will not be able to harm them.'

And yet, as we stood and stared, we started to realise that that golden cloud was not heading towards us at all. It was veering away, as if the great general who controlled it had decided that it was not worth throwing more of her minions into the fight for Jupiter and its moons.

You should have heard the shout of relief which went up from the assembled ships as word spread among the sailors that we were not to face the moths again. 'We've beaten them!' cried an officer, scooting past the *Sophronia* in a solar

punt. 'We've shown 'em we can sting and they are steering clear of us! Huzzah, and God Save the Queen!'

But Jack Havock still looked grim. 'Nip,' he said, 'skip below and bring me my copy of *Crevice*.'

The land-crab (who was much recovered from his cutlass wound and sported a large patch of sticking plaster on his shell) did as he was asked and was soon back aloft with *Crevice's Almanac* clutched in his pincers. Jack took it and leafed through the useful maps which Mr Crevice has provided, showing where each and every planet lies at each season of the year. He frowned a moment at the map marked *November 1851–January 1852*, then snapped the volume shut and looked up at the rest of us with a strange expression on his face.

'It looks like we have persuaded 'em that Jupiter's not worth the taking,' he said. 'They're ignoring us and heading for a greater prize.'

'The asteroids?' asked Colonel Quivering.

'Mars?' suggested Charity.

Jack shook his head. 'The asteroids are barely worth their time, and Mars is right on the far side of the Sun at present. No, the course they're on will take them straight to Earth, and at the speed they're travelling I'll warrant it won't be long before they get there.'*

---

* Jack was correct, as we later learned. Surprised by the fierce resistance we put up, the Mothmaker had decided that the way to crush us would be to capture or destroy our Queen. She knew of Queen Victoria, of course, from her conversations with her captives, and her Snilth had told her how, 'mid battle's heat, they'd heard brave British tars shout, 'God Save the Queen!' and 'For Queen and Country!' as they fired their aether cannon or bravely boarded Snilthish ships. 'It seems,' she hissed, striding about inside her moth-bone house in a perfectly dreadful fit of rage, 'that although these foolish creatures have no Shaper to lead them, they still know somewhere deep inside themselves that they should honour and obey some great female ruler. I shall rid them of this puny Victoria and give them a new and greater Queen to serve!'

There was silence for a moment as the awful import of his words sank in.

'What are we to do, Jack?' I asked.

Before he could reply, a shout went up from our friends the Threls. From the star deck of their ship they had been scanning the heavens for further signs of moth attack, and now they were all pointing excitedly to the distant flanks of the Mothstorm and leaping up and down in a most passionate and warlike manner. We looked at once to see what had so exercised them and beheld a tiny silver dart streaking out of the storm.

'A Snilth ship!' shrieked Charity.

'And coming this way!' I declared.

Of course, we were not the only ship, or even the first, to spot this fresh threat. All about us ships were manoeuvring and running out their guns, hoping to have the honour of getting in the first shot. On a hundred star decks a thousand elegant naval gentlemen unfolded their telescopes and trained them on the approaching ship, and on the *Sophronia*'s star deck Jack Havock did the same. And all of them saw the same thing at the same instant.

'Hold your fire! Hold your fire!' the shout ran through the fleet. 'She flies a British flag!'

It was true. After a while I managed to persuade Jack to lend me his glass, and I saw it for myself. Upon one of the spines which sprouted from that ship's strange armour flew a tattered, stained and ragged British ensign.

'It must be the flag from the *Actaeon*!' I reasoned. 'Our friends have stolen that ship and escaped in her! Oh Jack; Myrtle and Mother may be aboard her!'

The fleet scintillated with signal lamps, all twinkling and blinking to ask the same question: was that fish-ship friend, or was she foe? And back came the flashed response: the officers and men of the *Actaeon* were reporting again for duty and requested permission to come alongside the flagship!

'You're right, Art!' cried Jack, with a laugh. 'I knew those mothfolk could have no prison which would hold your mother for long! She'll tell us how to stop this thing! Let's hurry now and greet them!'

He hailed the Threls, who relayed his message down to their human alchemist, and soon the *Sophronia* was being towed through the fleet. A few self-important officers on other ships tried to stop us going near Admiral Chunderknowle's flagship, but Colonel Quivering barked so fiercely at them that they let us by, and we drew alongside HMS *Unflappable* as the fish-ship came in.

Naturally the *Unflappable*'s snooty officers and prideful tars objected terribly to having an old hulk like the *Sophronia* moored to them, but Captain Moonfield stood beside the admiral on their poop, and he must have explained who we were. They grudgingly ran out a gangplank and let us go aboard, with Colonel Quivering and his antiquated warriors marching behind us like an honour guard.

Meanwhile, on the *Unflappable*'s other side, the great Snilth fish drew up, and down her gangplank came walking Mr Cumberbatch, Dr Blears, Midshipman Bradstreet and several other of the *Actaeon*'s officers, along with the Burtons and my own dear father and Myrtle.

'Father!' I cried, bounding across the *Unflappable*'s star deck to greet him, and the fact that the flagship had its own Trevithick generators and operated under British Standard Gravity seemed not to matter for a moment: I leapt into his fond embrace as if there was no gravity at all. 'What ho, Myrtle!' I said, and I felt quite pleased to see her again, which just goes to show that it is true what they say: absence really *does* make the heart grow fonder.

Yet still I kept searching among the faces of those who had emerged from the fish-ship, and still I did not find the one I was looking for. Where, I wondered, was Mother? And a Dreadful Sense of Foreboding began to steal over me.

'Oh Art!' said Father. 'I am so relieved to find you safe and well!'

'But where is Mother?'

'We had feared you lost upon Georgium Sidus . . .'

'Well, I was, but it is quite all right. Where is Mother?'

'Art,' said Myrtle, with two tears starting to cut channels through the silvery moth dust which smeared her cheeks. 'I am afraid that you must brace yourself for some rather terrible news . . . Our mother is dead.'

You may well imagine how this affected me! I reeled

backwards, and might have fallen had Jack not supported me. But before I could speak, Father assured me, 'Don't worry, Art! We have reason to believe that her condition may be only temporary!'

'Temporarily dead?' cried Dr Blears, turning from a hurried conversation with Admiral Chunderknowle to peer quizzically at us through his spectacles. 'What mawkishness is this?'

'Before the Mothmaker overcame her,' said Myrtle, 'she told me that we must travel to the Tin Moon.'

'We presume that she means the Tin Moon of Mercury,' Father explained excitably. 'It is one of the oldest and most mysterious bodies in the Solar System, and perhaps it is connected somehow with your mother and her ancient race. We must do as she said and travel there with all haste. If we can restore her to life, I'm certain she will be able to think up a way to defeat the Mothmaker.'

'Nonsense!' objected Dr Blears. 'Balderdash and flapdoodle, my dear sir! We cannot afford to dispatch a ship on some wild-goose chase to Mercury, when every last one is needed to defend England! For Admiral Chunderknowle has just told me that it is for Earth that those Godless insect-herders are now bound, and I have no doubt they mean to assail the very heart and seat of the Empire! Besides, it would take months to get there!'

'Not in the *Sophronia*,' I cried angrily. 'Why, she has been all the way to – ulp!'

I added the last bit, you understand, because Jack abruptly clamped his hand over my mouth. He saw at once what I in my grief and anger had neglected to think of: that if Dr Blears knew of the speeds the *Sophronia* could now reach, he would commandeer her at once and go flying off to Earth, or at least demand that we hand over the special mix of alchemical powders which had been Ssilissa's Christmas present from Mother.

'What Art means to say,' he explained, 'is that he's sure the *Sophronia* could be spared, if only you could loan us an alchemist to work her.'

'What!' growled Dr Blears, looking most displeased to see Jack there. 'I thought you had an alchemist already, Captain Havock. A blue creature, as I recall, of the very type who now threaten us all!' He turned to the *Unflappable*'s officers and marines, crying, 'Clap him in irons! He's a rebel and a pirate, and his alchemist is a blue-skinned spy for the Snilth!'

'I say,' exclaimed Captain Moonfield (who was standing near and heard him), 'that's not fair, sir! Jack Havock saved my bacon out there in the trans-Georgian aether, and Ssil's a sweet girl, quite above suspicion!'

'She's gone, anyway,' said Jack. 'Lost overboard in the heat of battle and dead for aught we know.'

'Oh, how very *convenient*,' sneered Dr Blears.

Poor Admiral Chunderknowle blinked at us. He was a mild old gent, whose greatest interest was the cultivation of his magnificent side-whiskers,* and the battle with the Snilth had quite upset him. He did not know what to make of this bitter argument which had broken out upon his star deck.

'Arrest Havock and his cronies!' demanded Dr Blears, signalling furiously to the file of marines who stood at attention behind the admiral. But since he was only a civilian, and they did not know him from Adam, they stoically ignored him.

'Jack,' said Myrtle, stepping to his side, 'a few days since,

---

* Naval officers of Admiral Chunderknowle's generation, who have spent so much of their lives in low gravity or in none at all, often sport the most extraordinary whiskers and mustachios which would collapse in an instant were they ever to return to Earth.

you asked me to come with you aboard the *Sophronia*. You phrased it rather rudely and behaved quite churlishly afterwards, but I forgive you. I *shall* come with you, and if you will entrust the *Sophronia*'s alembic to my care, I am fairly certain I can take us all to Mercury.'

'Oh, what fiddle-faddle!' expostulated Dr Blears. 'Arrest them, or I shall have you *all* arrested!'

The marines nervously started towards Jack and the rest of us, but Colonel Quivering stepped into their path. 'Keep your distance!' he ordered. 'These good folk are under the protection of the Verdant Meadows Retirement Colony Militia!' And all his elderly comrades-in-arms, looking very pleased to be of use at last, stood or sat behind him with their muskets ready, forming a thin red line between the

Sophronias and those who meant them harm.

'Well,' said Jack, one hand upon his cutlass hilt, 'that's good of you, Myrtle. I ain't standing about here to be insulted, that's for sure. So who's for a pleasure trip to Mercury? Once around the planet and a stop at the old Tin Moon . . .'

I sprang to his side, of course, as did all the other Sophronias. So, too, did Myrtle and Father, and Charity Cruet. Together we turned about and strode across the *Unflappable*'s decks to the foot of the *Sophronia*'s gangplank.

'Good luck!' called Colonel Quivering, still holding the marines at bay.

'Good luck!' shouted Captain Moonfield, breaking off from a long defence of Jack's character which he was giving to the admiral.

Naturally Dr Blears was not going to give us up so easily. He squirmed past the Militia's guns and hurried after us, demanding querulously, 'What did Moonfield mean by claiming that you saved him in the trans-Georgian aether? That old tub of yours could not have flown to Georgium Sidus and back in the brief time we have been away!'

'Oh, couldn't she?' said Nipper.

Dr Blears scowled. 'What did the crab say?' By that time

we had started up the *Sophronia*'s ramp, and the pull of the *Unflappable*'s gravity generator was growing weak. Dr Blears clung to the handrails, and moved cautiously, looking a little like a crab himself.* 'Look here, Havock, if that unnatural minx Mrs Mumby gave you some of the same potion she used to boost the *Actaeon* to such speeds, then you shall hand it over! It is a vital weapon that must be used by Britain to defeat these blue devils. If you try to keep it to yourself, I shall have you and your whole ungodly menagerie taken up as traitors and shot!'

Jack's crew paused and looked back at him. But it was Father who took the action they were each considering. Father has a very peaceful nature, but that unkind reference to Mother had angered him. He turned to Dr Blears and said sternly, 'I do believe, sir, that we have all heard quite enough of *your* opinions!'

So saying, he grabbed the good doctor by the collar of his shabby frock coat, turned him about and planted a forceful kick in the seat of his trousers. I think he meant to send the fellow hurtling back down the gangplank on to the

---

* But a crab of the nasty, creeping sort, you understand, not a bold, heroic crab like Nipper.

star deck of the *Unflappable*, but, as I have said, the pull of the flagship's gravity was faint, and instead of falling down Dr Blears shot straight up into the aether, flailing his arms and legs and shouting, 'Help! Murder!'

There was a great deal of laughter and some happy 'Huzzahs!' from Colonel Quivering's men and also from Mr Bradstreet and other midshipmen assembled on the star deck, and a great many stern rebukes from their officers. I could see Admiral Chunderknowle looking quite outraged that a gentleman should be thus assaulted in his presence. I think he might have ordered his marines to stop us leaving, but Sir Richard Burton stepped forward and said something firm and urgent, and no action was taken against us.

We piled aboard the *Sophronia*, where the crew crowded round Father to pat him on the back and tell him, 'Well done!' and do comical impressions of Dr Blears's indignant shrieks.

'So this is your ship, Jack?' Father said, polishing his spectacles upon an end of his cravat and looking about him in a sort of wonder at the splintered holes in the hull and the scattered and tumbling debris.

And already Myrtle, showing unusual forward thinking, was at work in the wedding chamber, adding a little of

Mother's recipe to the alembic; already the walls and decks were trembling and the alembic starting up its song. Jack manned the helm. Charity took my father aside and heard from him the sad news about Rev. Cruet's enslavement to the Mothmaker. And I looked back from a porthole as we soared away into the aether.

The last I saw of our victorious British fleet was a puntload of able spacemen silhouetted against the face of Jupiter as they tried to catch the drifting Dr Blears with a boathook.

Chapter Eighteen

MADAME MILDMAY'S
PETTICOAT
and
PARASOL
PARADE

SILK MERCERS TO THE QUEEN

IN WHICH I, MISS MYRTLE EVANGELINE MUMBY, SHALL
TAKE UP THE REINS OF THIS NARRATIVE, SINCE ART WAS
TOO AFFECTED BY THE SAD NEWS I BROUGHT FROM
MOTHSTORM TO OBSERVE ANYTHING WHICH HAPPENED
DURING OUR VOYAGE TO MERCURY.*

I know what you are thinking, gentle reader. I know all
too well the burning question which has troubled you
since the middle of Art's previous chapter. You are

* Oh no I wasn't, you beastly fibber! — A.M.

wondering, was it proper for Myrtle to go aboard Jack Havock's ship again, having parted from him amid such angry and tearful scenes not one week previously?

You are right to wonder. I wondered that myself as the *Sophronia* pulled away from Jupiter and the British fleet. And all that I can say in my defence is that there are times, such as, for instance, when one's solar system is threatened by the moth fleets of a deranged demi-god, and one's mother has been killed, yet some hope of restoring her still lingers — there are times (strange as it may seem and much as it pains me to write it) *when questions of etiquette and decorum may have to be set aside*, at least until the greater good has been served.

So I considered it proper that I should board the *Sophronia*, and I imagined that I should be so busy using my alchemical talents to carry us to Mercury that I should never have to make conversation with Mr Havock at all. Indeed, the wedding chamber was in a terrible mess, and for the first few hours of the voyage there was so much tidying to do that I barely had time to think of him.

I scrubbed and polished and went about with a butterfly net, scooping up little drifting clouds of sawdust and oakum and the alchemical powders that had spilled during the battle (which appeared to have been an exceedingly messy one). And I tended to the alembic and found that it ran very happily on Mother's special mixture (which sat in a nice zinc jar at the front of Ssil's element rack, with a label saying, *To dear Ssilissa, wishing you a happy Christmas and GOD SPEED, with all my love, Emily Mumby*). And I thought sadly of how, since that was writ, both Mother and Ssilissa had been lost to us: one snatched away by death, the other simply snatched away.

And as I sat there in the dark of the wedding chamber, the bulkhead door was quietly opened, and Jack came in.

'It is strange not to have Ssilissa here,' he said, looking about and not making any remark at all about how much cleaner and tidier the wedding chamber was now that it was in my care.

'I am sorry that she is lost,' I said, 'but I trust that I can convey us all to Mercury with almost as much ease.'

'How goes the alchemical wedding?' he asked.

'Oh, swimmingly, thank you,' I replied. 'Though

Mother's special mix is rapidly being used up, and we may have to resort to ordinary elements to fuel our return from Mercury.'

'Let's get there first,' said Jack, 'and worry later about the return trip.'

'Quite.'

'Very well, then.'

I waited for him to leave me, but he lingered. It was rather awkward, as you may imagine. How is a maiden to address a young man who has Flung Away her Devoted Affection, and Trampled Upon the Bower of her Girlish Dreams?

Naturally, I decided to behave politely yet coolly. 'Tell me, Mr Havock,' I said sweetly, 'do you know anything of this Tin Moon for which we are bound? I have heard it mentioned, I believe, but I never paid it much attention until now.'

Jack looked surprised, as if he had not expected me to be quite so cool or polite. But he mastered himself and said, 'I've never been there, but I've heard stories told of it in every port in the system. They say it's the oldest object in all the worlds of the Sun. Though I suppose Larklight must be older, when you think of it.'

'And is it really made of tin?'

'Oh yes. Bright, shiny tin. A perfect sphere of it, hanging in space above the sun-baked plains of Mercury. There used to be a race that lived on Mercury, tho' they vanished long before any earthly explorers set foot there and left behind nothing but odd ruins. It's always been thought the Tin Moon was something of theirs. Many and many an expedition has tried to explore it, but no one has ever been able to get through its tin skin and find out what lies inside. Captain Cook tried blasting it with cannon, Mungo Park set to work on it with black powder charges and a man named Grambley Scraggs tried to hack his way in with a gigantic patent tin-opener. Not one of them so much as made a dent.'

'Then what use can there be in going there?' I complained. 'Are we really to travel clear across the Empire simply to sit staring at an impregnable ball of metal?'

'There must be some point,' said Jack. 'For your mother told you to go there, and I can't think she'd say something like that without good reason.'

I started to weep, which is never a good idea in zero BSG, for the tears, instead of running down, go up or sideways, and hang about one's head like little glass beads.

Some drifted against the alembic and the hot exhaust pipes, where they sizzled and turned into steam. 'Do you think there is *really* any hope?' I whispered. 'Is Father right, or is he just deluding himself? Do you think it possible that she may yet live?'

'I think where Mrs Mumby is concerned, anything's possible,' said Jack. 'She's wise and good and beautiful, and she knows a great deal more than she lets on. And you know something else? Her daughter takes after her.'

'Oh Jack,' I said, both touched and annoyed, and I felt myself blush hotly, which invariably makes my spectacles steam up.

'Oh Myrtle . . .' he said.*

At that moment the *Sophronia* suffered some sort of lurch or wobble – one of those minor disturbances which pass almost unnoticed by those of us who sail the aether seas – and I was flung against Jack, who caught me in his manly arms and would not release me. Instead, he removed my steamed-up spectacles and gently kissed me.† And we stood there together, looking out of the mullioned porthole at the

* Oh good grief, I hope this is not going to unfold as I fear it might — A.M.
† Yuck! — A.M.

Sophronia's sparkling wake, shining in the golden light of Sir Isaac Newton's roads, and I knew that the rift between us had been healed and that we never more must part . . . *

---

* This really is too much! — A.M.

The *Real* Chapter Eighteen

OUR VOYAGE TO THE TIN MOON, AS TOLD BY ART MUMBY,
WITH NONE OF THE SLUSHY BITS.

O h, honestly! Enough is enough, don't you think?
It is all very well to let Myrtle lend a hand in the
recounting of our adventures, but who wants to
read about her and Jack spooning, when the whole Empire
was riven by war and the fate of entire worlds hung in the
balance? Nobody, that's who, so I have resolved to put a
stop to her horrid whimsy and tell you what *really* happened.

Of course, sailing across those war-torn stretches of the aether was not at all the uneventful pleasure trip that Myrtle has made out. We were all busy repairing the ship and making plans for what to do when we reached Mercury. And Father was telling Charity about her father's sad condition and assuring her that if we could just find a way  to dispose of that nasty Mothmaker, he was certain that rest and loving kindness could restore Rev. Cruet to his former self. Meanwhile, the ship rolled and bobbed and lurched about so violently that Charity turned quite green, and Nipper was actually space-sick. Myrtle does not mention that, you'll notice! The truth is, she is not nearly so good an alchemist as she likes to pretend, and it was a wonder we did not fall off the Golden Roads entirely, or crash straight through the heart of an asteroid.

Naturally, when Jack gave the helm to Mr Munkulus and vanished into the stern cabin, we assumed he had gone to tell Myrtle off for the skittish way she had the engines behaving. And when he spent so long in there we imagined he was keeping an eye on her to make sure she did not blow us all up. So it came as something of a shock when they emerged together, hand in hand, looking shy and foolish. Myrtle's spectacles had steamed up, and there were tears shining like pearls in their hair.

'Father, Art,' she said, taking Jack's hand, 'Jack and I are engaged to be married.'

I believe she was expecting Father to object on the grounds that they were both far too young and that Jack was a sworn enemy of Britain. But his rough handling of Dr Blears had put him in an even sunnier mood than usual, and he just cried, 'A capital notion! Jack is just what you need, my girl. If only poor Shipton were here, he could perform the service right away!'

'Oh Heavens!' exclaimed Myrtle, looking most alarmed, for a wedding in space aboard a speeding aether-ship was not what she had in mind at all. 'We are prepared to wait, aren't we, Jack my dearest? I had thought of having the ceremony perhaps three or four years from now, in Port George Cathedral on the Moon. A simple little service, with just a few hundred well-connected guests. I shall need bridesmaids, of course . . .'

Father hugged her and shook Jack's hand. 'I shall look forward to the happy day,' he said. 'But what a pity it would be if your mother could not be there. So I suggest that before we make any detailed plans, we should concentrate all our efforts upon reaching this Tin Moon and getting inside of it. For whatever it is that Emily thought so important must be inside. It is well known that the Tin Moon's exterior is barren and featureless: a lifeless metal plain roasted by the merciless heat of the Sun.'

'Not altogether lifeless, Mr M.,' Grindle put in. 'It is one of the hunting grounds of the Twooks: the dreaded Sun Dogs, which ate up so many of Captain Cook's men and many other bold aethernauts since.'

'What do they look like?' I asked.

'Why, no one knows,' declared Grindle in a ghoulish tone. 'For everyone who's met one has been eaten up by it, and their friends caught only glimpses of the creatures as they scarpered. Some say they have the heads of lions, the bodies of snakes and the tails of shrimps; others, that they're more like jellyfish. Most likely, they look like nothing we've ever seen before.'

'Well, let us hope we never *do* see them,' said Myrtle

fervently. 'They sound most unsavoury! Besides, it would not be at all genteel to be eaten up. How would it look in the Obituary column of *The Times*?'

'We shall be ready for 'em, whatever they look like,' said Jack, seemingly glad that the talk had veered away from love and marriage and towards a subject which he knew more of, e.g. fearless battles against dreadful foes. 'Grindle, Munkulus, break out the weapons – pistols and cutlasses for all, and be sure the cutlasses are good and sharp and the pistols primed and loaded.'

And so Myrtle, with many a fond glance at Jack, went back to her post by the alembic, and the rest of the voyage passed in the business of checking and preparing the *Sophronia*'s little arsenal of weapons, and sneaking peeks at ourselves in the cabin looking-glass, and being astonished at how splendid we looked, bedecked with swords and shooting instruments. And also, I believe, we ate and slept, and all in all it seemed not so very long before the ship began to slow, and Myrtle emerged again to announce in tones of unutterable smugness that we were entering the Mercurial aether.

Indeed, we could have guessed where she had brought us to even without her announcement, for as the golden glow of alchemical particles faded from without the portholes it was replaced by another glow, equally intense and also golden, though of a redder hue; and through the *Sophronia*'s thick, space-weathered planking we felt a summery warmth come creeping, quite different from the usual chill of space. We had arrived in the gardens of the almighty Sun!

You would expect them to seethe with life, those regions of the aether where the great Sun rolls. I had imagined they would be like tropic seas, teeming with abundant shoals of many-coloured fish and groves of song flowers. But when Charity, Father and myself scrambled out on to the star deck, our eyes shielded by smoked-glass goggles, we looked about us at a sky almost deserted. Half of Heaven was taken up with the immense furnace of the Sun, a sphere of

blazing coals and towering fires so vast that it made Jupiter seem no bigger than a pea. It was a thousand thousand miles away, but still space was filled with the roar and rumble and crackle of its burning. No wonder we saw no fish, no flowers! Few are the forms of life which can bear for long the gaze of that great golden eye!

'Look!' called Charity. 'There is Mercury . . .'

And there *was* Mercury, a dusty, reddish sphere which swings around its brief orbit with the same scorched face turned always to the Sun. Dimly, in the shadow line between the bright and dark sides of the planet, I made out the forms of crumbled towers and the angles of walls half buried in baked sand: the ruins of one of the cities left behind by the great lost race of the Mercurians. And then, beyond the planet's curve, something caught the light and seemed to flare up, dazzling, like the burnished helm of some knight of olden times. It was the Tin Moon, rising behind the shoulder of its mother-world, and as it rose, so the *Sophronia* flew towards it, stirring the hot aether with the steady flap of her wings.

It is hard to explain the Tin Moon in words alone. It is a featureless sphere of metal, and that sounds somewhat dull. But when you see it hanging there in the orbit of that long-dead world, its surface rippling with the reflections of the nearby Sun, it is enough to make the breath catch in your throat. 'What is it?' you ask yourself. 'Who put it there? What is its purpose?' And you know that for a hundred years explorers have been asking those questions.

I could only hope, as we soared towards it, that we might shortly be provided with an answer!

Jack climbed out on to the star deck then, with Grindle, Nipper and the twins. It was Jack's intention that Myrtle and Mr Munkulus should stay aboard the *Sophronia* and keep her in orbit about the Tin Moon while we explored its surface and sought for some clue as to why Mother had sent us there. Nipper had hooked a great many lanterns over his claws and went about handing them out to us, for we were to land upon the moon's dark side.

We were close enough by then to feel its mild gravity

tugging at us. The dim band of twilight between its day and night sides filled the sky to starboard now, and we could see that its dully shining surface was not really featureless at all, but was pock-marked with the imprints of meteors and minor comets. I believe we all felt the same doubt creep into our minds then, though none of us spoke it . . .

How could we hope to find anything in that dimpled metal wilderness?

But while we all stood staring at it and wondering, we had quite failed to notice that the empty stretches of aether behind us were suddenly empty no more.

Charity was the first to sense a movement. She turned to look. I saw her eyes widen in surprise and heard her say, 'Is that a Sun Dog, do you think? Good Gracious, I had no idea they would be quite so large . . .'

And then it struck us. The silly creature must have sensed the ripples which the *Sophronia* had made when she first entered the Mercurial aether, and had tracked us ever since. But in its brutish ignorance it seemed to think that the ship was a living creature – and I suppose that with her aether-wings flapping like fins she did somewhat resemble a gigantic icthyomorph. At any rate, the Sun Dog came swooping down upon her, driving

*'Is that a Sun Dog, do you think? Good Gracious, I had no
idea they would be quite so large . . .'*

itself forward with great lashing movements of its vile transparent tail, and before we could do anything about it there was an almighty wrenching and a crashing of torn timbers, and those of us who stood ready on the star deck, waiting to go ashore, found ourselves thrown unceremoniously into space instead!*

Well, it was not the first time I had been flung into space, and I don't suppose that it shall be the last, so I did not worry overmuch at first. But then, as I turned a slow somersault and was able to look back whence I had come, I beheld a Very Dreadful Thing.

The poor *Sophronia*, which had borne us all so faithfully across so many leagues of space, had been torn quite in half! Weakened as she was by her recent hurtling to and fro about the aether, her aged timbers had not been able to

---

* I have no idea which bright spark decided to give the name 'Sun Dogs' to these great predators of the Solar Sea. They look not a bit like any dog I've ever seen. The one which attacked the *Sophronia* resembled much more closely a sort of gigantic, wingless dragonfly made out of living glass. Through its translucent skin all its internal organs could be viewed, like goods displayed in the window of a London store. Charity Cruet claims that as it swept past her she quite clearly saw into its see-through belly, where the carcasses of icthyomorphs and other aetheric life forms were slowly dissolving in the acids of its stomach. Eugh!

withstand
the dreadful
impact of the Sun
Dog. A spreading cloud of
splinters and smashed timber was all
that remained of her mid-section. A torn-off
aether-wing flapped feebly as it whirled away into the dark.
Mr Munkulus, looking most surprised, still clung to the
dismounted wheel. The bows were caught in the jaws of the
wretched Sun Dog, which was worrying and savaging them
like a terrier with a rat. The stern section, responding to the
gentle pull of the Tin Moon's gravity, was tumbling down to
the surface. Alchemical fire billowed in bluish veils from the
ruptured ducts and pipework of the wedding chamber, and
Myrtle was scrambling desperately across the wreckage,
trying to escape the flames!

'*Au secours!*' she wailed.*

The Sun Dog saw her too. It tossed aside the splintery remnant of the bows and flicked its tail, speeding towards the drifting stern. I saw Myrtle snatch up a floating jar of alchemical potion and heave it at the oncoming monster's face, and saw the creature flinch aside as the contents burst upon its nasty nose in a flare of green vapours. But it was not defeated; it merely swerved around the stern section and came at Myrtle from the other direction, and this time she had no weapons to hand, nor any way to escape or defend herself . . .

So I realised, with a horrible sinking feeling, that *I* was going to have to defend her.

'Raaargh!' I shouted (or something very similar – trying to sound fierce, you see). The Sun Dog, which I believe had no more brains than Myrtle herself, was distracted by the sound. It twitched its glassy head in my direction and flexed various barbels and feelers. 'Boo!' I told it. 'If you want to eat something, shrimp, come and eat me!'

Well, I was wrong to say it had no brain, for it appeared

* Myrtle has made a decision only to call for help in French, which she says sounds far less vulgar.

to understand that perfectly. What's more, as it whooshed at me, I saw its brain quite clearly, hanging in its transparent head like a pickled walnut trapped in a block of ice.

Luckily, that sight gave me an idea of how I might see off this nuisance. Kicking myself frantically out of its path, I drew my cutlass and drove it with all my might through the taut jelly of the Sun Dog's skull and clean through the middle of its brain.

Screeching in pain and fury, the creature lashed violently about and flung itself back towards the light of the *Sophronia*'s blazing stern section. 'Myrtle, jump!' I shouted, and she did and came swimming gracelessly through the aether. In another instant the Sun Dog had crashed headlong into the wrecked wedding chamber, to be consumed in a colossal blast of multi-coloured fire. For a moment I saw all my companions clearly, scattered across a mile of open space. In the light of that conflagration, I could read shock and distress upon the faces of those nearest to me and guessed that mine must wear a similar expression.* Then the light died, and in the dark that

* I only hoped that it suited me better than it did poor Myrtle, who looked more than ever like an owl who has just received bad news.

followed we all fell gently, gently towards the surface of that strange satellite.

We had survived the onslaught of the Sun Dog. I heard Jack calling out the names of the others as we fell, and there was none that did not answer. But what good had our survival done us? For we were shipwrecked and quite alone, marooned without hope of rescue upon the barren surface of the Tin Moon!

Chapter Nineteen

IN WHICH WE CONTEMPLATE OUR SAD PREDICAMENT, BUT
ARE SAVED FROM DESPAIR BY A DISCOVERY QUITE STRANGE
AND WONDERFUL.

It took several hours for us all to be reunited, for the
shipwreck scattered us across a broad portion of the
Tin Moon's face, and most of us had lost or broken
our lanterns. Very strange and eerie it was to hear that
ancient metal world echoing with familiar voices as we
sought each other through the inky dark. Luckily I had

fallen close to Mr Munkulus, and with his help I soon found Charity, and then Father, who, despite a few nasty bumps and bruises from his fall, was still enthused by our encounter with the Sun Dog. 'Magnificent!' he kept saying. 'A remarkable new species. The reports of earlier voyagers were all inaccurate and quite failed to do it justice! How does it hunt? What does it live on in this sparse, almost azoic aether? I can hardly wait to report on it to the RXI!'

'I am afraid you shall have to, sir,' said Mr Munkulus. 'Wait, I mean. For the dear old *Sophronia* is no more, and I can see no other way of getting off this nasty moon.'

That dampened everybody's spirits somewhat, and we went on in silence, finding our way by the sparks which Mr Munkulus's hobnailed space boots struck from the tin surface underfoot. After a while we saw two crackling lights away to our left and realised that they were the electric crowns of Yarg and Squidley. We hastened towards them and found that others of the ship's company had already homed in upon those amiable living beacons. Myrtle and Mr Grindle were there, and so was

Nipper (he had lost a leg in the wreck, but he said it did not matter, dear brave crab, 'for it will soon grow back, and in the meantime I still have seven others').

We all went on together, and it was not long before we came upon Jack, who sat on a shard of wreckage with his chin upon his fist, looking a perfect figure of melancholy and gazing out across a tin plain littered with the fragments of his beloved old ship. He looked up at us as though he was not sure that we would be glad to see him there, and I saw the tracks of tears shining quite clearly on his cheeks. He had lost first Ssilissa and now his ship, poor fellow, and he was feeling very low.

'I'm sorry,' he muttered. 'I should have seen that creature coming. I should have kept a lookout.'

'It's no fault of yours, Jack,' Mr Munkulus told him.

'How was you to know they grew so big?' agreed Mr Grindle.

'You and your crew had the tides of the Sun and Mercury and this Tin Moon to steer us through,' said Father. 'It was useless passengers like I who should have kept a better lookout.'

'Never mind whose fault it was,' said Myrtle, with that faint wobble in her voice which tells those of us who know her well that it is time to run to the bathroom cabinet and fetch the smelling salts. 'The question is, what shall become of us now? Who shall rescue us? Or are we to perish as castaways upon this metal moon?'

'First things first,' said Father, seeing that Jack was not yet ready to take charge of us. 'We must salvage whatever we can from the wreck and make a camp. Then we can begin exploring. Remember why we came here. This moon has some secret, otherwise Emily would never have sent us here. Maybe if we can discover what it is, it will help us to find a way off.'

He was being terribly brave, and all our spirits lifted a little at his words. Nipper portioned out the surviving lanterns, and we set off at once, in groups of two and three, to scour the surface of the metal moon for

fragments of the *Sophronia*. I went with Charity, and we had not walked far before we came to a crater where lay several spars, a puncheon of water and a barrel of ship's biscuits. In the moon's low gravity it was an easy matter to lift them up and carry them to where Yarg and Squidley waited, marking with their electric glow the place where Jack intended to make camp. By the time we reached it we found that Father and Nipper had brought in a great section of the larboard aether-wing, the very thing to make an awning from, and that many other useful fragments had been collected. We started to feel a great deal brighter and set out again with high hopes of finding even more.

On that second trip, however, we let our enthusiasm carry us away. It was not long before Yarg and Squidley were lost behind us, and we found ourselves in a darkness broken only by Charity's small lantern and the glow of starlight reflecting from the metal ground. But we could still hear the distant voices of our friends all calling out to one another as they searched, so we saw no reason not to press on, especially when we made out a shape lying a little way ahead. Imagining that it must be some large section of the wreck, we hurried towards it, making great strides in the low gravity.

You may imagine our alarm when we drew close enough to the object to let the light of Charity's lantern shine upon it, and saw that it was not part of the ship at all, but the carcass of the Sun Dog, draped in ruin across the brim of a deep crater. And if that was alarming, it was nothing to what happened next. For as we stood there, gazing upon the remains, two sparks of light flashed high above us, where the Tin Moon's shadow did not reach, and the aether was filled with sunlight.

'What are those?' asked Charity excitedly. 'Oh, they are ships! Some far-wandering explorers or prospectors must have seen our accident and are coming down to rescue us!' And she began to swing her lantern in circles, which made the huge glassy corpse beside us flash and flicker with reflected light.

Larger and larger grew those two sparks, and at last they blinked out as they plunged into the Tin Moon's shadow, but we could still see them descending as blobs of deeper darkness against the dark of space. *How odd*, I thought. *Those ships carry no lights*. And then I understood what should have been plain to me in the first instant that I set eyes upon them: they were not ships at all, but more Sun Dogs!

'Charity, put out the lantern!' I cried, thinking that its

light was certain to bring the creatures down upon us.

'What?' asked she, quite indignant, still thinking that they must be rescue ships.

There was not time to explain. I snatched the lantern from her and hurled it away. It spun slowly from my hand and smashed against the hulk of the dead Sun Dog, where its flame went out, and I heard a tinkle as its glass chimney shattered. For a moment there was blessed darkness. Then, to my horror, a great glow burst up from the body of the Sun Dog.

It is surprising how many of the alien monstrosities one comes across are highly flammable. I may have mentioned before how I managed to explode an impertinent squid in the wind-race of Jupiter, and how well he blazed. But you would think a creature like the Sun Dog, which lives all its days in the hot skies around our parent star, would want to be made of something fairly impervious to fire. Not so. A little spilled lamp oil, a stray spark and the carcass went up with a *woof* like a bundle of dry straw and lit the tin about it bright as day. A mile above us, those other Sun Dogs must have seen me and Charity standing there astonished, with our trembling shadows stretching out behind us as if drawn in charcoal. And they must have thought, *Dinner!*

Down they came. I could hear them whiffling as they lashed their tails to and fro. I saw the fire of their burning friend glimmer in their glassy hides and their mouthfuls of icicle teeth.

'Do you suppose there would be any point in running?' I asked Charity.

'I certainly mean to try,' she replied. 'Otherwise we shall end up stuck in their tummies like those poor creatures I saw earlier, being slowly digested. And that must be a perfectly horrid experience.'

So we set off running, and I must say we did pretty well, covering about a mile every thirty seconds or so. You can run jolly fast on low-gravity worlds, and faster still when you are being chased by airborne greenhouses which want to gobble you up and digest you in full view of the public within their see-through tums. Yet, fast as we were, those Sun Dogs were faster. And then it dawned on me why it was they were called dogs, for even when we were far from the flames of their fallen comrade and plunging blindly through the pitchy dark, they stayed on our trail. I began to think the whiffling sound that I could hear close behind me was the sound of the creatures sniffing. Whether or not that was the case, the fact was those monstrosities stuck to our trail like a couple of scent hounds, and we should both have been dogs' dinners had the ground not suddenly vanished from beneath our feet.

'Aaah!' we cried, falling through the blackness. And there was irritation as well as fear in those cries. Had we not been told, time and again, that the Tin Moon of Mercury was wholly featureless? And what was this pit or hollow that we were plummeting into if not a feature?

Luckily, it was not too deep. A mere ten or fifteen feet, I should say, although in the low gravity we fell slowly, which made it feel as if we were plunging for miles. We landed with soft thuds upon a floor of dented tin, and, looking up, saw the smooth walls of the crater stretching up to a circle of starlit sky above. Almost instantly it was blotted out by the dim shape of a Sun Dog. The vile whiffling noises sounded even louder as they echoed in the shaft, but the creature was too large to squeeze down after us, and so, for the moment, we were saved.

'Art,' said Charity at last, 'what would you say this place is?'

'I suppose it must be a sort of crater,' I replied.

'Yet it is perfectly round and smooth. Like a well.'

Charity is jolly observant, for a girl. I had to admit that she was right. It was difficult to believe that this shaft was a natural feature.

'And do you notice something strange about these depressions in the floor beneath us?' she asked then. 'They feel too regular to be mere dents. Each is a shallow dip, with five grooves leading off it . . .'

I struggled to see in the darkness. Luckily those Sun Dogs were still gruffling about above, and the reflections of starlight bouncing from their hides cast shifting gleams upon the floor of the shaft. Soon I was able to make out the marks to which Charity had alluded. She was right again: it was clear at a glance that they were not just natural dents, acquired during the Tin Moon's long and uneventful history . . .

They were the prints of human hands!

There were two of them: one large, one slightly smaller, yet neither big enough to be the handprint of an adult. And they reminded me instantly of a day at Larklight, long ago, when Mother amused Myrtle and I by making us press our hands into damp sand and taking plaster casts of the resulting prints. Just so did these prints look. It was as if two children, millions of years before, had pressed their hands into the still-soft surface of this metal world and left their prints there for eternity.

'Whatever can it mean?' said Charity.

'I cannot guess,' I replied.

'Do you think it is what your mother sent us here to find?'

'It is rather a coincidence if it is,' I said doubtfully. 'Just stumbling on it like this, I mean.'

'But what if it is not a coincidence?' Charity suggested. 'You are her son. Perhaps some inner knowledge guided you to this well, or whatever it is.'

Carefully, I reached out and set my hand upon the smaller of the two prints.

A deafening clang filled the well shaft. The hungry Sun Dogs up above drew back with wary whisperings. I looked at Charity and realised that I could see her clearly, for the shaft was filling with light!

Around the edge of the circular floor, where it joined the wall, a crack of blue-white light had appeared – and was steadily widening.

'What is happening?' I gasped.

'You've broken it!' wailed Charity.

We felt ourselves beginning to descend. It was as if the floor we crouched on had broken free of the shaft and was sinking slowly into a sea of light. Fresh air surrounded us, and we took deep, grateful breaths, realising how thin and unsustaining the air of the Tin Moon had been. And then the light faded, and something slid shut above our heads, sealing us off from the indignant Sun Dogs.

We were standing in a large, silvery room. High above was a domed ceiling, beneath our feet a floor covered in perplexing patterns of tiles, whose texture reminded me of the insides of sea shells. Around the walls, in strange, glassy pods, stood hundreds of people, as if watching us. None of them, as far as I could see, was alive. Very few of them were human. Some were not even people at all, but animals. Flowers of frost had formed on the insides of the pod windows, and some of those who stood there were obscured entirely, but I recognised a Callistan snapdragon, a

Venusian shrew and several other exotic species. And surely
that huge saurian must be one of the extinct reptilia of pre-
Adamite Earth?

Who were they? What power had brought them here?
And were Charity and I soon to join them, to be killed and
stuffed and mounted in one of those glass pods like
butterflies in a display case? For in my bewilderment, I
could only imagine that we had blundered into the museum
of some unearthly collector!

And then, in the domed space above us, something

moved. Something stirred and uncurled. Something made of light and darkness, and so large that I had at once to adjust my whole understanding of the room's perspective, unfurled long tentacles of shadow and sank down slowly until it hung in front of us and gazed at us with a thousand fiery eyes.

Charity and I had backed against the nearest pod when the thing came down on us, and Charity had drawn her cutlass, which she held out shakily in front of her. But I somehow sensed that we were in no danger, and I reached out and pressed Charity's hands so that she lowered the sword.

The golden eyes roared softly, circling like suns in the shadows of the thing which watched us. I thought at once of Myrtle's and Father's descriptions of the Mothmaker. Was this she? But no. The Mothmaker had been a being of immense power, and this thing before us was weak: the fires that were its eyes kept guttering and threatening to go out, and it seemed barely able to move; the fringes of its shadowy form lay listlessly upon the floor; its tendrils drooped.

I reached down and touched it. It felt like the ghost of a velvet curtain.

'*Mother?*' I said.

And inside that cloud of darkness, fresh fires ignited. The burning eyes whirled faster. The shadows deepened and grew crisper. 'Yes,' it breathed. 'Yes, now I remember . . .'

'Mother!' I said, wishing I could hug her, but not quite sure how to begin.

'Art,' said the darkness, gathering itself and ruffling my hair with a friendly tentacle. 'Oh Art! I'm afraid I am not quite myself this morning. But I am ever so glad to see you here, and your friend too. Is your sister with you, by any chance?'

Chapter Twenty

INTERESTING FLORA & FAUNA

Callistan Pygmy Pompom

№ 4

A MERRY CHRISTMAS, ONE AND ALL!

'M other!' I cried. 'What are you doing here? And why do you look so . . . well, I am not sure how to describe you.'

'I am terribly sorry, Art,' the strange cloud said. 'It must be a shock for you to see me like this. It is a shock for me as well. I had grown so used to my old body, and now that wretched Mothmaker has broken it. It was one of my favourites, too, and I had not nearly finished with it; I had planned to have so many more years with you and Myrtle and your father, and grow old, and oh, all *sorts* of adventures.'

'But you aren't dead!' I shouted happily. 'I mean, we none of us really believed you were, but even so, we couldn't help but be worried . . .'

'I am not dead,' agreed the cloud. 'My mortal body is shattered and I cannot return to it, but when it died, the essence of me, my Shaper self, fled to this little place that I prepared long millennia ago. The journey across the aether almost finished me; I have been waiting here, too weak to leave, barely certain of who I was. Waiting for you to come and find me.'

'So you weren't telling the truth when you said that you would die when your body did!' I exclaimed. 'I knew it!'

'I would not lie, Art,' said Mother reprovingly. 'Not to you. But it is no easy matter for a Shaper to die. My death was simply a promise that I made to myself. When Emily Mumby died, I always said, and my essence wound up here at the Tin Moon again, then I would do what I should have done four-and-a-half-thousand millennia ago. I would cease to be. But I can hardly do that with the Mothmaker still rampaging about in my lovely solar system, and without saying goodbye to you and Myrtle and your father, could I?'

I shook my head. I don't know if you have ever seen *your* mother transformed into a nebulous being of pure energy with innumerable eyes, but I found it a rather disconcerting experience. So many of my notions about who Mother was were bound up with her face and her voice and her little habits, and there was no trace of any of those things left in the cloud which hung before me. *And yet it was her.* I was certain of it.

'Now,' she said, 'what of Myrtle and your father?'

'They are out on the surface, with Jack Havock's crew,' I replied.

'Oh, well, that won't do! We must bring them in, and then you shall tell me all about the Mothmaker and we will try to decide what must be done about her.'

'But how can they find their way here?'

'Myrtle will lead them. She knows where the door is, just as you did – though, like you, she does not *know* she knows. I impressed the secrets of the Tin Moon on your minds when you were both ever so little, in case it might be useful one day. You would have found your way here eventually even if I had not had time to mention it to Myrtle before the Mothmaker so rudely interrupted me.'

'But there are Sun Dogs outside the door!' said Charity.

'I can see you have not known Jack Havock long,' said Mother, 'if you believe a few of those creatures will give him any trouble.'

I restrained myself from telling her of the trouble which a Sun Dog had already given us and of the loss of the *Sophronia*. It was a little like the loss of Mother's familiar mortal form: a sadness too great, for the moment, to even think about. Instead I said, 'But Mother, you must not let Myrtle see you as you now are!'

The cloud of fire and shade before me looked thoughtful – or, at least, as thoughtful as a cloud can look. 'You're right, Art,' she said. 'Poor Myrtle would think it terribly unladylike of me to wander about without a body. Help me to choose one, dear, before she arrives.'

'Choose one?' I gaped.

'Why, yes. Unlike our friend the Mothmaker, I have never learned the art of shaping myself into a human form. Such illusions do not interest me. When I want to live as a

Martian, or an Ionian, or an Earthling, I grow a proper, flesh-and-blood body and slip inside it. These figures who you see about you are all bodies that I have inhabited through the millennia. Now which one do you think would be most suitable . . . ?'

I walked with her down the aisles between the glass pods, where her former selves all waited, frozen by some science beyond my human comprehension. The room was not circular, as I'd thought at first; its shape was constantly shifting, and there were far, far more of the pods than I could count. In one I saw some hideous three-headed thing which wore its muscles on the outside; in another a Ganymedian aquabat floated in brine. A third bore nothing but a clump of moss. ('Those were a tedious few hundred years,' Mother reminisced, brushing a shadow-tentacle affectionately over the glass of that pod, 'but restful, in their way.') I looked up nervously at the bladed jaws of a mighty dinosaur and shuddered,

wondering what Mother had been like when she wore *that* form. I smiled down at a sweet little Callistan pygmy pompom. ('A charming body,' said Mother, 'but not particularly practical.') At last we paused before a pod where a tall and graceful woman stood – almost human, she seemed, and yet the cast of her features and the tone of her skin marked her as something quite other.

'Who is she?' asked Charity.

'She was me as I looked when I lived upon Mercury and watched the empire of the Mercurians stretch out to Venus and the infant Earth,' said Mother.

'She's very beautiful,' said Charity.

'Why, thank you! She is the body I wore when I dwelled in the Mercurian colony of Atlantis and went picnicking upon the lost continent of Mu. But the Mercurians grew tired of their empire, and in time a great white ship came sweeping through our solar system, a starjammer making some endless voyage between the suns, and the Mercurians all joined its crew and flew away, and I was left alone.' Her veils of shadow rippled sadly. 'I was so upset that I became a small Venusian shellfish for several thousand years.'

This Mercurian lady looked very like Mother, I thought, but not *quite* like her; she could perhaps have passed for the half-sister or the cousin of the Mother I remembered.

'Do you think she will do?' asked Mother.

'I think she will do very well,' I replied, 'although her clothes are rather out of fashion.'

'Good quality never really dates, Art,' Mother assured me.

She reached out wisps and tendrils of herself. She smoothed her shadows over the glass of the pod. The air – or whatever it was in there – grew smoky, and my cloud mother seemed to fade, her eyes of drifting fire dwindling to pinpricks in her depths. Then she was gone, and the door of the pod slid silently open, letting out a faint breath of cold. And the Mercurian woman inside opened her eyes, and she was Mother.

'There!' she said, blinking her new, golden eyes. 'A little stiff, and I could eat a horse, but I think this will suit me very nicely for the time being.'

And so it was that when Myrtle brought the rest of our shipwrecked company to the secret door, she found someone who looked very much like our own dear mother waiting there, and so never saw Mother in her true cloudy Shaper form.

The others did not want to follow Myrtle, of course, as they told me later. They were busy making a camp out of sundry sections of the poor old *Sophronia* when my sister suddenly started to wonder what had become of Charity and me and had the idea that they should all go looking for us in a north-easterly direction. Father agreed at once, of course, but the others were reluctant, because they were tired, and the camp they were constructing was one that would have done credit to any shipwrecked mariner. But you know how impossible Myrtle can be once an idea finds its way into that tiny mind of hers, and at last they set out, waving their lanterns in a desultory manner and crying out, 'Hulloa! Art! Charity! Ahoy there!'

There came no answer, save for the gentle whiffling of the solar wind as it gusted across that drear moon's tinny plains – and then the not-so-gentle whiffling of two ravening Sun Dogs, who had grown weary of snuffling and slavering over the pit where we had vanished, and were eager to eat up these new arrivals instead. But the Sophronias and their friends were wise to those beasts' tricks by then. Munkulus and Grindle hauled out their largest firearms and let fly a perfect storm of shot, which pierced the Sun Dogs' translucent hides and found their brains and hearts and other squelchy, pulsating inner parts, and brought them crashing down in ruin. Huzzah!

A little time was wasted then, as Jack and the rest went to and fro, shining their lanterns in through the glassy walls of the dead monsters' bellies, very fearful that they might see Charity or myself trapped inside and already part-digested. (It was such a horrible prospect that Myrtle fainted before they even started looking, just in case.) But when they had satisfied themselves that their lost lambs (e.g. us) had not been eaten, and Myrtle had been revived with a whiff of Mr

Munkulus's pipe tobacco (in the absence of salts or *sal volatile*), they pressed on upon their former course and shortly saw the circular opening of that well-like shaft before them. Shining down their lanterns, they spied the handprints in its metal floor, at which Myrtle, just like me, felt a strange compulsion to float down and set her hand over one of those prints. And in another minute, she, Jack and Father and all the others were descending in the shaft of light and looking about in great awe and perplexity at the secret chamber and the ranks of Mother's former selves. And a very pretty reunion we had there, with fond good wishes expressed on every side, though I believe Father and Myrtle were a *little* troubled (just as I was) by Mother's new form.

'Now,' she said, when we told her how we had been reunited in the Jovian aether, and how the battle had gone, and how Ssilissa had been stolen and the *Sophronia* wrecked. 'Where is the Mothmaker? For if there is one thing I am certain of, it is that we must deal with her before she causes any further unpleasantness and inconvenience to the races of this system.'

We all started telling her at once, in a great din, but she quieted us down and had us speak one by one and soon understood where the Mothmaker was bound – and why.

'Naturally, she will see the Queen as her chief enemy now that I am gone,' she said (tilting her new head thoughtfully on one side in the same old, Motherish way). 'She will betake herself to London, and may be there already.'

'But if our friends among the Snilth continue to spread their influence,' said Father, 'she may find that her legions are too polite to do any fighting by the time they reach England and will only curtsey when they meet the Queen.'

Mother clapped her hands, delighted at the vision he conjured up of the fearsome Snilth o'erwhelmed by genteel good manners. 'But alas,' she said, 'the Snilth are many, and it is too much to hope that *all* of them will have escaped the Mothmaker's control. And even a few of them, with those great ships and tame moths, would be more than a match for Britain's fleets. We must go at once to London.'

'No,' said Father, 'to Scotland! The Queen and her family are spending Christmas at Balmoral Castle; I remember reading of it in the Court & Social columns of *The Times* before we left Larklight.'

'To Balmoral, then!' declared Mother.

'But how?' asked Jack. 'Don't you recall, Mrs Mumby – the poor old *Sophronia* is ash and matchwood? I don't see how we can ever get off this moon, unless you have an aether-ship stashed somewhere about.'

'No, I haven't,' said Mother, but she had a twinkle in her eye, and I knew that she had something 'up her sleeve'.

'Mother,' I said, casting a glance at all the motionless bodies which had once been hers. 'How did all these beings come to be here? When you wearied of life as a Callistan snapdragon, for instance, did you flap your wings and fly back here before you abandoned that body and put it in its pod? And likewise, when you abandoned the body of that Mandarin lady I see standing over there, did you simply climb into an aether-ship and sail back to this moon? Surely such behaviour would have raised eyebrows in medieval China?'

Mother laughed. 'Of course, Art, I did none of those things. I come and go from the Tin Moon just as I please.'

'But how?'

'I use the door, of course.'

We all looked up at the door we had come in by. It had vanished neatly into the eggshell dome of the ceiling, and only the faintest circular crack showed where it was.

'That door does not only open on to the surface of this moon,' said Mother. 'It can lead to any place within my

Solar Realm. It may take an hour or so to arrange it, for the Shaper device which powers it is *very* old and *very* complicated, but we should be able to step through it and emerge in the hills above Balmoral. With luck, we may even get there before the Mothmaker.'

'Impossible!' cried Myrtle.

'Remarkable!' gasped Father.

'Nice one, Mrs M.!' chuckled Grindle.

'I shall begin the process at once,' said Mother. 'And while we are waiting, I suggest we have a little something to eat. Did you salvage any food from the *Sophronia*? Good! Then some of you hurry back and fetch it before those nasty Sun Dogs find it. I seem to recall that we missed Christmas, what with one thing and another. But it is a complicated business working out the date on all these different, whirling worlds we flit between. Whatever date it is on Earth today, I am almost certain that it must be Christmas Day upon this Tin Moon.'

And so we made it the best Christmas that peculiar little world has ever seen. Munk and Grindle scurried back to camp and returned bearing a barrel of grog and a crate of table wine as well, and several jars of pickles from Mother's hamper, along with some well-salted chunks of that space fish which had swallowed Captain Moonfield, and fruit cake, chocolate, ship's biscuits and other delicacies rescued from the wreck. And Mother, by some scientific magic, caused all her pods of cast-off bodies to fold themselves away, and a neat little kitchen and dining room with a table set for dinner materialised in their place. Sat around that table we enjoyed the jolliest Christmas dinner you can imagine, with toasts and carols and jokes and food a-plenty. And if there was no goose and no pudding and no tree, it hardly seemed to matter. For, as Myrtle said, 'Christmas is about goodwill and good cheer and good company, and not about mere outward trappings, don't you think?'

And for once, dear reader, we all agreed with her.

But all good things must come to an end, and once our long meal was finished Mother clapped her hands again and said, 'Well now, I think a quick bout of Saving the Solar System from an All-Powerful Enemy would aid our digestion uncommonly well.'

'Oh, do we have to?' grumbled Grindle, who I believe had taken a little too much table wine. 'What about another glass and some poetry? I know some grand limericks, I do.'

'Or we could play Charades,' suggested Nipper.

'Dear Mr Grindle,' said Mother, looking fondly at him, 'I can too well imagine the sort of limericks you know. And Nipper, Charades is a capital game, but it is hardly *exercise*, and *exercise* is what a young crab needs if he is not to grow stout around the middle in his later years. Now what could be better exercise than a

nice brisk walk across the Scottish Highlands, followed by pitched battle against the legions of the Snilth?'

Was I the only one who thought she might have grown a little over-confident? Gingerly, I raised my hand.

'What is it, Art?'

'Well, Mother, it is just that last time you met the Mothmaker, she killed you. How do you mean to make sure that the same does not happen again?'

Mother laughed. 'Oh, that,' she said. 'I was not ready for her last time. This time I shall go prepared.'

She waved a hand. The plates and centrepiece vanished away, along with the remains of our dinner (much to the perplexity of Father, who was reaching out for a spare bit of ship's biscuit when it happened). In its place there stood upon the table top a sort of box, made from the wood of some tree which I don't believe ever grew in the light of our sun. The box was open, and within it, on a cushion of some silvery fabric, there nestled an egg-shaped object which I thought at first was made of a shiny black substance. Then I realised that it was a small vial or bottle of the clearest crystal and that within it a seething darkness swirled and stirred.

'Whatever is that?' asked Myrtle, awed.

'It is Dark Energy from before the Dawn of Time,' said Mother. 'Every Shaper who is sent to build a star system brings one of these with them. It is the means by which we are supposed to extinguish ourselves once our work is done. It is the means by which I had always intended to extinguish myself when my old body died. But now it seems to me that there may be another use for it.'

'To kill the Mothmaker!' I cried (for I catch on fast, you know).

Mother looked grave. It is an awful thing, I believe, for one Shaper to plot the utter destruction of another. No doubt that was what she had been contemplating while she waited in her cloud-form for Myrtle and I to meet her in that place. Perhaps she had thought she did not have the right. And perhaps our arrival had changed her mind and decided her. At any rate, she took the ampule of Dark Energy from its box and tucked it into a secret pocket of her dress.

'Well, then,' she said. 'Is everybody ready?'

We were. Even Myrtle made no mention of how unladylike she would feel, rushing into battle. I believe she had been changed by her adventures and now saw that it did not matter *all* that much if you perspired a little, or lost your bonnet, or accidentally allowed a stranger a brief glimpse of your ankles, so long as it was in the service of Queen and Solar System. We gathered up our weapons, Mr Grindle drained a wine bottle which had been left behind when the dinner things dematerialised and Mother led us towards the door, which opened, letting in a dazzling shaft of light upon our upturned faces.

We rose through that unearthly light, and somehow it turned into the more familiar brilliance of winter sunlight reflecting from snow. I breathed in deeply the fresh, cold air of Earth, and looked about. Behind me, my companions were blinking as they stumbled out of Mother's shining door, which now led like a miners' tunnel into the side of a snow-speckled bank of heather. Above it a steep hillside

rose, and on the summit, high above, a magnificent stag stood framed against the sky, just as if it were posing to have its portrait done by Sir Edwin Landseer.

'We are in Scotland!' I cried.

'Did I not promise as much?' said Mother. 'Balmoral is a half-hour's brisk stroll in that direction . . .'

'Couldn't you have landed us a bit closer?' grumbled Grindle, looking unenthusiastically at the steep path which she indicated, leading over the shoulder of a nearby mountain.

'Really, Mr Grindle,' snapped Myrtle. 'Mother has carried you instantaneously across ever so many millions of miles of space, and all you can do is grumble.'

'If I had been able to spare a few more days to let the machine adjust itself,' said Mother, 'it might have set us down in Queen Victoria's own drawing room. But I felt speed was of the essence in this case. It is my hope that we may be here before our enemies and that we can help the gentlemen who defend Balmoral Castle to prepare themselves for the coming of the Snilth.'

Yet even as she spoke, a chilly shadow fell across the glen. The stag turned and fled, and looking up we saw a great cloud darkening the sky above us – a cloud of dusty, fluttering wings, thrashing feelers and furry insect bodies, sweeping out of space to whirl and churn above the Scottish hills! And looking still higher, we saw stretching across the high wintry blue of the western sky a pale band or arc, shining in sunlight in just the way that the Moon sometimes does on a winter morning. The Earth had rings now, like Saturn's, and they were made out of moths! Among them we could see faintly the lumpish home-made planetoids of the Snilth and the Mothmaker's midget star, glittering like a diamond, pitting its silvery light against the golden rays of Earth's own sun.

Our race was lost! Despite Mother's magical doorway, the Mothmaker had beaten us, and we had reached Scotland too late to prevent the coming of the Snilth!

Chapter Twenty-One

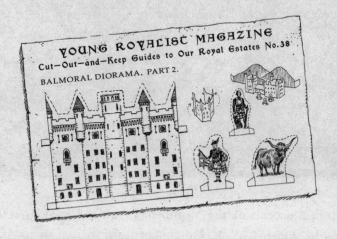

IN WHICH THE READER IS GRANTED A RARE GLIMPSE INSIDE ONE OF OUR ROYAL FAMILY'S COUNTRY SEATS AND WITNESSES SOME SURPRISING HAPPENINGS THEREIN.

Perhaps there is no need for me to describe to you the scene which awaited us as we came, panting, over the shoulder of the mountain which stands behind Her Majesty's home at Balmoral. Everyone has now seen the pictures which appeared in *The Times* and the *Illustrated London News*, showing the castle surrounded by squadron

upon squadron of the Mothmaker's winged minions. The moths which had already landed were drawn up on the heather-covered hillsides in battalions, with the cool Scotch breeze riffling their fur and trembling their feelers. They covered the landscape for several miles about Balmoral, like a sort of living quilt. And these were not the moths we had met before, but larger ones, darker in hue, for the Mothmaker had unleashed her elite battalions from deep within the Mothstorm. On the folded wings of each there was a pattern of markings which looked like a death's head.

Down from these monstrosities were climbing hundreds of Snilth, armed with their bagpipe dart-guns, which they

held ready as they moved towards the castle. We lay in the scratchy dead bracken on the mountain slope and watched them, hoping that our travel-stained clothes would help to hide us from the riders of the moths which were still airborne and whose wing beats echoed ever and again across the valleys. Everything cast two shadows: one a dark natural shadow made by the Sun, the other a pale and ghostly umbra cast by the Mothmaker's silver sunlet. Southwards, the atmosphere was streaked with conden-sation trails, marking the place where Britain's home fleet struggled against the main body of the Snilth armada in the skies above London. No help would come from there to wrest Balmoral from the enemy's grasp!*

'It's all up!' said Father. 'We cannot hope to fight so many Snilth!'

'They must already have overcome the Queen's guards,' said Mr Munkulus. 'For I can hear no sounds of battle.'

We listened. He was right. No shot or clash of steel on steel was borne to us upon that Highland wind – only the mournful lamenting of a solitary piper playing 'Scotland the Brave', as if in defiance of the otherworldly invaders. And after a few seconds a dart from a more sinister set of bagpipes must have found him, for the sounds gurgled and squawked and died away, and thereafter all was silence.

Silence, but for the beating of a pair of wings mightier than any we had yet heard!

* I saw nothing of this battle, which is a pity as it sounds jolly spectacular. But I visited London a few weeks later and saw for myself the vast heap of dead moths piled up for burning in Regent's Park and the wrecked Snilth warship which had fallen upon Parliament Hill Fields. And I have read accounts of how the brave citizens of London fought off the moths which landed in their midst and made captives of the Snilth who spilled from them. Luckily, little damage was done to the city during the fighting, since most of it was still in ruins following the Crystal Palace Disaster of the previous spring.†

† See *Larklight*, available from all good booksellers, price one penny.

We looked upward, shielding our faces from the low winter sun. Down from out the dome of Heaven a huge moth came flapping. Black as midnight were its pinions, and plates of black armour hid its head and thorax. It landed with a ground-stirring thump just in front of the castle, in a space made by the other moths, who shuffled meekly aside to make room for it. From a fortified howdah on its back there uncoiled a swirl of shadows, lit with drifting fire.

'The Mothmaker!' squeaked Myrtle, edging backwards.

'What vanity!' said Mother crossly. 'She doesn't need that great insect to carry her about. She is simply showing off!'

The evil Shaper was sweeping quickly up the drive towards the castle now, with squads of Snilth falling back on either side to let her pass, and after a second or two she was hidden from us by the trees in the gardens.

'We must make our move,' said Jack. 'It is now or never.'

'Might it be best if Charity, Ssilissa and Miss Myrtle were

to remain here, safely out of harm's way?' suggested Father.

'Oh no, Mr Mumby!' cried Charity. 'I haven't come this far just to hide in the heather like some droopy heroine in a melodrama! I want a chance to get even with those beastly Snilth, and so does Myrtle, I am sure! We can fight as well as any man, can't we, Myrtle?'

Myrtle looked for a moment as if she was about to say that she would be quite content to hide in the heather. But before she could, she was interrupted by an unwelcome hissing voice, which said, 'Ssstand and show yoursselves! You are captives of the Sssnilth!'

From behind a craggy sort of boulder twenty feet away emerged a Snilth warrior, and then a dozen more, all training their blowpipes on us. I glanced at Jack to see if he

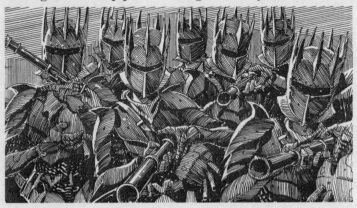

thought it worth trying to fight, but apparently he did not. With a rueful look upon his face, he scrambled to his feet and threw his revolving pistol down into the bracken. The rest of us, one by one, did likewise. But how bitterly disappointing it felt to have come so far, only to be captured so easily!

The Snilth came closer, closer, and then halted, forming a loose ring about us. One stepped forward, raised her visor and said suddenly, 'Oh, Misss Mumby!' And then all of them began sketching clumsy curtsies and running up to hug Myrtle and saying, 'We thought we had lossst you for ever!' and, 'Forgive usss for appearing in sssuch unladylike garb; She *makesss* usss wear it.'

I began to realise that these must be some of the Snilth who had fallen under Myrtle's spell at Mothstorm: the ones who thought her such a treasure and had resolved to model themselves after her example. I suppose it was jolly lucky that we got captured by them, instead of by their more warlike sisters, but I still could not help thinking that they were all as mad as hatters.

Myrtle, however, flushed pink with pride. She returned the curtsies of the Snilth and began introducing us. 'This is my father, and this lady is my mother . . .'

'Your mother?' cried the genteel Snilthess, quite amazed, before Myrtle could even mention her dashing younger brother. 'The other Shaper? Then she isss not dead?' And she and all her comrades fell in the bracken at Mother's feet, probably expecting her to blast them to ash for their impertinence in daring to invade her worlds.

Mother laughed and helped the leader to her feet. 'No, no,' she said. 'I am not like your Mothmaker. I haven't quite her power, or her love of power, and even if I had, I should not seek to harm you. But I should very much like to stop your mistress. Will you help us? I know it is asking a great deal of you, to betray your Shaper and your people . . .'

'No! It isss not!' declared the Snilth captain passionately. 'We hate Her! And we would be serving all Sssnilth if only we could free them from Her tyranny, so that they too may come to underssstand the joys of needlework, flower arranging, polite converssssation and other passstimes suited to young ladiessss.'

'Then will you help us to get inside that castle?' asked Jack.

'But how, Jack?' asked Mr Munkulus. 'Even with the help of these ladies, there's still about a thousand Snilth outside the front door, and *they* don't look ladylike at all.'

'Then we should go in at the back,' said Myrtle. 'If we cut through the vegetable garden there is a small turret door which leads in through the west wing.'

'Aaah!' sighed all the Snilth admiringly, delighted to find that Myrtle combined a keen tactical brain with her perfect manners. But the rest of us were taken aback by the notion that Myrtle had a brain of *any* sort. Why, even Mother looked astonished.

'I declare, I cannot imagine why you all stare so,' said Myrtle, sticking her chin in the air in that infuriating way she has. 'Art is not the only one who reads journals, you know. I have been a subscriber to *Young Royalist Magazine* since I was little, and I remember the floor plans of Balmoral quite distinctly. It was number thirty-eight in their series of *Cut-Out-and-Keep Guides to Our Royal Estates*.'

Nobody had any better ideas, so we set off towards the castle, following Myrtle's directions to the vegetable garden. At first we talked among ourselves as we went. My father said to the Snilth captain, 'I'm terribly sorry for the rough way you were handled by our companions when they seized your ship.' And she told him that it did not matter, none of the Snilth had been badly hurt, and the small injuries they had suffered had helped to convince the Mothmaker that they had been overpowered and done all they could to prevent the escape of Myrtle and Mrs Burton.

'It disstresssed uss terribly to lose Myrtle, without even ssaying goodbye,' said one of her companions. 'But ssoon after you departed, ssomething wonderful happened. A ship returning from the battle besside the gasss-planet brought in a Ssnilth named Thsssss Sixspike, and with her came another, whom she had ressscued from an Earthlet ship . . .'

'Ssilissa!' I cried excitedly.

The Snilth looked startled, in their Snilthish way. 'How did the male hatchling know?' one asked.

'Because Ssilissa was taken from *our* ship,' said Mr Munkulus. 'She is our particular friend.'

'We should have known she was a friend of Missss Mumby!' said another of the Snilth. 'She has sssuch exquisssite manners and was wearing a charming dresssss.'

'But is she all right?' asked Jack.

'As far as we know,' said the Snilth captain. 'We hid her at once, lessst the Mothmaker learns of her presssence in Mothssstorm.'

'But why did Thsssss take her from the *Sophronia*?' asked

Father. 'Was it simply misguided kindness? An attempt to reunite her with her own kind?'

'Do you not know who your friend isss?' asked the Snilth, wondering at our dimness. 'Thsssss recognised her tail-club insstantly! She is of the clan of Hammertail, which was thought to have been extinguished many thousandss of yearss ago.'

Myrtle gasped. 'You mean she is related to your brave, tragic queen from the olden days? The one who stood up against the Mothmaker? But I thought all her friends and family had been killed . . .'

'They were,' said our Snilth friend soberly. 'But her eggs, her unhatched eggs, were taken from her nessst and buried in the heart of a comet which the Mothmaker hurled far out across the gulfss of ssspace, sso that we could not hope for one of her hatchlings to grow up and lead a new rebellion.'

'Great Scott!' cried Father. 'But Ssilissa hatched from one of a clutch of eggs found in a comet!

The others were broken, but hers was whole, and my colleagues at the Royal Xenological Institute were able to incubate it . . . Could it be that it was one of those same eggs?'

'Something of a coincidence if it were not, I'd say,' said Mother, smiling at the neatness of Providence, which must have guided that comet with its cargo of eggs through all the wilderness of space to her own sun.

'Yesss!' agreed the Snilth. 'Ssilissa is one of the lossst hatchlings of Queen Zssthss! Her return is a sssign that our rebellion against the Mothmaker shall sssucceed.* While the Mothmaker busies hersself with the attack upon thiss blue world, thousands of usss are preparing to rise up againsst

* Good old Ssil! It came as a terrible shock, of course, to find herself thrust suddenly among millions like herself and to learn that she was born to be their queen. She is a modest, unassuming person and was quite distressed at first by the excited way that the Snilth stared at her and whispered about her, and how Snilth fathers came and lay their babies at her feet, as if her touch would be enough to bless them.

From a high gallery in Snil-ritha, where Thsssss and some other friendly Snilth had hidden her, she looked out across the silvery void at the planetoid which they called 'the Death Star' and wept sad tears to think that that mass of bleaching bones was all that she would ever see of her own family. But she consoled herself with the thought that after so many years of wondering who her. And when it is over, we shall have a polite and ladylike queen to rule uss, jusst as you do.'

'Ssilissa? A queen?' said Nipper.

'Rule over all them moths? Our Ssil?' exclaimed Grindle.

'*Queen* Ssil!' Munkulus grinned.

The Tentacle Twins cooed with incredulity.

'I always thought Ssilissa was a rather superior sort of person,' said Myrtle, who had never thought anything of the sort, of course, but is always awfully impressed by anyone with a Title.

But we could talk no more of it, for we had to pass just then through a great cordon of Snilth sentries. We concealed the weapons we carried beneath our clothes, and

and what she was, she now knew who her mother had been and that she had been both brave and beautiful. And it was a comfort to find herself surrounded by others of her kind and also to know that she had a family of sorts outside Mothstorm too, in the form of Jack Havock and his crew, whom she was resolved to save if she could from the wrath of the Mothmaker. So, like the sensible lizard that she is, she did not give in to melancholy or despair. Instead, with the help of Alsssor and Ssoozzs, she began laying plans to overthrow Mothstorm from within.

Thus it was that even as the Mothmaker was marshalling her legions for the final assault upon our empire, the rebellion against her was already gathering strength inside the Snilth planetoids.

our Snilth walked behind us with their dart-guns trained upon our persons and called out to their comrades in their own fierce, hissing language, telling them that we were prisoners who they were taking before the Mothmaker for questioning. And by this clever ruse, we managed to pass through their lines unhindered, and through the avenues between the mighty moths, and were soon crunching over the frosty earth in the very shadow of the castle walls.

'The castle is not quite finished,' explained Myrtle to anyone who cared to listen. 'Work on it only began two years ago. But it will be most genteel when it is completed. Over there beyond the ha-ha lies an ornamental loch which has been stocked with trout and a pair of Ganymedian water serpents. All the best Scottish lochs contain a monster.'

We looked where she pointed, but the water serpents were sensibly keeping out of sight beneath the water. Low over the pewtery waves the watchful moths hummed by.

The royal vegetable garden was sparse and bare at that season, with crusts of snow upon the dark earth in the raised beds and frost on the panes of the greenhouses. A gardener, who must have been pulling up leeks for the royal supper when the Snilth arrived, lay insensible beside his barrow, felled by a dart. Father cast his coat over the poor fellow to save him from being frozen as he slept, and we went on, through the turret door which Myrtle had suggested and up a winding stair, into a passage where soldiers in the uniforms of a Scottish regiment lay sprawled about, struck down by darts which had flown in through the windows as they leaned out to train their rifles on the attackers. A smell of powder smoke still hung in the chilly air. From somewhere ahead we heard a strange voice, both shrill and booming. It made our Snilth protectors flinch.

'The Mothmaker!' said Mother.

'She is in the ballroom!' said Myrtle, frowning as she consulted her mental map of the castle. 'No doubt the Royal Family were gathered there when she assaulted the place. Oh, I do pray she has not harmed them!'

I looked at Mother, but she said nothing. She simply

reached inside her gown, as if to reassure herself that the dreadful ampule of Dark Energy was still there.

We walked on along corridors lined with stags' heads and speckled trout in glass-fronted cases, our feet falling silently upon thick carpets woven with patterns of Gothick thistles. We passed rooms where many ladies and gentlemen lay in postures of abandon, sleeping off the effects of Snilth darts.

'It is like Sleeping Beauty's castle, in the fairy tale,' whispered Charity.

Ahead loomed a great carven door, where two Snilth stood guard. They hissed a challenge when they saw us coming, and our 'captors' responded in the same harsh tongue and hustled us through the door into Balmoral's magnificent ballroom, where paper-chains and Christmas wreaths hung from the stout oak beams and from the carved railings of a sort of minstrels' gallery which spanned the room. A fire crackled cheerfully in a huge hearth and a beautifully decorated Christmas Tree reached almost to the ceiling. It should have been a scene of festive bliss, for all the Royal Family were present; I recognised Prince Albert and little Prince Edward among the various courtiers and ladies-in-waiting. But not one of them was conscious. They lay in heaps upon the floor or spread-eagled over chairs and sofas, some of the gentlemen still clutching the swords and pistols with which they had sought to defend the Family against the Snilth. Snilth warriors stood all around the edges of the room, so motionless that they might have been no more than suits of ornamental armour.

On the rug before the fire was the Mothmaker. She had made herself into human form: a tall and stately lady, not unlike Mother in her looks. But I guessed at once who she was. There was something shadowy and flickering about her still: a sense of vast power pent up inside a shape which could not quite contain it. She had raised one arm, one slim white hand, and she was pointing at Queen Victoria, who hung suspended in mid-air a few feet away.

I had never seen the Queen before, though Myrtle had of course (indeed, Myrtle once sat upon her by mistake). She is a surprisingly small and portly person, very cosy-looking in her tartan dress, and I must say she was behaving with great courage, for most people might be a trifle alarmed if a demi-god barged into their living room, rendered their whole household unconscious and lifted them six feet off the carpet by means of some unnatural science. Her Majesty, however, seemed quite unflustered.

I suppose you learn how to deal with such situations if you are the Queen.

'I do not know who you are, madam,' she was saying, as our party entered. 'But I am *not* amused! You will kindly put me down and explain yourself.'

'Explain myself?' cried the Mothmaker, in that voice which Myrtle has already described to you, which seemed to have an invisible choir chanting behind it. 'I am so far beyond your feeble comprehension that I doubt it can be done! I am the Mothmaker! I am your successor, the new ruler of your empire, and all your subjects shall henceforth be my slaves. I was merely curious to see who you are and how you rule and what it is that makes them love you so and put pictures of your head upon coins and stamps and dinnerware. I think I should like pictures of *my* head upon such things when I rule in your place.'

Then she turned and saw us filing in. Her eyes flashed (and I do not mean that just as a figure of speech; they really did, as if some glimmer of her Shaper fire showed suddenly behind them). 'What is this?' she hissed. 'How dare you interrupt me when –'

And then she recognised Myrtle.

And then her eyes slid past Myrtle and she saw Mother.

'I am the Mothmaker! I am your successor, the new ruler of your empire, and all your subjects shall henceforth be my slaves.'

And for a moment the two Shapers stared at each other.

'So,' the Mothmaker said softly. She made a quick movement with her upraised hand and Queen Victoria went soaring upward as if on an invisible string until she collided with the topmost branches of the Christmas Tree, whereupon various strands of tinsel seemed to come to life and writhed about her like serpents, lashing her securely to the treetop.*

The Mothmaker forgot her royal captive then and came towards us, the edges of her skirts all blurring into fires and shadows. 'So you lied,' she said, still staring at Mother, as though the rest of us did not exist. 'You lied to me, and to your creations too. Even to these children of yours. When I broke your mortal body your essence did not perish, but fled away to some hiding place and to a new form. Coward! You hadn't the courage to die after all!'

'Not if it meant leaving *you* in charge of my worlds,' said Mother, reaching inside her gown for the Dark Energy ampule. But the Mothmaker turned to her waiting Snilth,

---

* And should you ever tie a fairy or an angel to your Christmas Tree, you might stop a while to remember where this custom came from, for it was started by Prince Albert to celebrate his own Dear Angel's bravery, when she found herself in that uncongenial position.

hissing a command, and they sprang to life.

In the next instant the great ballroom had become a battlefield! Snilth darts whooshed everywhere, spiking into priceless paintings and upsetting valuable vases, instantly striking down both Yarg and Mr Grindle, whose blunderbuss went off as he fell, blasting a splendid stag's head off the wall. It dropped on Mother, knocking her to the floor, and the precious ampule rolled from her grasp and went skittering away across the carpets. Meanwhile, Myrtle's Snilth admirers, apologising profusely for such unladylike behaviour, shot back, but their darts could not pierce the armour of their comrades; they rebounded, causing danger and inconvenience to the rest of us.

Jack and Father dragged an armoire in front of the door to stop other Snilth coming to their mistress's aid. Squidley, leaping to protect his fallen twin, thrashed his crackling tentacles, and six or seven of the armoured villainesses were flung aside, stunned by his electric touch. Then he too went down, positively pincushioned with darts, his tentacles sparking fitfully as he lapsed into unconsciousness. Mr Munkulus with his four strong arms sent armoured Snilth flying like rag dolls, and Mother went on hands and knees through the mêlée, hunting for the lost ampule.

Jack had his pistol out; I saw him put five bullets through the Mothmaker's heart, and when none took effect he aimed instead at the great iron chandelier which hung from the centre of the ceiling, directly above her. It came smashing down, crushing and trapping her beneath its spokes. But she could not be trapped for long; she restored herself to her true form and came flowing from beneath the chandelier like smoke. A writhing tentacle reached out from her, its tip condensed into something as hard and dark as flint, and Jack ducked as it swept over his head. It swatted one of the Mothmaker's own Snilth aside and hurled Mr Munkulus out of a window.

All these things I saw in flashes, like scenes glimpsed by lightning, for I was busy myself. A Snilth had seized me from behind in the first seconds of the battle and I had to struggle to break free of her. At last my flailing feet found a portion which her armour did not protect; she doubled

over with a muffled, 'Ooof!' Then Charity
Cruet, grabbing a marble bust of Nelson
which stood upon a nearby table, landed
a ringing blow upon her helmet and laid
the Snilth senseless on the carpet.

'Huzzah!' I cried, drawing my cutlass –
only for it to be dashed from my grasp by a
swiping shadow-tentacle! The Mothmaker now filled the
centre of the room like a great ghostly octopus, darting
blows at us with all her flinty fists. Nipper was hit between
the eye-stalks and collapsed with a clatter. I myself was
batted into the path of a Snilth, who raised a vicious knife
and would have cut me in two had not another Snilth struck
her down with the butt of an ancient musket seized from a
display on the wall. 'I'm mosst dreadfully ssssorry,' she
started to tell her victim. Then a blow from the Mothmaker
flung her with a crash against the wall, where her spiny
armour quite spoiled a portrait of Queen Adelaide.

'Art! Myrtle!' It was Mother, beckoning us into a nook
behind a large leather sofa. We crept in with her and found
that we were hidden from the fray. Better yet, she had
discovered the ampule! Unharmed, it had rolled beneath the
sofa, and now she held it in her hand once more. But how

could she use it, with those shadow-tentacles weaving just above our heads and the air above the sofa singing with flying darts? The tip of one spiked clean through the horse-hair stuffing and almost scratched me.

'This is *not* going as well as I might have hoped,' Mother confided, and she hugged each of us. 'Thank you both so much for helping to bring me here and keeping that creature distracted, but the rest I shall do alone. You stay hidden here until it is all over.'

I guessed at once what she meant to do. Why had I not seen it before? It was so like her! She meant to show herself and let the other Shaper seize her in those tentacles again. Then she would open the ampule and the Dark Energy within it would destroy both her and the Mothmaker at once.

'Stop her!' I hissed at Myrtle.

'What?'

'Don't you see? Mother means to sacrifice herself!'

'Oh!'

For once, Myrtle showed a flash of quick thinking. She pinched the shaft of that dart I have mentioned – the one that was sticking through the sofa-back – between finger and thumb and pulled it free. Careful not to scratch herself with its envenomed tip, she used it to prick Mother's bare white shoulder as she wriggled past us on her way out to do battle with the Mothmaker.

'Myrtle!' gasped Mother, half turning, her free hand moving to the place where the dart had touched. She looked at us and understood. 'Oh you dear, foolish children!' She tried to rise, to lift the ampule which she clutched, but she could not. Her eyelids drooped; she swayed towards me and I caught her. 'Blast!' she said, as she slid down into unconsciousness. 'I *knew* I should have chosen the dinosaur . . .'

I raised my head and gingerly peered over the chair-back. The room beyond was full of pistol smoke, and the floor was hidden by the heaped-up bodies of friends and foes and minor royalty. The Snilth had all fallen. Of my companions, only Jack and Charity were still on their feet. Jack's pistol was empty, but he was brandishing a massive antler which he must have wrenched from the fallen stag's head. Charity had armed herself with some Highland clansman's age-old shield, which was quite porcupined with the Snilth darts she had warded off. They stood side by side

near the middle of
the room, facing
the Mothmaker,
who hung above
the hearthrug,
rumbling and
flickering like an indoor thunderstorm.

'Where is the Shaper?' boomed her
cathedral of a voice. She lashed at Jack
with a shadow-tentacle, and he sidestepped and whacked it
with his antler, striking sparks from the flinty tip. 'Where are
her puny mortal children? I shall show her again what death
means!'

'Here I am!' said Myrtle brightly, standing up behind the
chair.

The Mothmaker's dark form swung towards her. The
whirling fires whirled faster. 'Girl!'

'Young lady, if you please,' said Myrtle. 'My mother is
unconscious; look, here she lies, behind this sofa. And I
believe those are my father's feet I see poking up from
behind that chest or ottoman. So, as my parents are both
indisposed, I wonder if I may be of any help to you?'

I was reminded how jolly plucky my sister can be

when the occasion calls for it. But there was not time to stand and gawp. Behind the chair, where only I could see, Myrtle was making fierce little gestures with her hands, and, though she was not using Cruet's Universal Sign Language, I guessed at once what they meant. While she was distracting our enemy with polite conversation, *I* was to strike the fatal blow!

I must confess, it made me a trifle nervous. It was not the first time that the fate of our empire and solar system has depended on me,* but always before there have been others there to help: Mother, and Jack, and the Sophronias, and people much more grown-up and capable than yours truly. Now Mother lay insensible behind the furniture, Jack was cornered and, apart from Myrtle, I was all alone. If I went wrong, the races of the Sun would live for evermore as mere serfs of the Mothmaker, and doubtless down all the miserable centuries of their captivity they would tell their children, 'This is all the fault of that dunderhead Art Mumby.'

With trembling hands I prised the ampule from poor Mother's grasp. Luckily, unconscious courtiers and small

---

* Indeed, it was the third time that year.

royal children lay in a sort of slumbrous drift beside our sofa, so it was easy for me to remain hidden as I crawled out. I quickly made my way to a quaint little spiral stair which led up to the minstrels' gallery. I was fearful that at any moment the Mothmaker would see me with one or other of her myriad eyes and lash out a flint-tipped limb to end my games, but she did not. She had other matters to consider: namely, Myrtle.

'I wonder that you have the gall to face me, Miss Mumby,' said the rogue Shaper, looming over my sister like a typhoon with a sore head. 'What shall I do with you to teach you manners?'

'You may do whatever you wish,' said Myrtle primly. 'My manners are already quite perfect. Many of your Snilth think so. They have grown very tired of the way you lead them rampaging about the Universe with no regard for their feelings and no time to enjoy the refined things in life.'

'What is this nonsense?'

'They hate you, you know,' said Myrtle sweetly. 'And I think they will be rid of you in the end, however many of them you kill. Because decency and genteel behaviour always triumph over brutality in the end. And that's what you are, I am afraid. I don't mean to be unkind, but you are a brute.'

All this I heard as I crept along that carven gallery above the Mothmaker, and it was a wonder to me that the Mothmaker did not crush Myrtle like a fly. (Heaven knows, *I* have often wanted to crush Myrtle like a fly and I am not a deranged entity with god-like powers.) When Myrtle called her a brute, a great *basso-profundo* rumble came from somewhere deep within the Mothmaker, and I thought, *This is it; now the poor, silly goose is a goner for sure.*

But at that moment, Queen Victoria, peering at the gallery from her perch atop the Christmas Tree, saw me sneaking along it and cried out, 'Oh, well done! Huzzah! Go it, noble paragon of British boyhood!'

Which was all very flattering, but not particularly helpful, since it served to draw the Mothmaker's attention to the gallery, and to me.

'Art!' shrieked Myrtle.

'Over here! Over here, furnace-face,' screamed Jack and Charity at the Shaper, Jack jabbing his antler at her, Charity rattling her shield.

But they could not distract the Mothmaker. Perhaps she sensed the danger above her. Perhaps some Shaper instinct told her what it was that sloshed and coiled inside the ampule that I held. Her shadow-tentacles, which had been poised to pulverise poor Myrtle, lashed upwards instead. One punched through the gallery rail a foot ahead of me, another a foot behind. Others gripped the mountings which held the whole structure to the walls and wrenched it sideways, and suddenly I was falling down and down amid a storm of splintered wood, while the Mothmaker beneath me seemed to open a vast, shadowy maw!

I had just sense enough, as I plunged into her blackness, to grope with one hand for the ampule that I still clutched in the other and pull out its stopper.

'Oh crikey!' I heard myself exclaim.

There was a blinding light, and then only the darkness.

Epilogue

BY MISS MYRTLE MUMBY.

I am told that the explosion was so loud that it could be heard all over Scotland and shattered windows as far afield as Edinburgh (and probably in Glasgow too, though they are used to that sort of thing there and noticed nothing untoward). How strange that such a mighty blast could emanate from such a tiny bottle, but that was no doubt down to Shaper science, which contains so many mysteries.

Naturally, you will be wondering why I was not blown into pieces? (I am very glad that I was not, incidentally, for I think it would be most impolite to have bits of oneself scattered all over the landscape, where total strangers might trip over them.) It seems that the energy released by the uncorking of the ampule was of a sort which is harmful only to Shapers, and so all that the rest of us suffered was a mild dizziness and a ringing in our ears. My brother Art, it is true, was somewhat injured by his fall from the minstrels' gallery. As the light and dizziness of the blast faded, we found him lying in the middle of the room, clutching his ankle, which turned out to be broken, and employing some most unsuitable words which I believe he must have learned from Mr Grindle. However, since he had been so very brave, I decided not to chide him.

Of the Mothmaker, nothing remained except for a nasty black substance, rather like dried seaweed, which was plastered over all the walls of the room. We few who were still conscious after the dart-battle stood amid the ruin of our enemy and looked at one another: myself, Jack, Charity Cruet and poor, wounded Art. But before any of us could speak a word or unburden ourselves of the many passionate emotions which seethed within us, we became aware of a great din outside and, running to the window, looked out through a large Mr-Munkulus-shaped hole in the glass to behold extraordinary events unfolding in the sky above Balmoral.

The moths which had surrounded the castle were all taking flight, blundering into the sky in the most senseless, clumsy, mothy way you may imagine. Not all the efforts of their Snilth handlers could persuade them to stay upon the ground, and I saw many Snilth leap from their mounts' backs as they rose, jumping down into the heather.

'The creatures must have been controlled somehow by the mind of the Mothmaker,' Jack reasoned, looking up from splinting Art's ankle. 'Now that she is no more, they are simple moths again.'

'Well, I hope they do not eat all our clothes!' I said sharply, placing a protective hand upon my bodice.

Jack grinned at me, his dear face flickering in the shadow of a million wings. 'They're leaving, Myrtle. Bound back to space, where they belong.'

And then, coming down through the flocks of fleeing insects, we beheld several of the great Snilth fish-ships, which extended skinny landing-legs and settled in the castle grounds. Their mouths opened and their hatches gaped, and out raced a veritable army of Snilth, armour shining redly in the light of the westering sun.

'Reinforcements!' gasped Charity. 'Oh, they'll kill us!'

But they did not. Some of the Snilth about the castle – loyal soldiers of the Mothmaker, I imagine – flourished their bagpipe-guns and went running to meet the new arrivals, and a battle broke out, Snilth versus Snilth, with dozens on each side falling unconscious into the shrubbery, and green explosions hurling armoured figures high above the hedges.

But the newcomers from the ships were so many and the defenders of the castle so demoralised by the passing of the Mothmaker, which I am sure they could sense, that the battle did not last long. And as it ended, a strange noise arose, like a great rustling wind rushing from the ships towards the castle.

'They are cheering!' said Jack.

'Oh, look!' exclaimed Charity.

And up the drive, with a bodyguard of armoured Snilth about her, came Ssilissa. And it was wonderful to see the way in which even those Snilth who had been fighting against her supporters a moment before seemed to

recognise her natural breeding and knelt on the grass as she went by, acknowledging her right to rule them!

A moment later she was in the castle, and I helped Jack unbar the doors and rushed out into the hallway to greet her.

'Myrtle! Jack!' she shouted, seeing us, and broke into a most unqueenly run and hugged first him and then myself. I sensed that she had much to learn about genteel behaviour and resolved then and there that I should be her teacher.

Another Snilth now presented herself to Jack. 'Why, Miss Thsssss,' he said, and she apologised for the precipitate way she had fled the *Sophronia* in the midst of the battle, leaving him without an alchemist. 'But when I realised that Ssilissa was a hatchling of Queen Zssthss, I knew that I mussst take her sswiftly home, for many Sssnilth have long awaited her. There was no time to explain. You would not have believed me anyway.'

'That's all right,' said Jack. 'No harm was done, and I admire the sly way you got off the *Sophronia*.' And he looked with what I thought was rather too much admiration at Miss Thsssss's pretty blue face, so I took his arm and led him back into the hall, leaving Art and Charity to listen to the tale of how Ssilissa found herself in Mothstorm and how the rebel Snilth hid and protected her and raised an army about her while the Mothmaker was besieging Earth.

Back into the great hall went Jack and I, and soon we were joined by all the rest. The rebels had a Snilthish lady doctor with them, whose mothskin case contained an antidote to the bagpipe poison. Soon our fallen friends and family were waking, with many sleepy groans and so many mutterings of 'Where am I?' and 'What happened?' that I grew quite weary of explaining how we had triumphed. And meanwhile, Jack scaled nimbly up the Christmas Tree and unfastened Her Majesty from its top, then lowered her down into the helpful blue hands of many Snilth; and there upon the hearthrug the Queen of Great Britain met the young Queen of the Snilth and congratulated her very prettily on her accession.

The sun went down and twilight deepened around the castle. The water serpents sported in the loch, and on the mountains all around us the highlanders lit their victory bonfires.

'It is not quite the Christmas I had planned,' said Mother, as we Mumbys and our friends took a stroll in the frosty garden before supper. 'But it is a good end to the year, I think.'

'An end to it?' asked Art, hobbling along at our side, leaning upon a crutch Prince Albert had kindly whittled for him out of the wreckage of the minstrels' gallery.

'Why, yes,' said Mother. 'I consulted a copy of *Crevice* in the castle library, and today, on this portion of the Earth, is the thirty-first of December. Tomorrow will be New Year's Day.'

'1852!' said Charity Cruet.

'1851 certainly held its share of surprises,' said Father. 'I wonder what this new year may bring?'

'School,' said Art, sounding doubtful.

'A cure for the Tree Sickness, I hope,' said Jack, who had spoken of his family's predicament to Her Majesty when she graciously thanked us for our part in her deliverance and asked us what we might like as reward.

'A new ship,' I said. (For that was the reward I asked for: a small but sturdy barque or aether-brigantine to replace the *Sophronia*. And a well-stocked wedding chamber aboard her, and a good alembic, and a comfortable cabin for a lady alchemist.)

'Father's wits restored to him,' said Charity, whose father had been brought to Earth aboard Ssilissa's ship most confused and quite unable to recall anything that had happened since he went out for a walk upon the cliffs one night in Cornwall, more than a year before.

'No more surprises,' said Father fervently.

'And you, Mother?' asked Art. 'What do you hope for from 1852?'

Our mother looked sorrowful and did not answer him at first. Then she said, 'I am not sure that I should hope for anything. My dears, I made a promise. I vowed that I would cease to be when my old body perished. Perhaps I was right to break that vow in order to defeat the Mothmaker, but now that *she* has ceased to be, perhaps it is time that I too followed her into oblivion.'

'But you can't!' said Father. 'I mean, the stuff that destroyed her is all used up, isn't it?'

'There are other ways that I could cease to be,' said

Mother. 'If I opened a pathway for myself into the heart of the Sun. Or if I left this Solar Realm entirely and flew out across space to seek oblivion in the depths of a dark star . . .'

'But you must not do any of those things!' I expostulated. 'They both sound quite horrid!'

'I am sure they would be, Myrtle,' Mother replied, 'but have I really the right to linger on in mortal form? Am I not as bad in my own way as the Mothmaker? I have interfered again and again with life upon these planets of the Sun. Your empire is my doing, and people have fought and perished because of me. Perhaps it is time for me to go.'

'No, no, no!' we all three cried. 'You can't! You mustn't! We need you!'

Mother turned to Father, taking his hands in hers. 'But don't you think people will say it is odd, Edward, that you went into Mothstorm with one wife and now have another who looks quite different?'

'Not at all!' said Father staunchly. 'Why, Emily, you are looking more like your old self every moment; and who will really notice? Only our closest friends, and they will understand that you are the same woman.'

'And you, my dears,' she went on, looking now at Art and me. 'You coped so well when I was a prisoner of the white spiders all those years and you thought me dead. You would get on well enough, I think, were I to leave.'

'No, we wouldn't!' Art declared.

Mother shook her head. 'Oh, what am I to do? My heart tells me that I should stay with you, but my head tells me that it is my duty to cease to be. What *am* I to do?'

And we stood beside her in the heather and waited for her to decide.

Another Epilogue

What sort of epilogue was that? I ask you! Even Myrtle must understand that our story cannot be left hanging like that, with everyone wondering what happened next.

Well, Mother decided, and I am jolly pleased to say that she decided to listen to her wise old heart and not her head. She is with us still and will be, we hope, for ever. And if people sometimes look askance at her and remark, 'How you've altered, Mrs Mumby', well, what does that matter? *We* know.

As for the rest of 'what happened next', I'm afraid it would make for dull reading. There were many months of tidying up and setting straight, and I had little part to play in any of it, for I was by then a pupil at Vermiform's Academy for the Sons of Space-Faring Gentlefolk, which turned out to be a top-hole place after all – perhaps I shall tell you about it one day.

Anyway, while I was puzzling over my Latin verbs and

trying out for the Low-Gravity Cricket XI, all manner of changes were afoot in space. Sir Richard Burton, who had been appointed Britain's Ambassador to the Snilth, arranged with Sir Waverley Rain to have the Mothmaker's silver sun towed out to the far reaches of the Solar System, where it now hangs in orbit about Hades, one of the lonely, lifeless worlds beyond Georgium Sidus. Apparently, all that world needed to make it pleasant and habitable was a little sunlight, and the Mothmaker's pocket-size sun suits it admirably. The Snilth have changed its name from 'Hades' to the far more cheery 'Snil', and under the wise rule of Queen Ssilissa they have settled there and are building a pleasant city for themselves. Not only that, but they are trading with their neighbours, the gentle mer-people of Georgium Sidus, with whom they have become firm friends.

In fact, they are becoming so polite and civilised that nowadays, when children behave well in company, people say, 'What a little angel; he has the manners of a Snilth!'

As for those hordes of mighty moths, the greater part of them went blundering aimlessly into space until, just like earthly moths drawn to a candle flame, they flew into the furnaces of the Sun. Indeed, for the first several months of the new year the sunlight was noticeably dimmed and had a greenish hue, due to all the moth ash that hung about it. But a few flocks survived and went with the Snilth to their new world, where they are farmed and bred much as they once were within the Mothstorm.

And someone else who has gone with the Snilth is our old friend Captain Moonfield. Sent out with Sir Richard's mission, he renewed his acquaintance with Miss Thsssss; they are to be married next June and we are all invited!

But now let me bring you to the present. It is the Easter hol, and I am spending it on the planet Venus, whither we travelled in Jack's new pride and joy, a lovely little

aether-ship called *Teasel*. She is not the *Sophronia*, but she is in every other way as trim and swift a ship as you could hope for, and Myrtle, pottering about in the wedding chamber, managed to carry us here from Larklight jolly smoothly.*

The *Teasel* rests behind me now, upon the long sward of blue Venusian grass which stretches down the hill above New Scunthorpe. Her crew and Myrtle, Mother, Father, Charity and I are gathered on the little headland where Jack once told me his life's story, on an evening which seems very long ago. We are quite familiar with this headland now, for we have spent much of our time here in the few days since we arrived. It was dark then (the Venusian night is very long) and we all held lanterns while Jack went among the three trees which stand in that little dell and injected into each a little of the serum that he was sent by the RXI upon

---

* Naturally, it would not be proper for Myrtle to live aboard the *Teasel* and be Jack's alchemist full-time, so when she is not available her post is filled by the Rev. Cruet. Charity's father is quite recovered from his brain fever, but very ashamed that he allowed himself to be used by the Mothmaker, poor gentleman. He has given up being a clergyman, declaring that it is far too dangerous an occupation, and was delighted when Jack offered him the post of alchemist and accommodation for himself and Charity aboard the *Teasel*.

the express orders of Queen Victoria.*

We have come back often since then, wondering if the trees are really changing or whether it is just a trick of the light as the sun slowly rises. But today the change is plain enough. Their upper branches have fallen away, their leaves lie in rustling drifts in the dell and they are people: a man, a woman and a child, standing like sleepers there.

'Oh!' cries Myrtle upon seeing them. 'They are all in the nude!'

'Well, what did you expect?' I ask.

'Their clothes must have torn away when they first turned into trees,' said Mother.

'Quite,' says Myrtle, hiding her eyes, but peeking through the gaps between her fingers. 'Even so . . .'

I am afraid that when Jack's ma and pa awake, the first thing that they will hear is Myrtle scolding them for being

---

* Her Majesty has ordered that enough serum shall be produced to restore all the Venusian colonists to their former state. Dr Blears objected strongly, of course, but Dr Blears has been dismissed from his post and appointed Keeper of the Royal Water Serpents instead, so who cares a fig what he thinks? If you ever visit Balmoral, you may generally find him up a stepladder on the shore of the loch, tossing bucketfuls of salmon to his charges. Huzzah, and God Save the Queen!

improperly dressed.

We all hang back and let Jack be the first to go to them. As his footsteps rustle through those fallen leaves, the former trees stir. They raise their heads and open their eyes and look about – a tall, good-looking young Scotsman, his pretty black wife and a little boy, no more than six, who was once Jack's older brother.

They have been trees for twelve whole years, so it is no wonder that they seem confused or that they look startled and even alarmed to find this handsome young aethernaut stood before them, bedecked with cutlasses and firearms.

It is Mrs Havock who is first to guess the truth. 'Jack?' she whispers. And she hugs him, and then he turns to hug the others as the rest of us look politely away or pretend suddenly to be very interested in the ground or the sky, and Mr Grindle wipes a tear from his eye and quietly blows his nose.

And now Jack is leading them towards us. I see their faces properly and they are all so like Jack in different ways, despite their leafy hair, that it is as if we finally have the key to him and he makes sense at last.

'Ma, Pa, Sid,' he says gently, 'I am your own Jack and these are my friends.'

We mumble, 'Pleased to meet you', etc., and I pull off my hat, but we do not quite know what to do or what to say, confronted by these revenants from 1839.

And then, to everybody's surprise, Myrtle steps forward and takes off her cloak and places it around Mrs Havock's shoulders. And that is the cue for Father to offer his coat to Dr Havock and for Mr Munkulus to wrap his pea-jacket round young Sid.

'We are delighted to make your acquaintance,' says Myrtle kindly. 'Jack has told us so much about you! And we have such a lot to tell you. But first, I think, we all need some jam scones and Devonshire cream, and a nice cup of tea.'

Art Mumby
Aboard the *Teasel*
Venus
1852

Mr Reeve and Mr Wyatt release a flock of Leaping Sphagnums into the Bonehill Rocks Vivarium.

TWO GENTLEMEN OF DEVONSHIRE

Mr Reeve is the author of the *Mortal Engines* quartet and the Carnegie Medal-winning *Here Lies Arthur*, as well as the illustrator of many children's books and co-writer of a musical, *The Ministry of Biscuits*.

Mr Wyatt is one of the leading illustrators of his generation, and his work has graced the books of Professor Tolkein, Mr Pratchett, Mrs MacCaughrean and many others.

Anxious to avoid the indolence or excesses that most successful creative persons fall victim to, Mr Reeve and Mr Wyatt have plunged their vast fortunes into the Babylon Endeavour, designed to promote a taste for knowledge and an acquaintance with the works of Nature. Several hectares of Mr Reeve's estate upon Dartmoor have been sealed within a great glass canopy (visitors can be assured the edifice will not suddenly up sticks and lay waste to the nearest city!*), in which flora and fauna from the Deepest Reaches of the Aether have been installed to provide a remarkable and informative attraction for the discerning gentleperson.

* See *Larklight*.

ACKNOWLEDGEMENTS

The Authors' uncouth demeanour and flimsy grasp of our fine language should have barred them for ever from good society were it not for the sterling education which they have received at the celebrated BLOOMSBURY finishing school. Their most particular thanks are due to Miss Szirtes (Eng.), Mrs Brathwaite (Art) and the strict but fair headmistress, Miss Elena Fountain (B.Sc. Physiol.).

The Pudding Worm was first Captured and Described with the help of pupils at St Aidan's C of E High School, Harrogate.

ACKNOWLEDGEMENTS

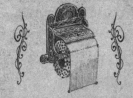

THE FANTASTIC
LARKLIGHT
SERIES
(IN READING ORDER)